CINDY DEES

started flying airplanes, sitting in her dad's lap, when she was three, and she was the only kid in the neighborhood who got a pilot's license before she got a driver's license. After college she fulfilled a lifelong dream and became a U.S. Air Force pilot. She flew everything from supersonic jets to C-5's, the world's largest cargo airplane. During her career, she got shot at, met her husband, flew in the Gulf War and amassed a lifetime supply of war stories. After she left flying to have a family, she was lucky enough to fulfill another lifelong dream—writing a book. Little did she imagine that it would win the RWA Golden Heart Contest and sell to Silhouette! She's thrilled to be able to share her dream, *Behind Enemy Lines,* with readers, and she would love to hear what people think if it, at www.cindydees.com or P.O. Box 210, Azle, TX 76098.

Annie stared at her unwilling patient. "What would it take to get you to stay in bed where you belong?"

"There *is* one thing I might like enough to stay in bed for...." His grin took on a suggestive slant. "You. If I can have a taste of you, I might stay in bed a little longer."

She felt hot all of a sudden. "And just what constitutes a 'taste' of me?"

"A kiss."

It was tempting. "You'll stay in bed if I play along with this foolishness?"

She did her best to sound resigned. It was better than letting on how her heart was racing like crazy and her breath was suddenly short.

"This is blackmail," she murmured. "But I'll do it. For your own good...."

Dear Reader,

It's always cause for celebration when Sharon Sala writes a new book, so prepare to cheer for *The Way to Yesterday*. How many times have you wished for a chance to go back in time and get a second chance at something? Heroine Mary O'Rourke gets that chance, and you'll find yourself caught up in her story as she tries to make things right with the only man she'll ever love.

ROMANCING THE CROWN continues with Lyn Stone's *A Royal Murder*. The suspense—and passion—never flag in this exciting continuity series. Catherine Mann has only just begun her Intimate Moments career, but already she's created a page-turning military miniseries in WINGMEN WARRIORS. *Grayson's Surrender* is the first of three "don't miss" books. Look for the next, *Taking Cover,* in November.

The rest of the month unites two talented veterans— Beverly Bird, with *All the Way,* and Shelley Cooper, with *Laura and the Lawman*—with exciting newcomer Cindy Dees, who debuts with *Behind Enemy Lines*. Enjoy them all—and join us again next month, when we once again bring you an irresistible mix of excitement and romance in six new titles by the best authors in the business.

Leslie Wainger

Leslie J. Wainger
Executive Senior Editor

Please address questions and book requests to:
Silhouette Reader Service
U.S.: 3010 Walden Ave., P.O. Box 1325, Buffalo, NY 14269
Canadian: P.O. Box 609, Fort Erie, Ont. L2A 5X3

Behind Enemy Lines
CINDY DEES

Silhouette®

INTIMATE MOMENTS™

Published by Silhouette Books

America's Publisher of Contemporary Romance

SILHOUETTE BOOKS

ISBN 0-373-27246-4

BEHIND ENEMY LINES

Visit Silhouette at www.eHarlequin.com

Printed in U.S.A.

Chapter 1

Air Force Captain Annie O'Donnell eased off the throttle and pulled back on the collective. She brought her helicopter smoothly to a hover over a featureless spot in the black ocean of jungle below them. The rendezvous point. Somewhere beneath her, a team of American soldiers was watching a rebel army prepare to go to war. And tonight that team was bugging out.

"What's the infrared scope showing, Rusty?"

Her copilot shrugged. "I've got an image of a clearing directly beneath us, maybe fifty feet across. No heat signatures, yet."

Five long minutes ticked by while they waited for the distinctive glowing blobs of human heat to light up the dark scope.

"Anything?" she asked yet again.

"Still nothing. You know, we can't sit here all night, boss. Somebody's bound to hear us eventually."

"Let's give it one more minute."

She was a sitting duck, hovering stationary like this. It didn't take fancy detection equipment to hear the distinctive thwocking noise of a helicopter. The back of her neck itched ominously.

She addressed the two crewmen manning the winch in the back. "Gentlemen, when we leave, I'm going to bank hard to the right and accelerate fast. Don't get dumped out the door."

"Roger that."

"Retract the forest penetrator seat and prepare for departure," she ordered.

"Yes, ma'am."

Annie's palms went slick with sweat on the control column. It was a good bet that missing this pickup would make her passengers' lives a heap more complicated for the next couple of days.

"Seat's retracted and stowed, Captain."

"And we're out of here in five, four, three…"

"Wait!" Rusty called out. "Got 'em. Two targets in the clearing, more moving in. They're transmitting the proper codes."

The winch motor whirred behind her, already lowering the cable and its heavy, steel seat back into the clearing some hundred feet below the canopy of leaves. The men behind her traded terse commands while one manned the winch motor and the other hung out the door, guiding the cable and reporting on the progress of the evacuation.

"Man in."

Annie heard the grunt of the first soldier as he landed unceremoniously on his belly on the Huey's floor. He was left to crawl out of the way and right himself while her crew continued the evacuation.

"Clear."

"Roger, winch away."

Metal hissed as the steel cable hurtled down into the belly of the beast once more.

"Two's on the seat."

"Hoisting him. Ten feet per second."

That was pretty fast. Whoever was hanging on that cable was getting a heck of a ride and probably getting the dickens scratched out of him as he tore up through the trees.

Two more soldiers landed in the helicopter.

"Winch away."

"Cap'n, I've got movement on the scope."

"Talk to me, Rusty," she ordered.

"I've got the last two men center screen. I paint four, maybe six more people just coming into range."

Annie frowned. They weren't expecting company. "You copy that, back there?"

"Yes ma'am. We're hauling 'em up like bats outta hell back here."

"Range, Rusty?"

"Five hundred feet. Ten hostile targets now."

"How are we doing, gentlemen?"

"Number five on the cable, ma'am."

"Max out the winch. We need to go. Now."

"Already doin' it. Fourteen feet per second."

"Cable's at forty feet. Thirty. Twenty! Slow the winch!" Frank shouted.

"Relax, Frank. I got it." Arty groused.

A thump as the fifth man hit the floor.

"Clear."

"Winch away."

"One more to go, ma'am. Damn, Arty. You 'bout slammed the last one's head into the skid!"

Annie interrupted. "Cut the chatter, guys. Rusty, report."

"Hostiles at two hundred feet. Closing fast."

Annie glanced over at the radar screen, then back at her own controls. A sudden warning tone made her jump.

"Trouble!" Rusty yelled. "They've got antiaircraft weapons! Looks like some sort of surface-to-air missile."

"Have they got lock on?"

"Not yet, Cap'n."

"Where's the last man, Frank?" she asked tersely.

"Climbing on the seat now."

"Get him out of there. He's about to have company."

"Cable's winding, ma'am."

"How far to lift him, Frank?"

"Eighty feet."

Rusty's voice was clipped, desperate. "Weapon activation, Annie." His voice rose. "They're gonna shoot as soon as they get lock on."

"How far, Frank?" she called.

"Fifty feet!"

Ping. Ping, ping, ping. Annie flinched and ducked. There was no other sound quite like bullets tearing through metal.

"Winch is hit! Motor's jammed!" Arty yelled. The warning tone in the cockpit changed pitch, became louder, more insistent.

Lock on. Her gut turned to water.

"We gotta go, Annie!" Rusty shouted.

Frank yelled from the back. "I got a man hangin' on my cable. 'Bout forty feet down. He's gonna die if we drag him through the trees."

They were *all* going to die if a missile hit them.

The next moment suspended itself around Annie in a slow-motion eternity where life and death hung in delicate balance. She could stay and try to retrieve the man hanging below her, thereby jeopardizing the lives of the nine people on board, or she could go, probably kill the man on the cable, and save everybody else.

"Hang on!" she shouted as she slammed the throttles forward.

She felt, rather than heard, the first thud when the man beneath her crashed into a tree. The scream of the engines wasn't loud enough to drown out the collective groan that issued from the five passengers in the back.

Dear God. What had she done?

Please don't let that man suffer. Please make his death swift and painless.

She climbed as high as she dared, right to the thirty-foot limit of the envelope over the jungle where radar couldn't paint her. The man on the cable was still in the trees, but hopefully the smaller growth at the top of the jungle would be less destructive than the heavier trunks and branches lower down.

The guy didn't have a chance in the world of surviving, but on the off possibility that some higher power owed him a miracle, she planned to give him all the help she could.

Every few seconds a shudder passed into her hands from the helicopter's control column as the body of the soldier beneath her hit another tree. She nearly moaned aloud as grisly images of his mangled form swam in her mind's eye, shredding her self-control. It took every ounce of her self-discipline to force her mind to the business at hand.

"Status report, Rusty. What did that ground fire hit?"

"Your VHF radio's out, the oil system's leaking."

"How bad?"

"It'll take an hour or more to run dry."

They could be back in St. George in forty minutes. Forty endless minutes for that man down there to bleed and suffer.

"The door window got knocked out, and the winch got hit," Rusty continued. "Beyond that, we've got bullet holes here and there. Nothing major."

Nothing major except a man dangling, dying, below her. A man who'd been counting on her to get him out alive.

The interior of the helicopter went silent, except for the steady scream of the engines and the deep pounding of the rotor blades beating the air.

Nine to one.

Nine lives for one life.

Nine devastated families or just one.

She talked to distract herself. "Frank, Arty, any suggestions on how I ought to set this guy down?"

"Yeah. Gently."

Frank cut in. "Shut up, Arty. You might want to radio the embassy, ma'am, and have one of the duty marines guide you down from the ground. We don't want to drop this guy hard."

"While you're at it, Captain, have them bring a cable cutter out to the pad."

"Why, Arty?"

"That guy's body is gonna be all tangled up in the cable. They're gonna have to cut him out."

Annie squeezed her eyes shut against the image his words called to mind.

"Right. Cable cutters. I'll take care of it," she choked out.

She took a quick glance over her shoulder at her passengers. They wore black close-fitting clothing devoid of any military markings. Special Forces, then.

"Arty, put one of our passengers up on headset, will you?"

"Okay, just a sec." There was a brief pause. "He's up."

"What do you need, Captain?"

The voice was tired, gruff.

"Your buddy's hanging under my helicopter and is no doubt, uhh, injured. I can proceed now to your planned drop-off point and leave him hanging. Or I can divert into

St. George, which is about thirty minutes closer, and get medical treatment for him there. I don't know anything about your team's orders, so it's your call."

"Stand by." After a brief silence, the voice came back up on the headset. "St. George."

Man, he sure was talkative.

"I'll have the embassy doctor meet us when we land. If anything can be done to help your buddy, I'll personally make it happen."

"He's got a name, you know."

The man's abrupt flash of anger startled her. But then why wouldn't the guy be mad? She'd killed his friend, after all.

She asked quietly, "What's his name?"

"Major Thomas P. Folly."

Tom's whole existence could be summed up in one word. *Pain.*

Grinding, unbearable pain ripping through his body. Just thinking about moving sent white starbursts of torture roaring through his brain. He'd have screamed if his throat muscles would cooperate, but they ignored his commands. He struggled against the sheer weight of the agony, fought for air, fought to open his eyes against the encroaching blackness.

He did his best to hold it off, but inch by anguishing inch, he gave way. He was almost grateful when the darkness closed over his head, blanking out the light, blanking out thought, blanking out all feeling.

He welcomed oblivion.

Light. Shining brightly in his eyes. Someone tugged at his eyelids and shone that damn light at him again.

Voices. Quiet, murmuring as if they stood beside a dead man.

"…patient's progressing extremely well, given the extent of his injuries…will maintain regimen of painkillers and sedation for a few more days…"

Days?

That was bad. But why?

Think, you idiot. What's so important about getting moving?

His men. That was it. They needed him. He was their leader. He was responsible for them. He had to get up, get moving, take care of them. They had to go.

Go where?

The answer refused to come.

A hand smoothed his brow with the infinite care of a mother's touch. It soothed him deep down, in his soul. So long since he'd been touched like that. He fed on the caress, a starving man at a feast.

And then the fingers slid into his hair. The touch was still light, but different somehow. It evolved into something sensual. Seductive. Female. A sudden, driving need tortured him. He wanted those hands all over him more than he wanted to draw another breath in this world.

He opened his eyes to beg for his heart's desire, and a fuzzy vision of a golden-haired woman swam before him. He couldn't make out her face. Had he died? Was she an angel?

Him in Heaven? No way. Not unless some celestial paper pusher up above had screwed up.

His angel's voice was throaty. Sexy. It flowed over him, hot and sweet. His body's most primal reaction kicked in with a vengeance, a pulsing, throbbing need that made him rock hard.

Surely people in Heaven weren't allowed to lust after angels. He must not be dead, after all. He'd never been so grateful for the discomfort of an arousal in his life.

Who was she?

"I've given you another dose of morphine. The pain will go away soon. Don't fight it."

His gut clenched at the sinful promise of her voice. He shook his head in the negative. Boy, was he weak. His head wobbled like a newborn baby's. He tried to lift his hand, to get the tube out of his mouth so he could tell her about his men, about his need to leave. About his need to have her touch him. His arm was so blasted heavy.

She subdued him easily, pushing his arm back down to the mattress. Her hands kneaded the unused muscles of his shoulder, sending a melting warmth coursing through him. He could lie here forever if she'd just keep doing that to him.

Something niggled at the back of his consciousness. He pushed it aside, but it kept intruding on the bliss of his angelic massage. Finally, reluctantly, he let the thought surface in his consciousness. There was something he was supposed to do…somewhere he had to go…

It came back to him vaguely. He was supposed to lead his men out of the country. To safety.

Man, her hands felt good.

He closed his eyes and let the pleasure break over him like warm waves lapping upon a sunny beach.

He awoke with a start. Something was different. He lay quietly and took inventory of his body. The respirator tube. It wasn't taped over his mouth.

He swallowed. His throat grated like sandpaper.

"Thirsty." It came out a croak, but at least his vocal cords worked.

The blond angel of his hallucinations appeared like magic at his side. He was learning to love the sight of her.

"Hi, there, handsome. How are you feeling today?"

Her smile lit up the room and sent warmth seeping

through him. Not the demanding lust from before, but just as beguiling.

"Thirsty," he repeated.

She disappeared from his field of vision and came back carrying a glass with a plastic, flexible straw sticking out of it. She put its end between his teeth.

He sucked and cool water flooded his mouth. It slid down his throat. Soothing. Every time he saw this woman she brought him relief.

"Where am I?"

"In a hospital in St. George, Gavarone."

Gavarone. A jumble of images flooded his head almost too fast to process. Rebels. Revolution. Reconnaissance. The jungle. His guys. A helicopter.

"Where are my men?"

"They're safe. They come to visit you when they can."

"They're still in-country? Why didn't they get out?" He frowned, trying to fill in the blanks. "I remember a helicopter..."

A shadow crossed the face of his angel.

"It was supposed to take us out. Fly us to—" He broke off. Good grief. They must really have him drugged up. He'd almost divulged classified information.

He lurched, or at least tried to lurch, upright. What if this woman worked for the Gavronese government? He'd just compromised his team. Holy smokes.

"How did I get here?"

"I drove you here in my car."

"No. I mean, what happened to me?"

"What do you remember?"

Dangerous question. She might be probing for information.

"Not much," he answered cautiously.

He did remember standing in a clearing in some of the thickest jungle he'd ever crawled through. He was watching his guys ride up a steel cable into a helicopter. Somebody was chasing them. No, a lot of people were chasing them. The memory stopped.

The blond angel was giving him a funny look. He'd better distract her.

"What's wrong with me? Why am I here?"

"You have a number of broken bones. Three cracked ribs, both your legs fractured, your left arm broken. That was your most serious break. They had to do surgery to set it. Both bones in your forearm had to be pinned. Your jaw was fractured, your right collarbone broken. You had cuts and scrapes all over the place, but they're mostly healed. A number of your wounds needed stitches. I insisted on a good plastic surgeon to stitch you up. You shouldn't get too many new scars out of it."

She said that like she'd seen his old scars.

"Anything else busted up?"

"One of your kidneys was badly bruised, but it's stopped hemorrhaging. The doctors say it's all right, now. I think you broke a couple fingers, too, but I lost track."

Geez. Maybe she should just list the things that weren't broken.

"How long have I been here?"

"Forty-five days."

"What?" Disorientation swirled about him. Six and a half weeks? All he remembered were a few snatches here and there. Mostly of this woman standing watch over him and promising to make the pain go away. She'd always kept her word, too.

"What's going on?" he asked.

"Going on where?"

"In Gavarone."

She smiled. "Why don't you get a little more of your strength back before you dive into Gavronese politics?"

"Is there war?"

Her features tightened, grew serious. "Not yet."

"But it's close."

"Very close."

He nodded. "Then you're right. I will need my strength. By the way. Is there something to eat around here? I'm starving."

She laughed. "I'll go see what I can find. I'm sure I can scrounge up something."

Scrounge. An imminently American slang word. And her accent. Not to mention she was the only true, Kansas-wheat blond he'd seen in this godforsaken place. She had to be American. Relief washed over him.

He tried to stay awake until she returned, but the drugs still coursing through his system called to him. He drifted off, cursing himself for his weakness as he fell asleep.

He hoped she was there when he woke up.

She was. Sleeping in the chair beside his bed. The room was mostly dark. A single small lamp burned on the table beside his head.

He smiled at the picture she made, curled up like a little girl, her feet tucked up on the seat, her head resting on her arm. Even in her sleep, she was alluring.

He caught sight of the water glass and tried to reach for it. He noticed for the first time that his arm was encased in a plaster cast. No wonder it felt so heavy.

His angel awoke with a jerk. She looked around for a second, trying to place where she was. He knew the feeling. A person with a job like his woke up that way a lot.

Her smile, when she noticed he was awake, was sleepy and sexy as heck.

"Hi, Tom."

Warning lights flashed wildly and alarm bells clanged in his head. How in the world did she know his name?

"Who are you, lady?"

She murmured under her breath, "My name's Ann O'Donnell. Most people call me Annie. I'm here to take care of you. To make sure the hospital does right by you, to translate if a non-English-speaking doctor needs information, that kind of stuff…"

She was babbling at him. Why was she so nervous? And why was she whispering? He stared at her speculatively.

"How did you know my name?"

She did an odd thing. She laughed.

"What a ridiculous…oh, I get it. Stop teasing me, darling."

His brows slammed together, and he opened his mouth, but she frantically gestured him to silence before he could speak. He watched, frowning, as she went to the door and opened it a crack, peeking out into the hallway. Then she went into the bathroom and did something to the toilet. It flushed, and continued to run.

Background noise. She was creating interference in case the room was bugged.

Who in the hell was she?

She came back to the bed and leaned close. Her golden hair swung down over her shoulder and brushed his cheek. It felt like corn silk, slippery and soft. And it smelled good. Like a field of wildflowers. His heart pounded all of a sudden. It had been a long time since he'd been this close to a woman. A very long time.

She pushed her hair back and tucked it behind her ear.

"Sorry," she whispered.

"Who are you?" he whispered back.

"I'm your cover. You had to have hospital care, but you couldn't exactly be admitted under your own name."

Now that was an understatement. In Gavarone, he was as illegal an alien as they came.

"The American Embassy worked up papers for you, saying you're my husband, and backdated a visa placing you in Gavarone before you got hurt. We told the authorities you fell in a rock-climbing accident.''

"They bought your story?"

"So far. But with the rebels getting more aggressive by the day, the government's getting pretty paranoid. There've been some questions asked about you. I'm glad you're getting better, because we may have to move you soon."

"You still haven't answered my question. Who *are* you?"

She jerked at the sharp tone of command in his voice. "Captain Ann O'Donnell, U.S. Air Force, Assistant Air Attaché, American Embassy in St. George to the principality of Gavarone. Do you want my serial number and date of birth, too?"

"We can skip those for now. I can't verify them until I get out of here. What level of security clearance do you hold?"

"Enough to know your name, rank, serial number and date of birth, mister."

"Is that a fact?" He grinned. Who'd have guessed angels had claws? "And do you know what I was doing here?"

She shrugged. "Not exactly, but it doesn't take a rocket scientist to guess what you were up to."

"Do you know how I got hurt?"

She opened her mouth to speak but stood upright abruptly. The door to the hallway swung open. A white-jacketed hospital employee stood there. He spoke in heavily accented English.

"Excuse me, ma'am. But the toilet, it stuck. I fix, no?"

Tom blinked as she smiled graciously and answered in Spanish as smooth and flawless as his own.

"That would be wonderful, *señor.* I'd have reported it, but I didn't think anyone in maintenance would be awake at this hour."

The man nodded and disappeared into the bathroom.

Interesting. That was certainly a prompt response to a running toilet. Two minutes at most. Just about as long as it'd take a guy to get from his listening post to this room. Somebody was suspicious about him, all right.

He and his angel, Annie, she'd called herself, waited silently until the man fixed the toilet and left the room. She sagged with relief when the door closed behind the guy.

So, she didn't make a habit of doing clandestine stuff. His adrenaline had hardly budged over the incident. Every now and then it dawned on him how different he was from regular people.

"Annie, I need to know. How bad am I hurt?"

"You were busted up pretty bad. But you're recovering great. Your legs, collarbone, fingers and jaw are about healed. Your left arm's still going to take some time to knit, and your ribs aren't quite there yet. But then, you probably know that, if you've tried to take a deep breath."

He thought about it for a second. His ribs did hurt. Right side, front. Three of them, she'd said. He hadn't noticed it in the underlying background of pain until she pointed it out.

"Can I walk?"

"Not in those casts."

He lifted his head off the pillow and discovered both his legs were encased in white plaster, the left leg from the knee down, and the right leg from the hip down.

He smiled wryly. "I'm a wreck, aren't I?"

Relief and a hint of…guilt maybe?…crossed her face. "It could've been a lot worse."

"You mean I could've died."

"Yeah."

"Nah, not me. I'm too stubborn to die by falling off some stupid mountain."

She blinked and then nodded in comprehension. His, or rather her, cover story for the benefit of the bugs.

"How 'bout a kiss for your long-suffering, wounded husband, honey?"

Annie's green eyes snapped, but her voice dropped into that sexy drawl he remembered from his waking dreams. "I don't think so, darling. The excitement of it might kill you in your weakened condition."

He smiled widely at her. "Later, then, when I'm stronger."

"Of course." She flashed him a look that promised hell to pay if he ever tried it.

Tom grinned. He never could resist a challenge. "I'll hold you to that."

Her response was dry. "Somehow I thought you might feel that way."

"How much longer till I'm out of here?"

"Hopefully, you'll only be here a couple more weeks." She leaned close and placed her luscious mouth practically on his ear. She whispered, "I don't think you'll have anywhere near that long before we have to get you out of here."

Oh, Lord. Her breath was warm and moist against his neck. How long had it been since he'd been with a woman? Not just sex with the nearest willing female to satisfy his craving, but real affection with someone who cared about him?

He shook off the thought. He was losing it. Here he was in the middle of a blown mission, thinking about a woman. He had much more important things to concentrate on right now.

Like how to get out of this hospital in one piece, and how to get his team out of Gavarone alive.

Chapter 2

Tom woke instantly, at full alert, when Annie touched his shoulder in the predawn hours a couple of mornings later.

She whispered in his ear, a bare breath of sound. "We've got to leave. Now."

He didn't bother to ask questions. There'd be time enough for that later, assuming they got out in one piece.

"It would attract too much attention if I pushed you out of here in a wheelchair. Can you walk if I take off your casts?"

"I'll do what I have to."

The men chosen for his unit were trained to be capable of nearly superhuman feats of strength and self-discipline. Walking on two broken legs sounded doable.

He watched in silence as Annie leaned over his legs. She used a wicked-looking pair of shears to start cutting away the plaster. Her hair swung over her shoulder the way it always did when she leaned down over him. His fingers sent the imagined feeling to his brain of it sliding beneath his hands.

He jerked his attention back to the task at hand. No wonder the military didn't send out women with teams like his. He was going to get them both killed if he didn't concentrate on business instead of her.

While she worked, he methodically disconnected the tubes and needles still taped to him in various places. The last piece of plaster lifted away, and Annie helped him sit upright. He steadied himself with a hand on her shoulder while the dizziness of being vertical for the first time in nearly two months passed. The bones beneath his palm were deceptively slender. Feminine.

Stop that, pal!

He swung his legs over the side of the bed and gently eased his weight onto his feet. Twinges of pain raced up his legs, as much from unused muscles as from protesting bones. But it was manageable.

Annie looked at him questioningly.

He nodded once.

She dug under her coat and pulled out some clothes for him. He sat back down on the edge of the bed and let her help him pull the slacks up over his bare legs.

Oh, boy. Her hands were warm and soft and felt so good easing up his legs under the edge of his hospital gown. His male parts leaped to instant attention. He must be well on the road to recovery to react like that. He pushed her hands away and finished pulling up the pants himself.

Tom noted with grim amusement the way her eyes went wide when he shrugged out of the hospital gown and reached for the shirt. Hopefully it was his physique and not his collection of scars that caused her reaction.

He tugged the polo shirt into place and flashed several hand signals at her. She stared blankly at him. What was he thinking? Of course she didn't know the Special Forces sign language.

Instead he swept his hand toward the door in the universal hand gesture for *You go first.*

She nodded and placed her finger to her lips.

Well, duh. Of course, he'd be quiet. He knew things about being quiet she hadn't even dreamed of. He could walk, stalk, even kill, in utter silence. He picked up the pair of loafers she'd brought for him and followed her to the door. He'd be quieter barefoot.

The hallway was deserted, and the nurse, a gray-haired woman, dozed in her chair behind the nurses' station. They glided past her, picking up speed farther down the hallway.

He flinched when a bell dinged to announce the arrival of the elevator. Before the door was barely open, he pulled Annie into the elevator and pushed her up against its side, out of the nurse's line of sight.

Annie's body felt luscious pressed against his. Pleasure welled up in his gut. But then she looked up at him with dark, frightened eyes. He mentally cringed. The worst missions were the ones involving civilians. They never could be counted on to keep their wits about them. He'd learned that the hard way a long time ago.

Although the smart thing to do was to drag her to the floor and clap his hand over her mouth without further ado, that would mean lying on top of her, belly to belly, with every inch of her pressed against him. He opted merely to smile reassuringly at her and to hope fervently that Annie recognized the delicacy of the moment.

The hall remained empty during the eternity it took for the door to slide closed. Relief and chagrin warmed his skin.

Dammit. He was going to get them both killed at this rate. And all because he was afraid of his reaction to a woman. This operation had disaster written all over it.

Tom closed his eyes. He wasn't a particularly religious

man, but he offered up a rare prayer for help in getting him out of this one alive.

When Tom finally relaxed, Annie closed her eyes and gave a deep, heartfelt sigh of relief. The elevator began its quiet descent.

"Thank goodness that's over! That was the hard part, Tom. Now we can just stroll right out the front door."

She'd spoken too soon. Two hundred pounds of bulky man abruptly sagged against her.

Her arms came up around him. Good grief, he was big— rock solid underneath the cotton shirt. He was also trembling.

"Hey. Are you gonna make it? My car's right out front."

"Yeah. I'm just a little dizzy." His voice was no more than a sigh. "I'll make it. I gotta collect on that kiss you still owe me."

"If you walk out of here under your own steam, I'll give you two kisses."

"Deal."

The elevator door opened. He dropped the shoes and slipped them on. Tom kept his word to her and resolutely walked out of the hospital. But he practically collapsed into the passenger seat of her car.

She had to help him lift his legs inside, and his head lolled back against the headrest by the time she got around to her side of the car.

"If you puke in here, you have to clean it up."

"Yes, ma'am." His lips curved upward faintly but his eyes stayed tightly shut.

She didn't want to think about the kind of pain he must be suffering. "Hang on. It's not a long drive to the place I've rented."

"What place?"

''I got us an apartment. The owner of the building does a little work on the side for us.''

''For Uncle Sam?''

''Yup.''

''Do you trust him?''

''Yes, I do.''

He shrugged. ''That's good enough for me.''

Annie blinked. ''Thanks.''

''For what?''

''For trusting me.''

''You're the attaché. You know this town better than I do.''

That might be true, but it didn't mean she'd ever done anything like this before. The enormity of having another person's safety rest entirely on her shoulders stilled her tongue for the rest of the car ride across town.

The next hour passed in a nightmare of anxiety and physical strain. Tom was grimly silent. He was obviously at the end of his strength, but he did what he could to help her. Somehow, she managed to half coax, half drag him up the stairs to the third-story apartment she'd rented.

To her vast relief he fell into an exhausted slumber the second she got him horizontal on the bed in the flat's single bedroom.

Drained, she slumped on a chair beside him and watched him sleep, the way she had for the past seven weeks around the clock.

By now she knew his features almost better than she knew her own. The smooth plane of his brow, the aggressive slash of his eyebrows, the sweep of his dark lashes against lean cheeks. She'd only seen his eyes on the rare occasions he was awake, but their smoky-blue color was unforgettable. Intelligence burned like a beacon in Air Force Major Tom Folly's gaze.

His personnel records verified her observation. Summa

cum laude from Texas A&M, fluent in Spanish and Chinese, top graduate in his Special Forces training. Heck, just finishing that grueling course was an accomplishment.

He stirred in his sleep, and she leaned over him to stroke his brow. It was the one thing that always seemed to calm him. His dark hair slid through her fingers, cool and sexy. It was wavy now that it was growing out from the buzz cut he'd had when she first saw him.

She shuddered at that memory. His body, mangled and bloody, wrapped in twisted steel cable, had sprawled awkwardly on the cement beside her helicopter. He'd lain so still, his limbs at unnatural angles. He'd looked dead. Doing that to another human being made her physically ill.

In fact, she'd been gagging on the far side of the helicopter when the embassy doctor had announced that the man was alive.

Alive!

She'd been so relieved she'd broken down and sobbed like a baby. But then Doc Clark recruited her to work up a cover story and get him to a hospital pronto. She'd promised his men she'd look out for him, so she pulled herself together and kept her word. And here he was.

His forehead was warm under her palm, but she was familiar enough with him to know it wasn't a fever. He always ran to the hot side.

Without the slightest warning his right arm snaked up around her neck. He yanked her down, twisting so she landed partially beneath him. She stifled a scream. Man, he was fast!

She stared up at that piercing slate-blue gaze of his. He blinked, looking disoriented. Holy mackerel! That was a heck of a wake-up reflex he had.

"Good morning to you, too. And do you always tackle people first thing like this?"

The corner of his generous mouth curved upward. "When they look like you, I do."

His heavy, solid body pressed her down into the sagging mattress.

"Any chance you could let me breathe, here?" she gasped.

His weight immediately eased off her, but he didn't release her. His thigh lay across both her legs, his foot tucked around her far calf in such a way she could barely move. One of her arms was trapped beneath him, and her free hand pushed to no avail against his muscular chest.

"Good grief, Tom. Be careful, will you? I haven't spent all this time nursing you back to health just to have you break everything again in some macho display."

Up close his eyes were the color of a stormy sky and more penetrating than ever.

"Let's talk, shall we, Annie?"

His voice was dangerously soft. It hinted at violence if she didn't give the correct answers. She gulped. He'd always seemed so harmless lying unconscious in a hospital bed. He'd responded like a puppy to her touch, eager, grateful even. Nothing had hinted at this side of his personality.

"What would you like to talk about?" she asked, doing her best to keep her voice even.

"The apartment's free of bugs?"

"Well, it's got a cockroach problem, but I've laid in a good supply of bug spray."

His eyes narrowed, and he stared at her with that saber-sharp stare of his. Suddenly he looked very much like the trained killer she knew him to be. And she was alone with him in a grungy apartment in a foreign city. A flippant attitude probably wasn't the wisest choice right about now.

She cleared her throat. "No bugs. What do you want to talk about?"

"Tell me everything."

Everything. Like how she'd nearly killed him? Like how she'd broken his bones and caused him weeks of suffering? Like how she was responsible for deciding his life was less valuable than her own? No way. She didn't have a death wish.

"'Everything' covers a lot of territory. Could you be more specific?"

"When and where did you first see me?"

"On the helicopter pad at the American embassy seven weeks ago." A glimpse of a heat blob on the infrared radar didn't really constitute *seeing* him.

"What exactly did you see?"

"You, lying on the ground with a steel cable wrapped all around you. One of the marine guards cut you out while Dr. Clark and one of your men did some fancy first aid to stop the worst of the bleeding."

"That would have been Joe Rodriguez. He's our medic."

"I wouldn't know. Your men haven't introduced themselves to me."

He leaped on her words like a prosecuting attorney. "I thought you said they came to visit me at the hospital."

"They did. But they didn't exactly observe the social niceties. They'd slip in, sit with you for a while, maybe whisper a word or two to you and then leave."

He nodded once. "Good."

Huh? She frowned, perplexed by his comment. He must've caught her expression, because he explained.

"It was a risk to come see me. The government could've been using me as bait to draw them out. Were they disguised?"

She cast her mind back through the days and nights of her anguish and guilt to those ghostly visits by his men.

"Come to think of it, I guess they were. They weren't wearing wigs and sunglasses, but they wore all kinds of different clothes. One of them came in limping once. I tried to ask him if he was okay, but he motioned me to be quiet before I could say anything.''

"When was the cover story for me put in place?"

"Before you left the embassy. While the doctor and your medic stabilized you enough to move, the paperwork was done.''

Skepticism laced his voice. "That's pretty damn fast."

"You were pretty damn hurt," she retorted.

"So then you stuffed me in your car, drove me and my fake visa to the hospital and strolled into the emergency room?''

"More like I ran screaming into the emergency room, but you've got it basically right."

"Then what?"

"Five hours of surgery to repair your kidney, set and pin your arm, fix the rest of your settable fractures and sew up the worst cuts that the doc and Rodriguez hadn't already gotten to. Then you slept for six weeks."

"When did my men come see me?"

"One of them came right after you got out of recovery and were put in your room. The tall, blond one."

"Dutch."

She nodded. The nickname fitted the guy. He was a solid six foot five of Nordic blond good looks. "He came in, read your chart, nodded at me and left. The next guy didn't visit for about a week. After that, one of them came in every couple days to check on you."

"That would've been enough time for them to establish covers. Excellent. They didn't lose their cool and do anything stupid.''

"I didn't think any of you Special Forces guys were stupid.''

"We're not. But we are intensely loyal to each other.

There's always a chance that emotion will rule a decision when one of our own is hurt.''

"You guys get pretty close, huh?"

"Yeah. You could say that."

The very flatness of his voice spoke volumes.

"Anyway, you woke up eventually, and you know the rest."

"I remember you doing things to me."

Discomfort blossomed inside her. She'd taken over most of his day-to-day care, not only to help out an overburdened nursing staff, but also because she'd gotten, well, possessive of him in the weeks of watching over him.

"What do you remember?" she asked hesitantly.

Surprisingly, he was the one who looked uncomfortable all of a sudden.

"You gave me massages."

She nodded.

"And you gave me medicine. Painkillers."

She nodded again.

"And sponge baths."

She winced and nodded a third time.

"Damn!"

His sharp expletive made her jump.

"And I *slept* through it all?" He sounded thoroughly disgusted.

"Well, if it makes you feel any better, I'm still going to have to help you until you get your strength back. The embassy doctor wants you to stay in bed for another couple weeks."

"Two more weeks in bed? Not a chance."

The absolute refusal in his voice alarmed her. "Tom. You were terribly injured. You've got to give yourself time to heal."

"I'm not staying in bed anymore. I'm sick of being laid out like a slab of meat."

She wriggled underneath him. When she pushed against his chest he gave way, rolling on to his back. She propped herself on her elbow to glare down at him.

It was hard to concentrate when his hand settled in the small of her back like that. And then he reached up with his other hand to tuck a strand of loose hair behind her ear. Electricity shot through her at his touch. That hand was capable of killing—had killed—yet it touched her as gently as if she were a newborn lamb.

"Tom." Drat. Her voice sounded as breathless as she felt. "You've got to stay in bed."

"And just how are you planning to make me do that?"

Plastered alongside of him like this, she was intensely aware of how much bigger and stronger than her he was. There was no way she could forcibly make him do anything.

"What's it going to take to keep you in bed?"

Sexy sparks lit his eyes, making them glow bright blue. "If you kept me entertained enough, I might be convinced to stay here."

To his credit his voice wasn't laced with sleazy innuendo when he said that.

She stared at him thoughtfully. "Entertained, huh? How do you feel about gin rummy? I play a mean game of it."

"Hate gin rummy."

"Cribbage?"

"Nope."

"Strip poker?"

A grin split his features. "Now you're talking."

She laughed back at him. "My father taught me never to gamble with strange men, especially when clothes are involved."

"Too bad. But he's right."

She stared at him thoughtfully. "Would you accept some sort of bribe to stay in bed?"

His grin widened, took on a suggestive slant. "What did you have in mind?"

"Outrageously expensive chocolate would work on me. How about you?"

He shook his head. "Sorry. I don't have much of a sweet tooth."

"Oh."

"But there is one thing I might like enough to stay in bed for…"

She perked up. "If it can be had in Gavarone, it's yours."

"Oh, it can definitely be had in Gavarone."

"Name it."

"You."

She blinked. He sounded serious. "Come again?"

"You. If I can have a taste of you, I might be convinced to stay in bed a little longer."

She felt hot all of a sudden. "And just what constitutes a 'taste' of me?"

He considered her for a moment. "A kiss."

It was tempting. How *did* a man's man kiss, anyway? With the prospect of finding out dangling before her, it was suddenly imperative that she do so. It also had the side benefit of keeping him in bed where he belonged.

She gazed at him narrowly. "What's the catch?"

"Just one thing."

She groaned. "I knew it. What?"

"I need a preview. To make sure you taste as good as I think you will. Besides, you owe me two kisses for walking out of the hospital."

"You'll stay in bed if I play along with this foolishness?"

He placed his mouth close to her ear to murmur, "Except for when I need to go to the washroom."

A shudder of pure delight whisked down her spine.

"Okay. Two kisses to pay you back for not making me carry you out of the hospital. Then we're square."

"Three kisses. You owe me one for staying in bed today."

She did her best to sound resigned. It was better than letting on how her heart was racing like crazy and her breath was suddenly too short.

"All right. You realize, of course, that this is blackmail and you're a bully. But I'll do it. For your own good."

He pushed her down gently to the mattress, looming over her, dark and potent.

"Poor little good girl," he crooned. "Always used to getting her way. And then a big, bad sinner like me had to come along and spoil everything."

The smile faded from his eyes, leaving them as bleak as a cold winter sky.

His mouth descended toward hers.

"Welcome to hell, angel."

Chapter 3

Tom was lost the second his lips touched hers.

Dark fury at her swirled through him. An urge to hurt her momentarily rocked him. He set aside the violence with some difficulty. She tore away his defenses, revealed his weakness. She made him *feel,* damn her. He'd closed off that part of himself years ago.

His first impression of her was gentle, innocent even. Her lips were silky, pleasantly resilient. Against his will he tasted her.

Sweet. Musky. Feminine. He'd forgotten how good a woman could taste. His anger drained away.

He sampled again at the nectar of her. So very long he hadn't allowed himself this pleasure. It was like…coming home.

She was a lush woman, but she was small against his frame. He supported his weight carefully on his left elbow, ignoring the ache under his cast. He tried to pull back to keep from crushing her, but she followed him, curling into him, kitten-like. He couldn't bring himself to draw away from her. Everywhere she touched him he burned—his chest, his belly, his thighs. Ahh, yes. The feel of a woman.

Memories of jungles and rebels, of death and the hunt, fell away from him like so many discarded bits of useless trivia. The razor edge of his habitual tension dulled, softened. Escape ceased to matter. Anything ceased to matter but this moment.

One by one his senses reawakened as she called forth memories from him of man and woman together. Slowly, reluctantly, he emerged from the chrysalis he'd lived in for so long. Too late he realized the damage was done. His cocoon was pierced, light already seeping in, calling to him to come out and fly. He could no more deny its summons than the butterfly.

Reluctantly he surrendered to their kiss, taking Annie with him, up, up into unfolding currents of air and warmth. He was exquisitely aware of the softness of her mouth, of her gossamer fragility.

He felt her shyness in the way she hesitated, in her awkward movements. He'd caught her off guard. His training and instincts urged him to capitalize on her weakness, to press his advantage. But he restrained the hunter in himself; he let her come to him.

She unfurled gradually beneath him, relaxing inch by inch. He massaged her neck with his right hand, kneading the knotted muscles there. Her eyelids fluttered closed, and on a sigh she gave in to the pleasure he offered.

His breath caught in his throat, forgotten in the enjoyment of her. He renewed their kiss. She came to him readily this time, trusting without question. His mouth opened against hers, asking for—and receiving—permission to take more.

This time she arched up into the embrace, her arms tightening around his neck. Her abandon spun him around like a carnival ride. A chuckle, or maybe a growl, rumbled in the back of his throat, and he loosed the hunter, closing in on his beautiful prey.

His arms formed a solid cage on either side of her, and he used his weight to trap her in place. His mouth slanted across hers, his tongue plunging and exploring at will. The sheer force of his abrupt desire startled him.

She turned her head to catch her breath, and he followed her, stalking her, granting her no escape. Surprisingly, she didn't evade him but rather met his pursuit head-on.

Annie gasped for air, stunned by the intensity of their kiss. This was no tentative, first-time exploration. This was lust, greed, covetousness and gluttony all at once. A single thought pierced her consciousness.

If this is hell, let me burn here forever.

She reveled in the surrender, gloried in the sensation of being the hunted one, weak and feminine for a change. So much of her life was spent in a man's world, being strong, suppressing her gender, quashing her feelings in the name of professionalism. But this. This was the epitome of being female.

She turned to her man, seeking his unyielding hardness. Seeming to understand her impulse, he drew her close in a protective gesture.

His lips wandered across her cheekbones, her eyelids, her chin, nuzzled her ear and nibbled her neck. His mouth returned to hers, confident this time, settling upon hers in a perfect fit.

In those endless nights beside his sickbed, she'd wondered sometimes what it would be like to kiss him. She couldn't fail to notice that, beneath his injuries, he was a gorgeous guy. Even unconscious, he'd radiated an aggressive male aura of sexuality. But her idle fantasies hadn't even begun to match the reality.

His neck was a warm, muscular column beneath her fingers. Enthralled by the feel of him, she caressed the short hairs at the back of his neck. The tendons beneath her palm tensed as if he would rise away from her, and she tightened her grip. He sank back into her once more, relaxed this time.

His mouth moved across hers with finesse, enjoying her as he would a fine dessert. Annie returned the favor, savoring the warm, male taste of him. After a delicious eternity, he lifted his mouth. She blinked and opened her eyes, gazing up into the loveliest blue-gray gaze she'd ever seen.

"Wow." He cleared his throat. "Uhh, okay then, Annie. I guess that counts as all three kisses for today."

He rolled onto his side, depriving her of his pleasing weight. His arm lifted away from her, freeing her.

She sat up abruptly, her face flaming with scarlet heat. Holy mackerel. She'd just flung herself shamelessly at a badly injured man. Was she so desperate she'd take advantage of a guy in his condition? She moved to get up, to escape from him. His arm snaked out and wrapped around her waist. Even in his weakened state, he pulled her back down easily.

"Don't go," he murmured. "Stay for a minute."

It wasn't right. Here he was, being nice to her, and he didn't even know she was the one who almost killed him. She pulled her tattered defenses around herself and reached for a light tone of voice.

"Long assignment in the jungle, soldier?"

He frowned. "Not especially. I just wanted to say thank you for helping me."

He was thanking *her*? During all those days and nights of watching over him, his pain had become her pain, his suffering, hers. Her guilt at choosing to sacrifice him rather than die herself had been boundless, and it rose up to choke her anew. Tears burned the back of her throat and she swallowed hard. She nodded, not trusting her voice.

His breathing gradually slowed into the unhurried rhythm of sleep. Carefully she slipped out from under his arm. He murmured a protest, but did not wake as she eased away from him.

Wobbly, she stood and looked down at him as he slept. What the heck had just happened here?

She'd been a big-time fool. That's what had happened. It was all well and good to fantasize about being swept off her feet by some big, strong, macho male, but she knew very well that the reality of guys like him was another thing altogether.

She'd only spent the last eight years in the military fending off guys just like him. Had she learned nothing? Some of them might come disguised in sheep's clothing like this one, but they were all the same. They wanted a little woman who'd stay home, clean up after them, tolerate their piggish drinking buddies and, of course, be a nymphomaniac on demand.

When she'd first joined the Air Force, she'd been young and naive, relatively inexperienced with men. Her father had been far too conservative to allow any randy teenaged boys to date his baby girl when she was growing up.

And then suddenly she'd found herself in pilot training, surrounded by the fast, confident, supremely arrogant personalities of wannabe fighter jocks. Talk about diving into shark-infested waters.

She'd fallen for a couple of them. But fortunately she'd wised up fast, before she got burned too badly, and before her reputation got shot to pieces.

To guys like Tom Folly the military was their life—their wife, mistress and true love—all rolled into one. They had neither the time nor the inclination to sustain meaningful emotional relationships. They weren't bad people. They just had different priorities from hers.

If those types of guys found a woman along the way

who was willing to spend twenty years stashed away in some cruddy base housing facility somewhere, waiting and worrying over them, the Tom Follys of the world weren't dumb enough to turn them away. But she'd seen plenty of those relationships head south when the men finally did retire—cynical, psychologically messed up and emotionally fried.

No, thank you very much. She was having nothing to do with a guy like Tom Folly. He might kiss like the Devil himself, but he could keep his priorities and his toy soldier life. She shook off the last vestiges of their kiss.

In the meantime she needed to stop by the embassy and make a few last-minute arrangements. Her boss figured it'd be at least tomorrow before the Gavronese government, which was a veritable model of inefficiency, came looking for her. She had to be in hiding by then.

She glanced around the dingy bedroom. It needed something to brighten it up. She and Tom were going to be stuck here for a while, and this depressing room wasn't going to help his frame of mind one bit. Oh, and she needed to lay in more food. She hadn't realized just how big a guy Tom was when she'd been shopping yesterday. He was no doubt going to eat like a horse.

Fortunately, the apartment had a working refrigerator. There'd been several biology experiments growing in it when she rented the place, and it had taken her a whole day to work up the courage to clean it out, but it was spotless now.

She tiptoed out of the bedroom and closed the door behind her. She took a critical look around the apartment's only other room, a combination kitchen-dining-living area, cataloguing items she'd need to make the place a little more hospitable.

She took a last peek at Tom before she left. He was sleeping soundly, one arm flung wide and dangling off the side of the bed. Satisfied he'd be unconscious for several hours, she eased out of the apartment, locking the door carefully behind her.

Tom woke up to the feel of an unfamiliar weight covering him. He blinked open his eyes and was startled to see a cheery quilt lying on top of him. Yellow tulips and dark green leaves twined over its white background. It looked like something his grandmother might've made.

A cool breeze blew across his shoulders, and he pulled the quilt up higher. A breeze? He opened his eyes again. The two tall casement windows stood wide open, admitting fresh air to the room. Between them, tottering on a rickety ladder was Annie, paint brush in hand.

Two of the filthy, grayish walls already sported a brand-new coat of yellow paint. It was nice—a bright, lemony color. A jar on the table beside his head was filled with daisies, their clean white heads nodding a greeting to him. Yards and yards of gauzy white cloth draped over a chair, and two iron curtain rods lay across the fabric, waiting to be hung.

The room already looked completely different.

"What in the hell are you doing?" he growled.

Annie lurched, startled. The ladder wobbled and gave an ominous squeak.

Crap. His reflexes took over and he leaped out of bed. In slow motion, the ladder gave way while Annie flailed her arms, trying to maintain her balance.

He caught her as the ladder toppled over. Her weight knocked him to the floor, and they landed with a thud. Paint splattered beside them.

She scrambled off of him. "Oh, my gosh! Did I hurt you? Tom, are you okay? Talk to me!"

"What do you eat, anyway? You weigh a ton."

"I do not. I weigh 125, and that's pretty good for a girl my height."

"You're 130 if you're a pound."

"Well, maybe I am, but it's rude of you to say so. I can't believe you did that! I'd have been okay, you know. I've had skydiving training, and I know how to do a parachute landing fall. Are you hurt anywhere?"

What was she mad at him for? He was the one who saved her butt.

"I'm hurt in a number of places, as I recall. But no, I don't have any new injuries. And you're welcome, by the way."

She scowled. "Thanks for the macho display, Tarzan. Now, let's get you back into bed." She stood up and began hauling on his good arm.

"Ouch! Stop that."

"You walk around on two broken legs without a whimper, but you complain when I pull on your completely uninjured arm?"

"It hurts my collarbone." He eased himself carefully to his feet. "While I'm up, I think I'll mosey into the bathroom—and no, I don't want your help."

"Fine. I wasn't going to offer, anyway. Besides, I've got to clean up this paint before it dries on the floor."

He looked at the yellow splat on the curling, filthy linoleum. "It's an improvement over the existing floor. Leave it."

He left her staring at the yellow spot while he made his painful way to the bathroom. Damn. He felt as if he'd been run over by a Mac truck. He'd been like this ever since he woke up in the hospital. Shouldn't he start feeling better soon? What if he didn't get better this time? Was this it? Was his career finished?

He stared at his beard-stubbled reflection in the cracked,

faded mirror over the bathroom sink. In a moment of bleak honesty he studied himself.

He wasn't getting any younger. Fine wrinkles were showing up around his eyes, and worry lines were permanently etched on his forehead. He was still hard and fit, but at what cost? It didn't come easy to stay this way anymore, and he sure as heck wasn't bouncing back from this injury like he used to.

He'd always known the day would come when he had to hang it up, but he wasn't ready for it yet. An unpleasant sensation tightened his gut. Surprised, he identified the feeling. Fear.

Dammit.

He stared himself down in the mirror, daring himself to be a coward and look away from his own hard-edged gaze.

An errant thought struck him. How had he been getting shaved for the past two months, anyway? He ought to have quite a beard by now. Had Annie been doing it for him? Maybe she had a razor and some shaving cream hidden somewhere.

He searched the bathroom, but the place was bare. He relieved himself and went back into the bedroom. Annie was already back up on the ladder, painting around the window. He sat down on the edge of the bed.

"Our cover story is that we're a married couple staying here until I'm recovered enough to go home, right?"

She stopped painting and looked over her shoulder at him. "That's right."

"Then where's all your stuff?"

"What stuff?"

"Your female stuff. You know, makeup and lotions and annoying soaps."

"Annoying soaps?"

"Those frilly things that don't lather up and leave you smelling like a flower."

"Sorry. I'm an Ivory girl."

"If the government was suspicious enough of me to bug my hospital room, they're gonna search this place if they find it. We need to make it look like we actually live here. Speaking of which, where's my stuff?"

"Your stuff?"

"Surely I didn't go on a mountain climbing expedition in South America without bringing a couple suitcases of clothes and doodads. And where's my climbing equipment?"

Her voice was dry. "I imagine it fell off the mountain when you did."

"Then where's the gear I had on me? I must have been wearing a climbing harness. And I'd have had extra rope, a hammer, maybe some crampons in my pockets."

"Okay, I get your point. I'll go shopping for some mountain climbing gear this afternoon."

"And speaking of equipment, where's my pack? The one I was wearing the night I got hurt."

"I suppose it's still at the embassy."

"I need it."

"Why?" Suspicion blossomed on her face. "Are you planning to mount a covert operation from your sickbed?"

"No. I just want it."

"Yeah, right. I wasn't born yesterday, soldier." She scowled at him. "Far be it from me to argue you out of doing something insane. I'll see if I can find it."

"Thanks."

"You're welcome."

He grinned at the grudging tone in her voice. He sympathized. Growing up with good manners stunk sometimes. He had the same affliction. Like the time he thanked the drug dealer who'd just beat him up for wiping the blood out of his eyes. His guys had given him grief over that for months. Ah, well. So what if they were known as the most polite Special Forces squad in the U.S. Armed Forces? They also got more women than any other squad.

He eyed the woman on the ladder in front of him. From this angle, he could see several inches up the cropped T-shirt she wore. Her stomach was tanned and firm. She might be a curvaceous woman, but she was also in good physical condition.

As she continued to paint in silence, he gazed idly around the room. Slowly something disturbing dawned on him. He hated to make his angel mad, but he owed it to her to burst her bubble before it grew too big.

"Annie, would you mind coming down from that ladder for a minute?"

"Why? I'm almost done with this section of the wall."

"I'm going to say something you're not going to like, and I don't want you to fall off the ladder again."

Frowning, she came down.

"Would you mind setting down that paintbrush, too?"

She glanced down at it and smiled wryly. "You don't want me armed, either, huh?"

"Nope."

She set the brush down.

"Look. I appreciate everything you've done for me."

"But…"

"But I don't want you to get the wrong idea."

"About what?" she asked curiously.

Long experience with women had taught him to be direct and brutal when it was time to let them go. "Annie, I'm in the middle of a mission. I don't have time to play house with you. All this…nesting…you're doing is sweet, but I can't let you get involved."

"With you or with your mission?"

"Either."

"Too bad. I'm already involved whether you like it or not."

"How so?"

"Tom, I'm an attaché. It's no secret to the Gavronese government that I'm trained to do simple espionage work. I just spent seven weeks by your side day and night, and you disappeared out of the hospital this morning. Don't you think they're going to come looking for me?"

He rubbed a hand over his face and looked up at her bleakly. "I really wish you hadn't jumped into the middle of this."

"Don't. I am a military officer, you know. I knew what I was getting into, and I can handle it."

"But you're a woman."

"So?"

"A woman can't handle what my men and I have to do."

Her voice took on a distinctly belligerent tone. "And why not?"

"Look, Annie. I'm not some chauvinist pig who thinks women are only capable of cleaning house and making babies. But what we do takes enormous physical strength and endurance."

"I'll grant you men are stronger than women, but that doesn't mean we're less intelligent. In my experience brains can usually accomplish just as much as brawn."

"Women are an unnecessary and dangerous distraction in the field."

"Oh, please. I've worked with mostly men for eight years, and I've managed not to fling myself at any of my co-workers so far."

"How many of them have flung themselves at you?"

That shut her up.

"I'm not going to debate the pros and cons of women in combat with you, Annie. The point is, I don't want you involved with me or my men."

"Tough. It's already a done deal."

Frustration coursed through him. He knew what he was talking about here. He'd played this game once, a long time ago, and it had cost one of his men his life. Annie was *not* taking him there again. He had to make her understand.

"Dammit Annie. I want you out."

"And how are you planning to take care of yourself until you're healed? Do you expect to stroll out the front door and go shopping without being noticed—assuming you could do it without passing out? Do you know who in St. George will help you and who'll sell you out? Face it, Tom. You need me."

He stared hard at her, and she glared right back at him. As much as he didn't want to accept her argument, she was right. He needed her help. For now. But that didn't mean he had to like it one bit. As soon as he was a little stronger, he was ditching her like a hot potato.

He sighed, resigned. "If you're going to be part of this operation for now, you need to understand the ground rules my team operates by."

She crossed her arms and raised an amused eyebrow. Too cocky for her own good, she was.

"First and foremost, I'm in charge. You do what I say, when I say it. No questions, no hesitation. Got it?"

A wide grin spread across her face. "Got it."

"I'm serious, Annie. In my line of work, lives hang on orders being carried out instantly. I'm the leader of this squad not only because of my rank, but also because of my field experience. You're going to have to trust me, quite literally, with your life. Can you do that?"

She tilted her head to the side, considering him. At least she finally seemed to be taking him seriously. "How good are you at what you do?"

He answered her quietly. "I'm the best. My team's the best there is, too. If you run with my squad, every one of them will die for you without a second thought."

"Let's sincerely hope it doesn't come to that."

"Agreed. So. Do you trust me?"

"Yes, I guess I do."

Why did it feel so good to hear her say those words? This is a job. It's just a job.

"Welcome aboard then, Annie. Your first assignment is to find me something to eat."

She saluted smartly. "Yes sir. Right away, sir."

She marched out of the room, her rear end twitching pertly. Realizing he was enjoying the view, the smile faded from his face. He had a bad feeling about this. A very bad feeling.

Chapter 4

"Where in the hell were you?"

Annie jumped. She managed not to drop the bags of groceries in her arms, but her keys clattered to the floor. She stepped inside the apartment and closed the door.

"Gee, hello. Nice to see you too, Tom. What are you doing out of bed? You agreed to stay there today."

He glared at her from his reclining position on the ancient, overstuffed sofa that had come with the apartment. "I was worried sick when I woke up and you were gone. I couldn't stay in bed."

A warm feeling crept into Annie's irritation.

"I went shopping. I picked up more food, and I had to get you mountain climbing supplies." She plunked one of the bags on the scarred coffee table beside Tom. It rattled metallically. "I managed to find some used gear, so you won't have to make it look broken in."

"Good thinking."

Tom's terse approval made her afternoon of foraging

through dark, dusty, cobweb-ridden pawnshops worth the hassle.

"I've got one more load to bring in from the car. Back in a minute."

She hauled her best find of the day out of the trunk of her car and heaved one of its black nylon straps over her shoulder. Although she exercised daily, she was huffing by the time she reached the apartment. How Tom managed to sneak all over the jungle carrying this bag full of rocks was beyond her.

Triumphantly she set his backpack on the coffee table. "Merry Christmas a little early, Major Folly."

"My pack!"

He reached out eagerly. His hand stopped abruptly in midair. He grunted and collapsed back on to the sofa, holding his rib cage. His eyes closed tightly as he waged a struggle against the pain.

Annie jumped forward. All her best intentions to keep her distance from him went right out the window. She bent over him in concern.

"Are you okay? Is there anything I can do for you? I picked up some painkillers from Dr. Clark today. Shall I get you one?"

"No. Just leave me alone. I'll be okay."

His voice sounded thin, not the rich tones of his usual speaking voice. It took all the punch out of his attempt to be stoic and macho.

She sat down on the edge of the sofa beside him. His eyes flew open and the expression in them shifted from annoyed to startled. She kept forgetting he'd been unconscious most of the time she'd been getting so intimately familiar with him. He looked away.

She spoke quietly to his averted face. "You must hate having anyone see you like this."

He didn't respond. But then she didn't really expect him to.

"I can only imagine how frustrating it must be for you to be accustomed to perfect health and then to find yourself in this situation. Give it a little time. You'll be back to your old self soon."

He turned his head and gazed bleakly at her. "Will I?"

His words cut like a knife. She was responsible for potentially ending his career and causing him all this anguish.

She reached out to smooth away the frown from his forehead. To her surprise he closed his eyes and accepted the comforting touch. And as usual her fingers couldn't resist straying into his dark, silky hair. She massaged his scalp gently.

As much as she savored touching his vital warmth, she had to stop this. He'd made it crystal clear earlier that he wanted nothing personal to do with her. She'd pegged him correctly. He was one of those men to whom the mission was everything. Reluctantly, Annie removed her hand.

"Are you sure I can't get you anything?"

He sighed. "Actually, you can. In the top pocket on the right side of my pack, there's a beeper."

She fished around and found a small black object that looked like a pocket pager. "Is this it?"

"Yeah."

She handed it over, watching while he punched in a series of numbers.

"What are you doing?"

"Seeing if my team has left a message for me."

"They probably don't know you're out of the hospital yet, let alone that you've got your gear back."

"They will soon. I just sent each of them a message to come here." He set aside the beeper. "In the big section of my pack, near the top, there's a little vinyl notebook. Could you get it for me?"

Annie found it and gave it to him. Interested, she watched him flip to several pages covered with a jumble of numbers.

"Do you have some paper around here?"

"Yes, sir." Annie got up and fetched a yellow legal pad for him.

He tore off a single sheet of paper.

"Never write on a pad of paper. The impression goes through to the pad and can be lifted for someone else to read."

"I'll remember that, Major."

Tom stopped and looked up at her. "What's all this sir and Major stuff?"

"Well, you do outrank me, and I am working for you now."

He scooted back on the sofa. "Sit down."

She sat beside him in the spot he patted by his hip.

"You and I are going to be living together in very close quarters, Annie. And as much as I hate to admit it, I'm going to need your assistance. I'd feel awkward accepting your help if you decide to stand on military ceremony with me."

Annie resisted the charm in his voice. She knew better than to become vulnerable to one of these gung-ho types. "I understand your point, but it wouldn't be proper to fraternize—"

"Hey, I'm the first person to shout about the danger of superiors and subordinates getting too friendly and blurring the lines of command. But you don't work for me."

"Then what was all that stuff about me following your orders without question?"

His voice went dead serious. "I don't give orders often, but when I do, it's because people are going to die if something doesn't happen pronto. If I ever do give you an order, I expect you to hop to it."

She nodded. "Fair enough."

"One of my team's missions is to pull civilians out of dangerous situations. That's essentially how we'll treat you, even though you're military. It'll be less confusing for everyone if we treat you as a non-combatant evacuee. Can you live with that?"

Annie considered him. She knew full well he was splitting semantic hairs with her, but he had made several good points. They were going to be living together in pretty intimate circumstances. And he was still going to need care and assistance.

She didn't for a minute believe the ridiculously hopeful expression he was throwing at her was sincere. He was a smart enough operator to try charming her into agreeing with him. But darned if that boyish smile wasn't hard to resist.

"You're just saying this stuff because you want another one of my massages, don't you?"

He accepted her surrender gracefully. "Darn straight, I do. In fact, I may even have to order you give me one on a daily basis."

"Oh, yeah? And who's going to die if I don't do it?"

He arched a dark brow at her. "My, my, we have led a sheltered life haven't we?"

Abruptly she blushed to the roots of her hair and jumped up off the sofa. "And just when I thought you might be turning out to be a gentleman, after all."

She hustled over to the kitchenette and fussed with putting away the groceries. "Are you hungry?"

"Now that you mention it, I could use a bite to eat."

Tom's answer was mild, but she definitely heard undertones of amusement in his voice. The rat.

While she cooked up pasta and vegetables, Tom fiddled with his notebook and paper. From her vantage point, it looked like he was encoding some sort of message.

He set aside the pen and paper to eat. Annie was dismayed when, a few minutes later, he handed her his plate still half-full of food.

"You didn't like my cooking, did you?"

"Yes, I did. It was a far sight better than the grub I was living on before the accident. I'm just not hungry."

"Once you get more active, maybe your appetite will pick up."

He put his hand on her arm as she bent down to pick up his glass. Her breath hitched at the feel of his fingers on her bare skin.

"Look, don't worry about it. I'll be fine. The meal was great, and I appreciate you making it for me."

Flustered, she sidled away from his hand. She'd finished washing and drying the dishes before she calmed down enough to breathe normally. How in the heck was she going to live with this guy if every time he touched her she got the vapors?

Tom's voice interrupted the stern lecture she was giving herself. "Annie, would you mind helping me for a minute?"

"Not at all."

He rolled on his side and gestured for her to sit down by him on the sofa. She did so and found her fanny wedged against his lean, hard stomach.

"What can I do for you?"

Resting his forearm on her thigh, he showed her the sheet of paper he'd been working on. The top half of the sheet was covered with what looked like random mathematical doodles. The bottom half of the sheet was covered with neatly printed rows of numbers. They swam in a jumble before her unfocused gaze.

His muscular power surrounded her. His clean, male smell filled her nostrils and made her light-headed. Or maybe it was the picture that came to mind of all those brawny, bronzed muscles she felt as he spooned his body around her that made her feel faint.

"You see here where the sequence starts with 924681?"

She swallowed to clear the lump from her throat. "Uhh, yes."

"Start there and read me the numbers in sets of six while I enter them in my pager."

The procedure took a couple of minutes. Somewhere along the way she found herself relaxing back against the warm wall of his body.

When they finished, she jerked herself upright once more. "So. Can you tell me what we just did?"

"We sent a status report to my superiors."

"How?"

"Digital satellite paging. When we're out in the field, headquarters monitors all the transmissions over our assigned frequencies."

"Now what?" she asked.

"Now we wait."

"For what?"

"For my team to arrive."

She nodded. "Pretty slick. And here I was wondering how my contacts in St. George were ever going to find your guys to let them know where you are."

He grinned. "We stand by the Boy Scout motto—Be Prepared. We have contingencies for all sorts of things, including teams getting split up."

"Very impressive."

His answering grin was downright boyish. Dang it. Why did he have to be so blasted appealing? Her plan to resist him was in a shambles, and they'd barely been together twelve hours. She was going to be a mess in a week.

"By the way, Annie. Do you happen to know how I've been getting shaved for the past seven weeks?"

His question knocked what little equilibrium she had

right out from under her. She managed to mumble, "I might."

"Uh-huh. I thought so. Is there anything you haven't done for me?"

Her face heated up. "Not really."

His eyes glinted. Suddenly he seemed a lot less bothered by their forced intimacy than she was.

"Do you want me to give you a shave, Tom?"

"What I'd really like is a bath."

Oh, Lord. There was no way in heck she was going to manage to give him a full-body sponge bath when he was wide awake and watching her.

"If you think you can make it into the bathroom, I'll run a bath for you. How does a long, hot soak in a tub sound?"

"Amazing."

"Great. Stay here, and I'll get it ready for you." Relieved to have dodged that bullet, she jumped up and headed for the bathroom.

While steaming water filled the tub, she tucked her serviceable bar of Ivory soap out of sight and laid out shaving cream, a new razor and a towel. Grinning, she set out the array of floral soaps in frilly packages she'd bought that afternoon.

She returned to the living room. "All set. Do you want me to put a plastic bag over your cast, or can you keep your arm dry?"

"I'll keep it out of the tub."

She nodded as he swung his feet to the floor.

"How do your legs feel?"

He grimaced up at her. "Like spaghetti. It's damn annoying. Did the doc say how soon I can start working out again?"

"You mean like exercising?"

"Yes. Like exercising, you know, getting my strength back? Becoming mobile and self-sufficient?"

"Tom, you've got broken bones all over the place."

"It's been seven weeks. They must be repaired by now. Besides, I've had broken bones before. I feel healed." And with that, he stood up.

Despite his brave pronouncement, there was a distinct wobble to his steps. Annie wedged her shoulder under his arm and steadied him as they walked slowly to the bathroom.

"That's just great," she griped. "You feel healed. You have no idea at all how hurt you were, do you?"

He stopped in his tracks and gazed down at her. His arm, which rested across her shoulders, abruptly tightened.

"I remember getting dragged through the jungle, slamming into tree after tree. I remember feeling each bone break, and I remember hoping the next tree would be the one that killed me. Believe me. I know exactly how bad I was hurt."

Annie felt positively sick to her stomach. She'd never dreamed he'd actually been conscious through that horrible ordeal. Dear God.

They made their way into the bathroom in silence.

"Tell you what, Tom. How about if I have Dr. Clark come take a look at you? Let's see what he says about how you're doing before you embark on any aerobics programs, okay?"

"I don't need a doctor."

"I'll blow your cover if you don't see him."

He gave her a deadly look. "I do not appreciate being blackmailed."

If she'd learned one thing in eight years of working with macho males, it was never to back down. Even though the look he was giving her turned her gut to Jell-O, she glared right back at him.

"And I don't appreciate seven weeks of my hard work

caring for you going down the tubes because you're too antsy to let yourself heal properly.''

He replied grudgingly. ''Okay, okay. I'll talk to the doc.''

''Thanks. Now, let me help you with your shirt.''

She eased the shirt off his shoulders, savoring the feel of his skin sliding under her fingertips. She guided the left sleeve over his cast and greedily devoured the sight of his back as the fabric fell away.

Despite the many times she'd seen his body, the sight of all that muscle never failed to impress her. And to see it moving, bending and twisting in all its supple grace, stole her breath clean away.

Then she noticed he was looking over his shoulder at her.

''Uh, the cuts on your back have healed up nicely. You can barely see the scars.''

He shrugged. ''I never cared much about having a perfect body. Another scar or two doesn't matter one way or the other.''

She refrained from mentioning that his body was as close to perfect as she'd ever seen. Instead she asked, ''Speaking of scars, where did you get this one?'' She touched a small round scar under his right shoulder blade with her fingertip.

He sucked in his breath, and she jerked her finger away.

''I'm sorry. I didn't mean to hurt you.''

He turned to face her. In the tight confines of the bathroom, they were only inches apart. His voice was little more than a husky whisper. ''You didn't hurt me.''

She stared up at him, startled by the sudden intensity of his gaze. The attraction between them flared, hot and thick. Slowly, as if against his will, his arms came up and surrounded her, drawing her close.

Ohmigosh. It was all she could do to keep her hands at

her sides, not to lean into him, and most especially not to return his embrace.

"That's an old gunshot wound," he murmured. "A woman gave it to me."

"A woman shot you?" Annie asked breathlessly.

"She led me into a trap, and her father's men shot me."

"That sounds horrible," Annie whispered, her heart aching for all he'd suffered in his career. First a trap and a gunshot wound, and now multiple broken bones and a possibly career-ending injury. No wonder he didn't like working with women.

His husky voice drew her back to the present. The very steamy present.

"I like it when you touch me, Annie. Do you like doing it?"

"Uhh," she cleared her throat, "sure."

"Good. Then here's your first order. Do it some more."

She replied nervously, "I don't think that qualifies as a lawful order under the Uniform Code of..."

His finger stilled her lips. "Remember what I told you about following orders?" he murmured. "Don't think about it. Just do it."

Despite herself, she smiled. "Make it a request, not an order, and I just might."

He smiled back, slow and smooth. "Touch me, please."

Her hands settled on his lean waist. Pure, sexual pleasure shot through her. This was wrong. Really wrong. But did he ever feel good.

"You have me at a disadvantage, Annie. You've had your hands all over me already, but I don't know the feel of you at all."

His hands began to move, roaming gently over her back. His fingers kneaded the muscles along her spine, melting her will to stand up. Only the knowledge of his injuries kept her from sagging against him.

She mustered enough strength to murmur, "Your bath's going to get cold."

He drew her closer and spoke against her temple. "Sweet Annie, there's always more hot water. Besides, I may be needing a cold soak, anyway."

She buried her face against his shoulder. "We've got to stop this."

"Why?"

"Because you're in the middle of a mission and don't need distractions, and we've got to work together."

He sighed. "You're right." He set her away from him, but his hands lingered on her shoulders. "But holding you makes me feel alive."

His hands slid down her arms, and with a final caress of her fingertips, fell away from her.

"Did you know there was a time in the hospital when I thought I had died?"

She shook her head in the negative.

"When I first saw you, I thought you were an angel, and I couldn't figure out how I'd ended up in Heaven."

"Me an angel? Not a chance."

"To me you were one. Every time you came to me, you took away my pain. And you let me know I wasn't alone. You have no idea how comforting that was."

The extent of his suffering made her ache inside.

"I'm so sorry, Tom…"

"For what? It's not your fault I got hurt."

His words were a knife straight through her heart. Only the sink at the back of her thighs kept her from staggering at the blow.

"But—"

"Are you all right? Annie? You look a little pale."

"It's probably all the steam in here making me light-headed."

"Why don't you go into the other room? I can handle

the rest of my bath, and I'll give you a holler if I need anything.''

He guided her to the door, gave her a gentle push into the bedroom and closed the door behind her.

She turned to face the wooden panel, leaning her forehead against it in misery.

She whispered, ''But it is my fault, Tom.''

Chapter 5

On the other side of the door, Tom scowled at the bath supplies she'd left him. "Hey! Where's some real soap, dammit?"

The sound of snickering drifted through the closed bathroom door. The minx. She'd left him with nothing but those girly soaps he hated. Ah, hell. Who cared if he smelled like vanilla orchid sachet?

He rested his head against the high back of the old-fashioned tub and let the water's heat soak away his aches and pains. If only his mind would relax like his body. But his thoughts stubbornly continued to race.

You're in trouble, buddy. One Annie O'Donnell has gotten way under your skin.

He had no business letting her get involved in his mission. It was dangerous to her, and moreover, it was dangerous to his men. Okay, so he did owe her a debt of gratitude. She'd taken care of him and given him a cover, and she'd put herself at risk to pull him out of the hospital. But his first responsibility was to his guys. What was he going to do with Annie?

He sure as heck knew what he'd like to do with her.

Guilt crept into his consciousness like the heat creeping into his bones. Here he was, relaxing in a hot bath with a beautiful woman waiting on him hand and foot, while his men were living on a razor's edge, undercover, out of their element, and one mistake away from dying. He was their commander. He ought to be out there with them, leading by example. What were they going to think of him when they showed up here and saw his plush setup?

Showed up here…

He lurched upright, sloshing water over the side of the tub. "Annie," he called urgently.

She answered instantly from the other side of the door. "Yes?"

"Could you come in here?"

She peered cautiously around the door frame. Skittish about seeing him naked, was she?

"I don't bite, you know. Well, at least not so it hurts." How did she manage to scowl and smile at the same time like that?

"What do you need?"

"I wanted to warn you. If any of my men show up while I'm still in here, let them in the apartment and come tell me, okay?"

"No problem."

"The guys might get a little jumpy if you answer the door instead of me. I'd suggest you move slowly around them and keep your hands in plain sight at all times."

Her eyes widened in alarm, but she nodded.

"I don't know which of my men will get here first. Their nicknames are Tex, Doc, Dutch, Howdy and Mac. If somebody knocks on the door, ask them in English what their handle is. They should give you one of those."

"Tex, Doc, Dutch, Howdy and Mac? Sounds like the seven dwarves. How did they come by those names?"

He grinned. "Remind me to tell you the stories some time when I'm good and drunk."

She returned his smile warmly.

"By the way, while you're here, would you mind washing my back?"

Her shoulders visibly tensed up, but she moved toward the tub. Reluctantly. He bit back a grin.

She seemed to relax when she saw the thick layer of suds covering the water.

"So what do you like? A good hard scrub or a gentle wash?"

"Today a scrub is in order. I feel like I haven't had a real bath in months."

Her voice was wry. "You haven't. I was only able to give you sponge baths."

A washcloth touched his back, and then moved in vigorous circles that were pure heaven. He closed his eyes and enjoyed the sensation. Eventually he gathered his wits enough to speak.

"Is there any chance you could shave me now? I don't have a mirror, and with one hand," he lifted his cast off the edge of the tub, "I'm a little awkward. I wouldn't want to slit my throat after having survived everything else."

He watched the way she moved as she sat down on the edge of the tub and dunked a washcloth in the water. Graceful. Quick as a deer. She wrung out the cloth and leaned over to press it against his beard. And then she looked up at him. The rich emerald color of her eyes was almost hidden behind the black of her pupils. Poor girl. She had the same effect on him, too.

The silky smoothness of her fingers spreading shaving cream over his face was too much for even his control. He shifted uncomfortably and accidentally bumped her chest with his arm. The springy flesh pressed against his biceps, a brain-scrambling sensation. His control shattered, and under the cover of the bath water, his body reacted violently.

He eyed the big old tub, calculating its volume. It would definitely hold both of them. He could already feel her naked body, soapy and slippery against his. He'd lower her down upon him, easing himself inside her heat. He'd thrust up into her—

Annie cleared her throat, and he blinked away the image. Thank goodness the water covered his reaction to her. She'd probably run screaming if she knew what lurked beneath those suds.

He noticed her hands trembled a little when she picked up the razor. Eyeing the quivering blade, he decided not to tease her about her agitated state.

Instead, he focused on her chest, watching it rise and fall in quick, short breaths under her damp T-shirt. As she carefully scraped his face, her fresh smell mingled with that of the scented bath water. It did nothing to ease his throbbing flesh.

She finished her task with the speed of long practice and wiped the last of the shaving cream from his face. She must have picked up on his discomfort because she jumped up immediately and began to fidget with his towel.

"Uh, is there anything else you need?" she asked.

He racked his brain but couldn't come up with a single excuse to keep her with him any longer.

Reluctantly he answered, "No."

She stood up to leave, and he savored the slender length of her legs.

"You might want to put on another shirt before my guys arrive."

She looked down at the wet spot over her right breast, and so did he. The white cotton clung to her, revealing a wisp of lace and a lot of flesh. It left very little to the imagination and was sexy as hell.

She blushed fiery red and raced out of the bathroom.

You idiot.

He should have kept his mouth shut and enjoyed the view a little longer. She might be off-limits, but he wasn't dead, yet. Then the thought of sharing that view with his team nixed any regrets.

He leaned back and willed his thoughts to the revolution at hand and to escaping St. George. Anything to calm his body down. He certainly couldn't get out of the tub in this state.

Annie stopped in the middle of the bedroom, panting hard. Sexual vibes had been pouring off him like the steam from his bath. It had been all she could do not to plunge her hand into that water to see if he was reacting to her the same way she was reacting to him.

This was nuts. She had to get control of herself.

In the meantime she had to get out of her wet clothes. She stripped off her T-shirt and bra quickly, eyeing the closed bathroom door. With her luck Tom would pop out of there right now.

A naughty corner of her heart wished he'd do just that. She'd fling herself into his arms and they'd have wild sex in the bathtub, just like she'd been imagining while she shaved him.

Stop that!

Furious with herself, she yanked dry clothes from the scarred armoire in the corner and scrambled into them.

She breathed a sigh of relief when she was safely clothed once more. Restless, she moved out into the living room and straightened up. She carried Tom's pack into the bedroom and set it on the chair beside the bed. Maybe tomorrow she'd have better luck keeping him in that bed where he belonged.

Her breath hitched and her body tingled all of a sudden. Tomorrow Tom might kiss her again in exchange for another day of bed rest. She craved the taste of him. Her palms itched to feel him, and her breasts ached for the weight of his body upon her.

She jumped as a sound intruded upon her fantasy.

Someone was knocking on the front door.

Her heart beat double time as she moved to the entrance. Without opening it, she spoke softly through the flimsy wood.

"What's your handle?"

A drawl she could cut with a knife came from exactly opposite her ear. "Tex, ma'am."

She opened the door and stepped back.

The man edged into the room fast, his back to the wall beside the door. Lean and darkly tanned, he closed it with a soft click and took a hard, assessing look around the apartment. Remembering Tom's advice to move slowly, she eased away from the dangerous looking man.

"And who might you be, ma'am?"

"My name's Annie."

"Hey, aren't you the lady from the hospital?"

"That's right. I'm Tom's cover. He's in the bathtub at the moment. If you'll excuse me, I'll go tell him you're here."

"No need."

Startled, Annie looked up. She hadn't heard him come into the room, let alone get out of the tub and leave the bathroom.

Her breath caught at the sight that met her eyes. Tom lurked in the doorway to the bedroom, a towel wrapped around his hips and a nasty-looking pistol held low in front of him. He looked every bit as dangerous as the man called Tex. With lethal grace, he waited, poised to do violence.

"Hey, boss, am I glad to see you!"

Tom's posture relaxed and he stepped forward. "Ditto, Tex. Any trouble finding this place?"

"Are you kidding? I know every inch of this miserable hellhole—excuse me, ma'am—of this town."

Annie noticed that Tom looked a little pale around the gills and was beginning to wobble. "Tom, why don't you get dressed, and I'll pour some iced tea for all of us."

Tex's eyebrows went up, but he made no comment as Tom nodded and retreated to the bedroom.

Tom emerged a few moments later, bare-chested and wearing green camouflage pants.

Annie groaned mentally. He probably couldn't get a shirt on by himself over his cast and wasn't going to ask for help in front of one of his guys. But how was she ever going to sit calmly in the same room with him semidressed like that?

Tex dragged a chair over from the kitchen table and plunked down on it while Tom eased onto one end of the sofa. Annie had no choice but to sit beside him.

"Where are the others?" Tom asked.

"Mac's working in a government warehouse across town. Dutch is posing as an American journalist because he'd never pass for a local. Doc's got himself a sweet job working as a medic for the rebels, and Howdy and I hang out here and there. I keep an eye on things and stay in contact with the other guys."

"What's the situation?"

"In a nutshell, the rebels are fixin' to bust out and attack any second now. They've got most of the roads sewed up and they control the airport. Nothing's moving in or out of the city without their say-so. There's a major player out there backing them hard. They've got more equipment than they can possibly use, and somebody's trained them on it.''

"What's the government doing?"

"Sitting around with its thumbs up its—'' he threw an apologetic glance at Annie ''—nose. The army's got tanks and howitzers rolling around for show, but it lacks the manpower to fight an urban guerrilla war. Desertion numbers are climbing fast. The government troops have lousy weapons, rotten training, and their morale's the pits. Not to mention their leadership sucks. They outnumber the rebels about two to one, but that'll be good for squat when it comes to a shootin' war.''

"So the government's going down?"

Tex nodded succinctly. Underneath his homespun vocabulary, Annie sensed a sharp mind at work.

"Timetable?"

"Like I said. Any second. There's been some house-to-house fighting on the east side of town the last couple nights. Mostly drunks brawling, but tension is high.''

"So what have you guys been doing while I was out of play?"

Tex leaned back with an engaging grin and stretched his legs out in front of him. ''Mostly whorin' and drinkin' and gamblin' all night long.''

Annie was intrigued when Tom merely raised an eyebrow and Tex sat upright abruptly, the grin wiped from his face.

"We've been waiting for you to get out of the hospital so we can bug out of this damn country and leave it to its revolution. And we've been prayin' for you, sir.''

"Thanks."

Annie watched the silent look that passed between the two men. Yup, these guys had been through rough times together.

Tom asked casually, "Have you given any thought to how we go about leaving Gavarone?"

"Actually, sir, we were waiting to see how mobile you were before we finalized a plan."

Annie suspected that if they had to carry him out on their backs, they'd do it.

"Any idea how soon you want to move out, sir?"

Tom answered quickly. "ASAP."

Annie interjected. "Not so fast, Tom. I want Dr. Clark to have a look at you before you go running off into the middle of a war. And you still need some time to get your strength back."

He shot one of those saber-sharp looks of his at her, and she glared right back at him.

"Tex, I don't believe I've introduced you to my nurse-maid and resident fussbudget, Annie O'Donnell. She's attached to the American Embassy here and has been helping me out since the accident."

"We sort of met in the hospital. But it's a pleasure to officially meet you, ma'am. Doc and Dutch said you took real good care of Major Folly, here."

She smiled. "I did my best. But you know what a cranky patient he can be."

"I can imagine, ma'am."

She sighed, calculating her chances at getting him to stop ma'aming her every other sentence. The odds weren't very good, but it was worth a shot.

"You can cool it on the ma'aming, Tex. It makes me feel like an old lady."

"Yes, ma'am. I mean, all right."

Tom grinned and Tex scowled at his boss.

Another knock sounded on the door, and Annie gaped at the instantaneous transformation of the two smiling men into deadly serious hunters.

One second they were sitting in their seats, and the next,

Tex was plastered against the wall by the door while Tom melted into the shadows of the bedroom. A series of hand signals flashed back and forth between the two men, and weapons appeared in their hands.

Tom gestured Annie to get the door.

Scared so bad she shook, Annie walked over to the door. In Spanish, she asked, "Who's there?"

The half-whispered reply was also in Spanish. "A friend, madam."

In English, she tried, "What's your handle?"

"Mac."

She opened the door to a black-haired, blue-eyed Irishman with killer dimples.

He took a quick look down the stairwell, then leaped into the apartment, shoving Annie out of the way in the process. He closed the door fast, slowing at the last second to ease the latch shut silently.

"Sorry, ma'am, but I was being followed. I had to get in here before they saw where I went."

Tex raced silently across the room, a pair of binoculars coming out of somewhere on his person as he moved. Annie lost sight of him in the darkened bedroom until she made out his silhouette half-hidden behind her freshly hung curtains.

As fast as Tex moved into the bedroom, Tom moved out of it and closed the door behind him.

Keeping her voice low, Annie asked, "What's going on?"

Tom answered her emotionlessly. "Tex is trying to spot whoever followed Mac. I closed the door so he wouldn't be backlit from the light in here. Don't worry, Annie. Tex is the best spotter in the Air Force. He's got the damnedest eyesight I've ever seen. He knows what he's doing."

She let out the breath she realized she'd been holding. On wobbly legs, she made her way to the sofa and sat down. Tom's transformation into a Special Forces commander had been instantaneous and complete. Gone was the smiling, relaxed man from the bathtub. In his place was this cold, hard stranger who knew his way around guns and dark shadows.

When he spoke again, Tom's voice was perfectly normal. It showed no signs of strain over the last few tense moments.

"Hi, Mac. Glad you could make it. Any reason you felt obliged to bring company to the party?"

"A government guy picked up my tail, and a rebel guy picked up his tail. I couldn't dump them both without being obvious about it, so I had to wait till the last second to get rid of them. I think they're following each other right now."

The door from the bedroom opened. Tex strolled out, as unconcerned as Tom, as if this kind of thing happened every day.

"All clear. Your tails are running around in circles trying to figure out who's chasing who out there. Nice misdirect, Mac. Not bad for a dumb, Irish kid."

Mac flashed a fast hand signal at Tex, and all three men chuckled. She had to get Tom to teach her that sign language.

"Macready Angus Conlon, this is Annie O'Donnell. I gather you've met already."

He nodded at her. "Yes. At the embassy and again at the hospital. Thanks for your help with our commander."

"My pleasure."

Annie wasn't surprised when Tom wasted no more time on pleasantries.

"Tex has given me a quick overview of the situation, Mac. We were just starting to discuss egressing Gavarone. Any thoughts?"

"Yes. I've been working in a government supply depot

the last month or so, and I pick up juicy tidbits now and again. In fact, we spent all day today issuing ammunition to the troops. Word has it the rebels are planning an all-out attack on the coast highway tonight.''

Annie gasped. According to her situation briefing at the embassy yesterday, that was the last major road into or out of St. George that the government still controlled. If it fell to the rebels, the city would be surrounded and effectively under siege.

Mac glanced at her and continued. ''If you were a little stronger, sir, I'd suggest we leave this minute and head for the ocean.''

''If we've got to go now, I'll manage.''

The Irishman frowned and his brogue abruptly disappeared. ''Major Folly, sir. With all due respect, don't BS me. I've been in this business nearly as long as you. You can't handle the trip, and you sure as hell can't swim twelve miles out into the ocean to get to international waters for a Navy pickup.''

Annie piped up. ''I second that. I've been at your side for seven weeks, Tom, and you're in no condition to move yet. You've only been conscious a couple days, and walking for less than one.''

Tex dived in. ''Well, then. We'll hunker down and wait this thing out until you're ready to go, Hoss.''

Annie looked at Tom. ''Hoss?''

''My handle. And don't ask.''

Tex and Mac grinned widely, but said nothing. Annie knew a challenge when she saw one. Sooner or later she'd get one of them to tell her where ''Hoss'' came from.

The conversation drifted into small talk. A few war stories were swapped, and Tex updated Tom on how the other members of the team were fairing.

Annie went to the refrigerator to get refills on drinks and was surprised when Mac joined her in the kitchenette.

"How much morphine is the major taking, Miss O'Donnell?"

"Call me Annie, and he's down to two pills every twelve hours."

"Do you happen to know the status of his injuries?"

"His ribs and the left forearm aren't fully healed yet, and he complained about his right collarbone a little while ago. But beyond that, he seems to be mostly healed."

"Hallelujah. We may just make it out of here alive, then."

"You mean that's in any doubt?"

He gave her a long look and then answered, his voice candid. "You were holed up in that hospital a long time. The situation has gotten very bad in St. George the last few weeks. There's going to be bloodshed and lots of it before this is over, and the rebels are fanatically anti-American."

"What about the government? Won't they help the Americans get out?"

"They're trying to gain support from the population and have taken up a new anti-American stance. Besides, they're too busy covering their own behinds to worry about ours. We're on our own."

Dread burst forth inside Annie. "We've got to get out of here before the lid blows, Mac. How much time do you think we have?"

"Hopefully a few days, maybe no more than hours. If this rumored rebel attack on the coast highway pans out, it's probably going to draw an all-out response from the government."

Annie stared, wide-eyed, at him. "I had no idea it was so close. What are we going to do?"

He shrugged and gave her a grim look.

"Hey, what are you two whispering about over there?"

Annie turned away. Hastily she poured a glass of iced

tea and carried it to Tom. "Mac was just telling me the rebels don't like Americans."

Tom nodded slowly. "That's a fact. They certainly tried their best to kill us in the jungle."

Tex commented, "You'd have thunk there was a big ol' reward for our scalps, the way they came after us. 'Coon hounds couldn't have chased us harder. Speaking of such things, I hear the American Embassy's pulling out all its folks day after tomorrow. You gonna be leaving us, ma'am…I mean, Annie?"

The embassy staff was pulling out? The gravity of her situation hit Annie so hard it knocked the breath out of her.

Tom answered for her. "She can't leave with the embassy personnel. Annie gave up her diplomatic immunity when she yanked me out of the hospital. She's coming out with us."

Tom's men were silent, but a dismayed look passed between them.

She cleared her throat. "Look, guys. I don't want to be a burden to you. Major Folly's going to be enough for you to handle when you leave. I can make my own way out of town. I know the area pretty well, and I have some contacts. I'll work something out."

Tom was on his feet in front of her in the blink of an eye. He grabbed her by her upper arms and glared down at her.

"That's enough of that. Don't you even think about leaving on your own. Got it?"

"But…"

"That's a direct order, Annie, with all the authority of the Uniform Code of Military Justice behind it. Do you understand me?"

Sheesh. He didn't have to get so worked up about it. "I understand."

"You're with us, and this team doesn't leave anybody

behind. It's why my guys didn't get out seven weeks ago, and it's why I'm not even bothering to ask them to leave without me now. We live or die together. Like it or not, Annie, you're part of that deal for now.''

Tex and Mac murmured their agreement.

She looked at the grim faces of the three men. It obviously wouldn't do any good to argue with them, but she was troubled by the arrangement. Their leader was already hurt, and she'd be yet another liability to them. But she had enough experience with stubborn men to know these three had dug in their heels and wouldn't be budged on this one.

She sighed. ''Well, I guess that's settled, then. I'm going with you guys. But just for the record, there's no way on God's green earth I can swim twelve miles to get to a ship.''

Tom grinned down at her. ''Wimp. I guess we'll have to get you a boat and the rest of us will swim behind it and push you.''

''Gimme a break.''

Tex shrugged. ''We've done worse before.''

The smile faded from Annie's face. Holy mackerel. Tom wasn't kidding. What kinds of superheroes were these guys?

Annie woke up abruptly sometime after midnight, unsure of what had startled her out of her sleep.

There it was again. A faint noise, like rain hitting a metal roof. Except it sounded like it was coming from far away. She lay on the couch for several minutes, staring at the ceiling. The refrigerator rattled and then settled down to humming quietly. She didn't hear the noise again.

Restless, she rolled over a couple times, trying to get comfortable in her uncomfortable bed on the sofa.

A sharp noise jerked her upright. It was much closer this time. Much louder. And it sounded like…

That was gunfire! Right down the street.

And then another sound, one that caused her to leap to her feet. Tom groaned as if he were in pain.

Ohmigosh. Was he hit?

She raced into the bedroom and found him tossing on the bed, fast asleep. She sat down on the edge of the bed and reached out to soothe his forehead.

This time she wasn't quite as startled when he jerked her down beside him and whispered, "Get down, for chrissake, Jackie. They'll shoot you."

"Tom. Tom, it's Annie. Wake up."

Slowly he roused from his dream. His eyes opened, and his gaze locked on to her face. Gradually his eyes focused on her.

"Annie. What are you doing here?"

"You were having a bad…"

She broke off as a burst of gunfire sounded practically outside the window.

He rolled completely on top of her, crushing her. "Stay down," he ordered.

Annie replied dryly. "I had that one figured out, thanks. Besides, I couldn't move if I wanted to."

With a flash of white teeth, he grinned and rolled off her and on to the floor before Annie could stop him. She watched him…slither was the only word for it…to the window. He eased himself up under the curtain and peered cautiously outside.

He slithered back to the bed.

"Get on the floor on the far side of the bed."

Annie rolled off the bed, doing her best to imitate his liquid movements. It was harder than it looked. He started to drag the mattress toward the living room. As soon as she realized what he was up to, she crawled over and pushed the clumsy mattress from behind.

Once they'd horsed the thing into the living room, they

stretched out side by side on the narrow double mattress, each lying very still in their mutual awkwardness. In the silence following another volley of shots, Tom pulled down her pillow and blankets from the sofa.

"We may as well get comfortable. Those snipers are going to be out there a while."

"There are *snipers* out there?"

"Welcome to the Gavronese revolution, Annie."

"What are you saying?" Her mind refused to grasp the implication of his words.

"Congratulations. You've just entered a war zone."

"Maybe it's just some of those drunks Tex was talking about."

Tom fluffed the lone pillow and drew her close so they could share it. He pulled the blanket over them and tucked her head into the crook of his shoulder.

"Sorry. Those are government and rebel soldiers down there firing at each other."

"You're sure of that?"

"I chased a bunch of rebel uniforms through the jungle not too long ago, and I don't believe the government has changed its markings recently. Yup, I'm sure."

"Good Lord." So. War had come. The realization was beyond sobering. It was chilling. Absolutely terrifying.

"Welcome to my world, angel."

She didn't know whether to laugh at the absurdity of finding herself in the middle of a war zone, or to cry at the tragedy of Tom living in this bizarre, dangerous world.

"What do we do now?"

"We rest, and we wait for morning. The shooting will stop when it gets light out. You may as well get comfortable. We're gonna be here the rest of the night."

"And you live like this voluntarily?"

He shrugged under her ear. "I don't like war zones. But somebody's got to do this job, and I've got the skills to do it safely." He paused while another burst of gunfire exploded outside. "Or at least as safely as is possible under the circumstances," he added.

Annie shivered against him.

"Relax and try to get some sleep."

"You're kidding, right?"

"No, not at all. There's nothing we can do but ride it out."

"There's no way I'll ever sleep with bullets flying outside my window."

Humor tinged his voice. "You'd be surprised. If you get tired enough, you can sleep just about anyplace, anytime, including the middle of a war. Besides, this isn't that bad. There aren't rockets and mortars exploding all around us."

"Gee, that's reassuring."

A silent chuckle vibrated his chest. She snuggled closer to him, grateful for the solid feel of him against her. Just knowing he was beside her was reassuring. As long as she was with him, she'd be safe. He'd promised to take care of her, and he would keep that promise.

He rolled on his side and gathered her against his chest. "I have to say, you feel a lot nicer to hole up with than any of my guys."

"You mean you cuddle with them like this, too?"

A snort of laughter escaped him. "Hardly. I may be close to my guys, but we're not *that* close."

"That's a relief."

The moment of humor subsided slowly as they enjoyed a lull in the shooting.

After a particularly prolonged and loud exchange of gunfire, Annie whispered, "Tom, are you asleep?"

"No."

"Do you mind if we talk some? Maybe it'd help keep my mind off the shooting."

"What would you like to talk about?"

She thought about it for a second. "You said the name Jackie in your sleep. Who's he?"

Tom's voice was ice. "She. Pick another topic."

Wow. She must have hit a raw nerve, there.

"You seemed really upset by your dream. I'm just trying to look out for your health and well-being, here."

"So you're a psychologist, now, are you?" he challenged.

"It doesn't take a Ph.D. to know when something's upsetting somebody," she retorted.

He exhaled hard. "You're not going to leave this alone, are you?"

"Nope."

His voice went dangerously calm. "Jackie is a woman who betrayed me and my team. She led us into a trap, and her father—a world-class drug smuggler—and his cronies shot the hell out of us. They killed one of my guys, ended the career of another and damn near killed the rest of us. We all got out of there with multiple gunshot wounds."

"Was she beautiful?"

"Now why would you ask a question like that?" he challenged.

"Call it female intuition."

She felt him shake his head in the dark. "Yeah. She was so beautiful it hurt to look at her. I think every guy on the team was half in love with her."

Including him? Annie gulped. Wow. Being betrayed by someone he fancied himself in love with must have been awful.

Her arms crept around him of their own volition. He'd suffered so much in his career. It was too much for his country to ask of him. If only she'd known him before she had to make that decision over the jungle. Maybe she'd have chosen differently. And maybe he wouldn't have been hurt. And maybe, a reasonable corner of her brain argued, they would all have died.

For all she knew, a stray bullet could ricochet into this room and she or Tom might die tonight. Nothing was certain in war. She cast about for another topic that would distract her.

"Okay. Here's another one for you, Tom. How did you get the nickname Hoss?"

He grunted. "We're not going there, no matter how scared you are."

"Aw, come on. There must be story behind a name like that. Are you named after the television cowboy?"

"No, and I'm not going to tell you any more about it. It's not fit for a lady's ears."

She couldn't argue with that. If he thought she was a lady, far be it from her to disabuse him of the notion.

He interrupted her thoughts. "Okay, it's my turn to ask a question."

"I suppose that's fair," she replied.

"Why this career?"

"You mean why did I join the Air Force or why did I become a pilot?"

"Both."

"I joined the Air Force to get away from home. I come from a teeny little town in Iowa. I was expected to marry my childhood sweetheart, become something safe and traditional like a schoolteacher, have some kids and die there of old age or boredom, whichever came first."

"So you rebelled against your hometown?"

"I rebelled against my father. He's a retired army colonel and controlled every detail of my life. He only had daughters, and he always complained about not having a son to follow in his footsteps. I suppose on some level I joined the military in hopes of gaining his approval."

"And did you?"

Annie sighed. "Not hardly. Girls don't belong in the military according to him."

"Why did you choose to fly?"

She laughed. "I like roller coasters."

"Come again?"

"I like being upside down and going the speed of heat with my hair on fire. Flying's fun."

He commented dryly, "Except when you're getting shot at."

His words were a cold slap across her face. Flying also was no fun when she was faced with life-and-death decisions that terribly wounded another human being.

They needed to change the subject. Now. She said lightly, "It's my turn, again. So, tell me about yourself, Tom."

"What do you want to know?" he asked cautiously.

"Where are you from?"

"Norman, Oklahoma."

"Brothers and sisters?"

"One of each."

"You're the oldest."

"How could you tell?"

Annie laughed. "You're joking, right? You've got responsible eldest sibling written all over you. Let's see. What else?" She adopted what she hoped was a breezy tone. "Are you married?"

"Nope."

"Ever been married?"

"Nope."

"Did you ever want to be?"

He answered indignantly, "You don't have to ask that in the past tense. It's not like I'm too old to get married, you know."

"Sorry. Do you want to be married someday?"

"Maybe someday. I can't see doing it with my present

career. It's not fair to ask a woman to love a guy who may die tomorrow.''

That silenced her. A girl would be foolish, indeed, to fall in love with a guy who might die tomorrow. But a guy like that wasn't bad to be with on the floor of a dark room, in the middle of the night, while a revolution raged outside the window.

Chapter 6

Sunlight shone painfully in Tom's eyes, bringing him abruptly awake. He shifted his arm under a strange weight and realized it was Annie's head.

He ached from head to foot, as if he'd been worked over with a baseball bat. He was really going soft in his old age. Sleeping on a floor had never left him feeling quite this lousy before. For the first time in his career, doubt coiled in his gut. Was he going to be able to get his team and Annie out of this one alive?

He suppressed the thought violently. Thinking like that would certainly get them killed. There was no room for hesitation in his world, no mercy for those who looked back over their shoulders. They *would* make it out...somehow.

But meanwhile he felt like death warmed over.

He must've groaned because Annie popped up on her elbow beside him.

"Are you all right? Did I hurt you?"

"No, I'm just a little sore this morning."

"I know the perfect cure for that."

"Oh, yeah?"

She started to sit up but stopped partway. "Is it safe to sit up now?"

"Yup. The shooting stopped a couple hours ago. All the toy soldiers have gone to bed. They won't come out again until tonight."

"Tonight? You mean we have to go through that hell again?"

"'Fraid so."

Her look of dismay was so cute, he nearly dragged her down on top of him to kiss it away. "Why don't you tell me about this surefire cure of yours for all these aches and pains of mine? You don't happen to have a bottle of whiskey stowed around here somewhere, do you?"

"No such luck. I had this in mind." Her hands settled on him, and she began kneading the muscles of his shoulder and neck.

His whole left side went warm and relaxed under her touch, and his eyes drifted closed. He pushed away the guilt of being safe and comfortable while his men were out there dodging bullets. Just this once he would let himself enjoy the moment.

"I've died and gone to Heaven. You could do this to every inch of me and I wouldn't complain."

Her hands paused for a moment, but she didn't answer.

He opened one eye to peer at her. There it was. That rosy shade her cheeks got when she was embarrassed. She looked down, concentrating on massaging his palm where it protruded from the cast. Who'd have guessed a hand was such an erogenous zone? But as her fingertips slid between the bases of his fingers and drifted across his palm, the tingly friction definitely influenced other parts of his anatomy.

"How can you be so sure there's going to be more shooting tonight, Tom?"

"Because the war has started. After you fell asleep, there were some bright flashes from the direction of the coast highway. The rebels undoubtedly shelled it last night, which means the city's surrounded and the government's cornered. The army's going to have to engage the rebels now. There's nowhere else to run."

Her hands stilled on his ribs, which was just as well. He'd die before he let on how ticklish he was.

"Then there's nowhere else for us to run, either."

He shrugged, feigning a nonchalance he didn't quite feel. "I've been in tighter fixes. St. George has a large civilian population for us to hide in. Besides, the rebels need the people's support. They're not going to start killing women and children anytime soon."

"So where does that leave you?"

That was a darn good question, and he didn't much like the possible answers. He opened one eye to peer up at her lazily as she started massaging his other arm. "Lying low."

She didn't respond to that. He tried to relax under her soothing touch. He had to get control of his jitters. Tom concentrated on the massage. It reminded him of having a cat perched on him, kneading him with its paws. The only thing missing was claws. Annie's were sheathed for now. At least, they were going to be until he asked her what he was about to.

"Annie, I need you to do me a favor."

"Shoot."

"I want you to go out and do some reconnoitering."

Her hands froze. "Me? I thought that's what your guys were supposed to do."

"They can't get into the American Embassy unnoticed."

"Neither can I. I'm probably a fugitive by now."

"We'll disguise you."

"I dunno…"

Her expression was doubtful, laced with apprehension. Normally he wouldn't remotely consider sending out one of his men who was in a mental state like hers. But this wasn't a normal situation. Everything about this mission was messed up.

"Trust me. It'll be all right."

"Why do you need me to go to the embassy?"

"To find out if we can count on the American government to help us get out of here. Plus, I need to send my complete mission report to the States."

"You can't use any of your fancy gizmos to transmit it stateside?"

"The material in it is too sensitive to risk having it intercepted."

"I don't think I can do it undetected…."

"Sure you can. I'll show you how. Do you have a dress or something that a local woman might wear?"

"Yes."

"Go put it on. And if you've got one of those increase-your-cleavage bras, put it on, too."

Her eyebrows shot up. "I beg your pardon?"

"Just do it. I'll explain when you get back. Oh, and bring me your passport." He turned to dig in his rucksack. "While you're at it, put on a little too much makeup!" he called over his shoulder.

He found what he was looking for and stretched out on the sofa to wait till Annie returned. He could still feel her hands sliding over him in that knowing way. It was almost spooky having a woman be so comfortable with his body. He never stuck around long enough in relationships for that kind of familiarity to develop.

It was seductive for damn sure. He could sink into that easy comfort with nary a struggle, just like quicksand. Annie would trap him the same way—all smooth and nonthreatening on the surface, but deadly dangerous to stumble into and impossible to get out of.

He blinked when he realized she was standing beside the couch, giving him a quizzical look. He jumped up, startled, and winced when ice picks of pain stabbed his legs.

"Okay, Sherlock, now what?" she asked.

A floral-print dress made of a clingy fabric swirled around her figure, caressing her curves outrageously.

Perfect. He grinned. "Elementary, my dear Watson. Unbutton your dress."

Incipient outrage gathered in her snapping green gaze. "Now look here, Tom…"

He cut her off briskly. "We need to work on this trust thing, Annie. I'm not going to take advantage of you." He held out his hand. "Give me your passport."

"You can forget me undressing for you."

He raised a single eyebrow and gave her his most intimidating "Oh, yeah?" look. "I swear there won't be any hanky-panky. Now hand over your passport and get going on those buttons."

She gave him the document, eyeing him suspiciously. While he folded two thin sheets of paper and slipped them between the pages of her passport, she reached for the top button in the row that traveled the length of her dress. He tore his gaze away from the erotic sight of her fumbling at her buttons, the cloth falling away tantalizingly beneath her fingers.

He picked up a self-adhesive gauze bandage and spoke as casually as he could around the thickness in his throat. "My report's inside your passport. There are two copies of it. One is for Ambassador Kettering, here in Gavarone. The other one needs to go by diplomatic pouch or secure fax to the address on the top of the page. It's Eyes Only stuff so don't hand it over to any old clerk, okay?"

"Handling classified documents is part of my job, Tom. I know what to do."

Annie's fingers fell away from her front, and the dress gaped open.

Hot blood surged in his loins, and his pants suddenly felt tight. The thin cotton fabric of her dress clung to every nuance of her body, and a vertical slash of tanned stomach promised unholy delights.

He dragged his gaze upward. She blushed shyly, her face averted. Didn't she know the curve of her cheek was exciting in its girl-next-door purity?

His zipper grated irritatingly against his throbbing flesh. Dammit. This was business.

"Lift your arms, please."

Surely his voice didn't sound as hoarse to her as it did to him. He cleared his throat.

Annie complied in silence.

He took a step forward. It brought him close enough to smell the fragrance of a frilly soap clinging to her skin.

"I'm going to tape your passport to you, now." He reached out, but paused, inches from her warmth.

She jumped when his palms contacted her sides. Ignoring her widened pupils and her sharp little intake of breath, he wound the bandage around her, securing the passport just below her bra.

"If the police arrest you and find this, stick to your cover. You're an American whose husband was hurt in a climbing accident. You're going to the embassy to arrange safe passage out of Gavarone. You're worried about the rebels and have hidden your passport so it won't get stolen."

"What if they look inside it and find your report?"

"It's encoded. Tell them it's secret directions from a treasure map, and your husband's paranoid that someone will get to the loot before he can go back for it. That's a weird enough story that they ought to buy it.''

Annie smiled, momentarily relaxing beneath his hands. Man, she felt good. He'd like to keep right on touching her, all over her body. The discomfort he was already feeling grew to outright pain at the thought. He dragged his unwilling hands away from her.

While Annie buttoned up her dress, he pulled his pager out of his pocket. His hands weren't quite steady when he reached for her neckline.

She started to recoil, then stilled herself. ''Now what?''

''I want you to wear this.'' He tucked the pager into the impressive cleft of flesh made by her bra. The backs of his fingers brushed the swelling fullness of her breasts. It was as smooth and tempting as he'd imagined it would be. His palms itched to cup her breasts in their entirety.

Discipline, my man. Discipline!

Yeah, right.

''So that's why you wanted me to wear a push-up bra! You wanted to hide that thing on me!'' She sounded inordinately pleased with her powers of deductive reasoning.

He forced his mind to the business at hand. ''Exactly. When you come back here, I'll be watching for you out the window. If you're followed, I'll page you. The pager will vibrate with three one-second bursts in quick succession. If that happens, keep walking. Lose the tail and then come back to this street and try again. I'll keep paging you until you're clean. Got it?''

She looked alarmed, but her voice was reasonably calm. ''Got it.''

''If you get into trouble, push the square button on the end of the pager. That'll send a panic call out to the rest of my team. You sit tight wherever you are, and they'll find you. This thing has a homing feature in it.''

''Is this your pager, Tom?''

"Yeah."

"What will you do if *you* get into trouble? You need this more than I do." She reached into her bra for the device.

He put his hand over hers, trapping it against her breast. "You keep it. I insist. I can take care of myself."

"But…"

"No buts. It's an order. I know what's best, remember?"

She scowled at him, but thankfully didn't argue.

"Now for the pièce de résistance." He pulled a bushy black wig out from behind him.

Annie took one look at it and burst out laughing. "Are you kidding? I'd look like a hooker in that thing. I'll stick out like a sore thumb!"

"Put it on and then go into the bathroom and brush it out. Maybe pull it back into a ponytail or put it up. Do some girl stuff to it."

"Not even girl stuff's gonna help that rug. Where did you get it?"

"I got it in Mexico. And it's a perfectly fine wig. It's saved my butt more than once, I'll have you know."

"Will you try it on for me after I get back?" she teased.

He scowled and didn't deign to answer.

Grinning, Annie took it and disappeared into the bathroom.

Tom sagged onto the couch. That woman was going to kill him if he had to look at her and touch her like that again. He was a disciplined guy, but he wasn't made of steel. Hell, a ninety-year-old priest would contemplate sin with a woman like that standing half-naked in front of him.

Now, if she could just get to the embassy and back in one piece. The thought was icy water on his libido. He closed his eyes and let his head fall back against the sofa. He could think of a hundred things that might go wrong, and every one of them had a decent chance of happening today. But he had no choice. He wasn't strong enough yet to do it himself, and time was of the essence. He *had* to get her out of Gavarone and away from him and his team. Still, he hated to put her at risk like this.

He argued with himself. Annie was a military officer, after all, and she did have rudimentary training for this sort of work. When it came right down to it, she had signed up to be put in harm's way. The job needed doing, and she was in line to do it.

He chewed the inside of his cheek.

He'd shoot himself if anything happened to her.

Annie stepped out of the bathroom. How she'd managed to create a nice hairdo with his wig he'd never know, but she looked great. He stepped back to survey her critically.

"You've got the hooker look almost right. Come here, and I'll make the last little adjustment."

She stepped close, looking up at him curiously.

Quickly, before he could think better of it, he took her face in both of his hands and kissed her.

She tasted of wicked temptation and sinful delights. He shouldn't be doing this. It was wrong. It was unprofessional. It was completely impossible for him to stop.

He opened his mouth, asking her to surrender to the kiss.

She didn't need much encouragement. She melted into him, pressing that body of hers against his, every luscious inch welcoming him. He groaned and slipped his arms around her, molding her more closely to his frame.

Her hands plunged into his hair, pulling his head closer. She tasted him as greedily as he tasted her, their tongues clashing and wrestling like lovers. The couch beckoned him to pull her down with him and take all of her. Hell, the floor would do right now. A rage to have her flooded him, driving him mindlessly onward.

Suddenly, he stopped himself. Business, dammit! His team needed to get out of Gavarone without a woman in tow, and he owed it to Annie to get her out of this hellhole alive, purity intact.

He released her and staggered back a step. "Sorry about that. You looked too perfect."

She stared at him in disbelief. "So you kissed me?"

"You needed mussing up. That seemed the most efficient way to do it."

She looked confused as all get-out, but at least he'd managed to distract her.

"Well then." She cleared her throat nervously. "I'm all for efficiency. So how do I look now?"

She looked like a fallen angel dying to sin with him.

"Uhh, fine. You look fine. And you don't look like a hooker, by the way."

"I'll take that as a compliment. I think."

"It was. Sort of."

She stuck her tongue out at him as he escorted her to the door.

"Stay calm and keep your wits about you. Don't take any chances. If you can't make it into the embassy undetected, don't push it. We'll find some other way."

He unlatched the door and opened it for her.

"And remember not to let your gaze dart around. Don't walk too fast or too slow. Go with the flow of traffic. Keep your shoulders back and down. And don't clench your fists or show tension...."

"Yes, mother. I'll be careful."

She was grinning at him.

He returned her grin ruefully. "Okay, I'll shut up. You be safe out there."

"I will. But thanks for worrying about me."

"You're welcome."

He shut the door and turned to look at the empty apartment. He sighed. He purely hated waiting. Especially when he'd sent one of his people into danger and was helpless to protect them.

Annie peered out a side entrance of the American Embassy. The street looked harmless enough. So why couldn't she force her feet to carry her back outside? Only after achieving the safety of her embassy had she realized how fear had been her constant shadow these past few days. She was loath to leave the embrace of American soil and venture once more into the dangers of St. George.

But Tom was waiting for her. He needed her. She had to return his beeper to him. A bead of sweat formed and rolled slowly between her shoulder blades, gathering speed and rushing down her back into oblivion. She dragged her feet forward, took a deep breath and crossed the threshold into peril.

Gavarone's muggy heat slugged her in the gut. She stumbled, then moved doggedly onward. Although she slipped into the pedestrian traffic, Annie got an instant feeling that someone was following her.

It was probably just paranoia. But she felt as if a pair of burning eyeballs were boring into her back. She repeated Tom's instructions over and over and prayed they would be enough.

Her steps followed, one after another, relentlessly carrying her farther and farther from the embassy and safety. A terrible certainty set in that she was going to be caught.

She had no business being out here. This attaché posting was supposed to be a cushy one in a tropical backwater with lots of sun, sand and exotic fruit drinks. Rebels and guns and arrests weren't part of the deal. Tom and his men were depending on her, and she was going to let them down.

As a kid she'd imagined how exciting it would be to get involved in some supersecret espionage operation for her country. But this was too real. Too frightening. She'd never realized what it would be like to work without a safety net.

She wasn't trained in an array of survival skills, nor was she ironman fit, with nerves of steel. Heck, she wasn't even a student of warfare. Tom was prepared to operate in this kind of environment, but she wasn't.

She'd gotten so caught up in her fantasy of being part of a wildly cool squad like Tom's that she'd waded in way over her head. And here she was, alone and completely vulnerable, her no-kidding life on the line. She'd made a dreadful, terrible mistake.

No matter what advice Tom had given her, Annie's hands began to shake uncontrollably. Her legs felt like Jell-O, and her insides ran like water. Despite herself, her stride lengthened and her pace quickened. After a few blocks she realized she was practically running. She slowed her pace, her breath heaving.

And then it began again, the insidious panic that spurred her to walker faster and faster until she thought she was going to explode.

Light-headed with terror, she slowed herself again.

And again.

It was an interminable nightmare, but she made her way across town without bolting completely. If someone was following her, they were letting her go to see where she led them. At least Tom would know what to do. He'd take care of whatever mess she'd gotten herself into.

She managed by a thread to hold herself together. Only the thought of Tom sustained her when her anxiety became unbearable. He was her safe port in this wild ocean of unseen dangers.

As she finally reached the street their apartment building was on, she forced herself to stop at a street market. While she picked out some fresh sea bass—the locals called it corvina—for supper, she checked for the person who'd followed her.

Over there. That man in the gray pants and white shirt. Had she seen him when she left the embassy? Or what about that man in the leather jacket? Surely it was too warm a day for a coat like that. Or maybe that elderly woman browsing at the fruitstand next door. She looked as if she was moving too nimbly for her age. Oh, God. Now what to do?

Annie's thoughts tumbled in confusion. Should she try to lose her invisible follower now or go straight back home the way Tom had told her to? As much as she craved his protection, she dared not endanger Tom. He wasn't healthy enough to take on anything really deadly that she might lead back to him. Now what?

Tom's voice echoed in her head. *We need to work on this trust thing.* Trust. Tom would know what to do. He'd said to go straight back to the apartment. Well then, that's what she'd do.

Her back tingled with imaginary knives burying themselves in her spine. Her hands still shook, but there was nothing to do about that except clench her purse tightly and hope no one noticed her white knuckles.

She hummed a song in her head and forced herself to walk to its rhythm. Every instinct begged her to run screaming for cover. But she knew without a shadow of a doubt that giving in to the impulse would get her and Tom killed. Strolling toward home was an exercise in the self-discipline of sheer terror.

How in the world did Tom do stuff like this every day? She'd have a nervous breakdown if she had to live like this. Of course, that's why she wasn't in the Special Forces and Tom was.

He could have this job.

So then, why in the world was she playing at it?

The answer stopped her cold in the middle of the street. Because of Tom. She was out here risking her neck for him. She wanted to impress him. It was the dumbest thing she'd ever heard of, but here she was. Incredulity rooted her in place.

A horn honked right behind her, and Annie all but jumped out of her skin. She lurched into motion and moved out of the middle of the street.

As she caught sight of the apartment building where Tom waited, her breathing quickened even more. He'd have her in sight by now. The feel of his intense blue gaze on her overwhelmed every other sensation. She was pulled toward it, drawn to Tom by a force too deep, too fundamental to ignore.

Tom's beeper felt heavy and hot in her bra, burning against her skin. It reminded her of his blunt fingers brushing her flesh as he deposited the device between her breasts.

The beeper was perfectly still as she walked down the street. A film of sweat covered her face. As casually as she could, she wiped it away. There wasn't even a hint of vibration from the beeper.

What if something had happened to Tom? What if the Gavronese Army had found him? Then he wouldn't be able to signal her if she was being followed. The sensation of being watched intensified.

She was definitely being followed.

Come on, Tom. Page me. Let me know you're up there watching and you see the tail.

Nothing.

Now what?

Did she proceed as if everything was okay, or did she assume something had happened to Tom and keep on going? What if the Gavronese Army was waiting for her in the apartment when she got there? If only she'd had more training in how to deal with situations like this.

The door to their apartment building was beside her. She stared at its yawning blackness, torn in two by doubt and paralyzing indecision.

What the heck. Tom had said to trust him. If he wasn't good enough to evade capture while hidden away in an obscure apartment, then he surely wasn't good enough to get her out of Gavarone alive. Better that she get arrested now while the United States still had a presence in the country.

She veered into the doorway and hurried up the three flights of steps to their apartment. Annie reached their door out of breath and knocked quietly.

A gravelly voice answered from inside in Spanish.

Annie's stomach did a spectacular flip. Oh, God, oh, God, oh, God. They'd gotten Tom. And she was next.

Her pulse exploded, and she panted in raw fear. She fumbled for the beeper's panic button as she spun around to flee.

The door opened. An arm snaked out and grabbed her upper arm. She started to scream as the arm yanked her inside, but a brutal hand slapped over her mouth, cramming the scream back between her teeth.

The door shut behind her, and she couldn't see a thing in the darkness. Someone had blacked out all the windows.

A powerful body pinned her facing the wall beside the door, and she struggled in animalistic terror.

"I'm an American citizen. I demand to speak to my embassy," she managed to force out past the hand over her mouth.

She was dragged backward and strong arms wrapped around her in a fierce bear hug.

"Annie, it's me, Tom. You're safe. I've got you now."

Thank God.

All the strength went out of her in a rush, and she sagged against him. His hand eased away from her mouth.

Tom hung on tight to Annie and rocked her close while she cried out her fear and relief. He'd always envied women their ability to let go of their emotions so freely. He was none too steady himself at the moment. He'd stood at that window waiting to see her come around the corner for what seemed like a year.

Thank goodness she was all right.

She turned in his arms and buried her nose against his chest. Her arms came up around him, holding on fiercely.

"Why didn't you page me?" Her muffled voice sounded waterlogged.

"Because you weren't followed."

"Are you sure? I could swear I was."

"I'm positive. It's just that you were scared. The same thing happens to me all the time. You did fine."

Her shaking subsided a bit, and she'd recovered enough to look up at him skeptically.

"What do you mean, it happens to you all the time? You have nerves of stainless steel. I bet you don't remember what fear is."

He grunted. "Huh. I was afraid—knees-knocking-and-nervous-sweats afraid—the whole time you were gone, Annie."

She ducked her head against his chest once more.

He buried his nose in her hair and inhaled the fresh scent of it. His hands roamed up and down her back as he reassured himself she was unhurt. The elegant indentation of her spine drew his fingertips, and he caressed the line of her back down to the first hint of her buttocks.

She drew a short breath and molded herself even closer to him, her body giving way under the gentle pressure of his hand. Her hips flowed into his, their bodies intimately and perfectly aligned to each other. The softness of her belly complemented the hardness of his, and her breasts burned against his chest like fire.

How could he have sent her out there by herself? She was too precious to have put at risk.

Too precious?

Oh, Lord. What had he gotten himself into? The sense of impending doom that had been hanging over him ever since he woke up in the hospital moved a step closer. A giant step closer.

He backed her against the wall so his hands could continue their explorations. They ran down her slender arms and raised fine goose bumps under his palms. His fingers twined with hers, and he lifted her hands up over her head, trapping them against the wall.

Their fingers still clasped, he leaned into her, savoring the length of her body against his. He looked down at her, and she stared back at him wordlessly.

Naked desire warmed the dazed expression in her eyes.

His gaze slid lower to the pulse leaping in her throat, and lower still to the rapid rise and fall of her chest. Each breath she drew pressed her breasts against him in sensual invitation.

He ached to bury his face in the shadowed cleft of her bosom, to smell her and taste her, to lose himself in her. With one hand he reached down to stroke from her collarbone toward the subtle valley of flesh.

His fingers encountered hard plastic, almost hot to the touch. He grasped his beeper and drew it slowly from its enviable nest.

Annie's breath wobbled, catching in a sexual way.

He pocketed the pager and let his hungry fingers return to the exposed flesh of her neck. Delicate tendons and a racing pulse danced beneath her satin skin.

She shifted, and he captured her free hand with his before she could move away. He pinned her hands overhead once more, sandwiching both of hers in the grasp of his left hand.

He leaned down, touching the base of her neck with his

lips. Her pulse startled and leaped like a deer. His mouth traveled upward, pausing to sample the feminine delicacy just below her ear.

She inhaled sharply, and her head rolled back, stopped only by the wall. He pulled away momentarily to look at her radiant beauty. It lit the gloom around them, a lighthouse in the storm-tossed darkness of his world.

Her lips parted, sweet and inviting.

She didn't have to ask him twice. He grasped her chin gently and lowered his head. His mouth closed over hers.

Annie groaned as Tom finally got around to kissing her. Stretched on a rack of agonizing anticipation, the torture of wanting him was so great she could hardly stand it. Helpless to move with her hands trapped high against the wall, she could only use her body to communicate her desire. She writhed against him, glorying in the hardness of his frame and in the way her body yielded to his.

She ached to hold him within her, to cradle his strength against her, to be safe within his embrace, to shield him with her love. All of this she poured into her kiss and into the sensual undulations of her body against his.

His response was immediate and overwhelming. One powerful arm went around her shoulders and another around her waist. He swept her up against him while they pirouetted away from the wall in a dizzying embrace.

She clung to him, her arms around his neck, supported by his broad shoulders. Their spinning kiss carried them across the room to the sofa. He guided her to the cushions, following her down, covering her in a blanket of potent male, all muscle and power.

His thigh wedged between hers, and she gave way before the pressure. An elbow on either side of her head caged her beneath him while he kissed her into mindless oblivion.

She ran her hands into his hair and pulled his head closer,

deepening their kiss until she couldn't tell where he ended and she began.

He groaned, and she relished the sound, taking it into her and holding it in her heart. In return, she wordlessly offered up her remorse and self-recrimination for almost killing this wonderful man. She poured it all into kissing him, into treasuring and cherishing him. If only she could make it up to him somehow.

Her arms tightened around him.

Tom grasped her tightly in return, and then suddenly he shifted his weight to one side.

Startled, she was dragged with him as he rolled off the couch and onto the floor. They landed with a solid thump. Annie sprawled across him in the most delicious fashion, body to body in a nakedly suggestive pose.

And then her hand contacted the cast on his left arm. Her ardor cooled abruptly as shame filled her. She rolled off him instantly, appalled by the thoughtlessness of her lust.

"Oh, no, Tom. Did I hurt you? Are you all right?"

"I don't care if you hurt me. Just don't stop, sweetheart."

She ignored his comment and continued her self-flagellation. "I'll kill myself if I hurt you again."

"What do you mean 'again'?"

She froze. Did she dare confess all to him? And take a chance on ruining what they had together by admitting that she'd decided to sacrifice his life to save her own and had caused him all these injuries? Could she bear to see rage and disgust in his eyes when he looked at her?

"Hey. Why so grim? I'm grateful for everything you've done for me. Really."

"You're too kind," she protested.

A faint frown creased his brow, but he said nothing.

Suddenly nervous, she wiped her palms surreptitiously

on her dress. "You've never told me the details of your accident. Do you know what happened before you got hurt?"

"Yeah. We were egressing from the jungle and had a rebel squad on our heels. The rest of my guys made it into our pickup helicopter, but the rebels got there before I could get pulled out. The rebels started shooting, and the helicopter pilot decided to get out of there. I ended up getting dragged through the jungle at the end of a steel cable."

She took a convulsive swallow before she could speak. "You must be angry at that pilot."

Tom stared up at the ceiling as though replaying the incident in his mind's eye. "Why do you say that?" he asked absently.

"Well, by rights you should have died. It's a miracle you survived, you know."

He gaze swiveled to her. "Yeah, I know." He was silent for a moment. "The only thing that ticks me off is that the pilot didn't drop me."

Annie blinked. "Drop you?"

"Yeah. If we'd had an experienced Special Forces guy in the cockpit, he'd have cut the cable and left me behind."

"Left you behind? But you said there were rebels on top of your position."

"There were. But they were mostly drug dealers and thugs. City slickers. They didn't know what they were doing out in the bush. I could've run circles around them in that jungle."

"Wouldn't you have been hurt if the cable got cut and you fell?"

"The jungle floor is covered with several feet of dead leaves and plant matter. It's pretty soft. I was only twenty or so feet up when the shooting started. I'd have been fine from that height."

Sick guilt roared through Annie like hot lava. She

wouldn't have had to hurt him. She could've spared him all those weeks of suffering. All she would have had to do was cut him loose. She had no doubt he could've outsmarted and evaded the rebels. She was so stupid! Why hadn't she thought of that?

Because she'd been more worried about getting out alive. About saving her own worthless hide.

"Are you all right, Annie? You look a little pale." His hand stroked down her back in concern.

"Uh, yeah. I'm okay."

"Look. I'm sorry if I scared you when you got back here."

"How did you know it was me?"

"Your step is light like a woman's, and I heard you panic."

"What does panic sound like?"

"Your breathing tripled in about one second flat, and your movements became clumsy. I heard you fumbling for something."

"The panic button on your beeper."

"Ahh." His hand paused in the small of her back. "I'm sorry I had to send you out there. And I shouldn't have taken advantage of your fear by kissing you, either."

"It's all right. You didn't take advantage of me. If anything, I'm the one who's taken advantage of you."

"Mmm, whatever."

He smiled and tightened his arms around her once more. Then he rolled until she lay on her back while he loomed over her.

"Now where were we before we were interrupted by your excessive concern for my fragility?"

Chapter 7

"Wherever we were, we can't go back there, Tom."

He pulled back and stared at her. "Why not? Because we technically work together? That's temporary. I'll fire you if it makes you feel better."

"That's not it."

"Is it because I feel grateful to you for saving my life? You think our relationship's lopsided? I can't change the fact that it happened. Tell you what. The next time you're about to die, I'll save you. Just put it on account, and call us even now."

Annie closed her eyes. It hurt too much to look at him. It wasn't the saving him part that yawned like a chasm between them. It was the killing him part.

"It's not that simple."

"Why not?"

He stared at her expectantly. She should tell him now, just get it off her chest before their relationship went any further. He'd hate her, maybe even kick her out. But she still had time to get to the embassy and evacuate with the other Americans.

She took a deep breath and steeled herself. ''Tom, there's something I need to tell you.''

''I'm listening.''

''It's about…''

A knock sounded in a complicated rhythm on the door. Annie jumped, and Tom's head jerked up.

''That's Tex. Hold your thought.''

He rolled away from her and pushed himself to his feet. Annie frowned at the grimace of pain that flicked across his face. He wasn't resting enough. He was going to push himself too hard and get hurt again. She had to get him into bed somehow.

The irony of the thought struck her, and she smiled wryly as she jumped up and straightened her dress.

The door opened to admit Tex and the tall blond man Tom had referred to as Dutch. They slipped in fast while Tom shut the door quickly behind him.

Tom's voice was terse. ''Were you followed?''

Dutch answered, ''No, but there's a squad of rebels coming down the street looking for someone to harass. We didn't feel like tangling with them.''

''They're out in broad daylight?'' Tom sounded surprised by that. So was she. It was brazen behavior for people who'd be killed on sight by the Gavronese Army.

Tex replied, ''Yup. As big as life. Cocky bast—buggers.''

Tom moved into the bedroom to peer out at the street below. Annie followed, curious to see this rebel menace.

They were impossible to miss. Six young men swaggered down the sidewalk like small-time thugs, while civilians scuttled out of their path. The rebels wore bits and pieces of military uniforms along with the distinctive red berets of the rebel forces pulled down over one ear.

Tom murmured from beside her. "Things are moving faster than I expected. We need more time to set up our escape. But from the looks of those kids, we're about out of time."

Annie followed Tom out into the main room. Dutch was examining the contents of the refrigerator, and Tex slouched on a chair, his legs sprawled out in front of him, his chin on his chest. His eyes were closed and violet shadows underscored them. The guy looked whipped.

Tom spoke from behind her. "Have you gotten any sleep the last couple nights, Tex?"

One eye opened balefully and glared in their general direction. "Sleep's for wimps."

Tom answered dryly. "I'll take that as a no."

Shaking her head, Annie joined Dutch in the kitchen, such as it was. She shooed him aside and poured iced tea while she heated up water for instant coffee. She carried a mug of the hot beverage to Tex.

"Drink up, Superman."

He looked up at her and grinned. "That's me all right. Good ol' Clark Kent himself. Ya wanna play Lois?"

Tom answered for her. "Hey, Superman. Put out the fire in your tights. The lady's not in play."

Tex might be exhausted, but he still gave his boss a steady, assessing look over his mug. A single eyebrow went up questioningly.

Annie watched Tom frown back. The silence stretched out until she couldn't stand it any longer. "What? Do you guys read each other's minds, too?"

All three men looked at her blankly. Tom voiced their thoughts. "Read minds?"

"You guys are staring at each other like you're using a psychic phone link or something."

Tex grinned. "It's an old Indian trick."

Dutch rolled his eyes. "Yeah, and he uses smoke signals, too."

Tex sat up indignantly. "Hey, they worked didn't they? You guys saw us on our side of the river from your side of the river. It would've taken us hours to find each other without my smoke signal that day."

Tom chimed in. "Yeah, and half the Bolivian army found us, too. That was one of the worst egresses of my career. I had to crawl on my belly through mud for three days because of your bright idea."

Tex shrugged. "We made it out, and that's what counts."

"Yeah, we did, didn't we? Speaking of making it out, what's going on out there?" Tom jerked his head in the direction of the street.

Tex answered him. "It's corn-poppin' hot out there. The Americans started pulling out of the embassy about a half hour ago. That's why we hoofed it over here. We thought y'all might want to know in case Miss Annie has reconsidered and is going out the easy way."

Annie jerked as if she'd been slapped. The Americans were leaving *now?*

"I was at the embassy not more than two hours ago and everything was fine! What in the world happened?"

Dutch answered her. "Rumor at the newspaper office has it the Americans got a big bomb threat. One of those get-out-now-or-you're-all-gonna-die things."

Tex nodded. "The Americans are loading their nonessential personnel into helicopters as fast as they can and doin' the boot-scootin' boogie on out of here."

Tom spoke thoughtfully. "Annie, did you see Ambassador Kettering today?"

"No, but I did see my boss, Colonel James. He didn't say a word about any evacuation."

"He'd have kept you at the embassy to leave with them

if he knew about this. Especially since you've lost your diplomatic protection. Whoever threatened the embassy must have done it in a big way. And it's someone Old Ironsides Kettering takes seriously.''

Tex nodded. ''The only serious players in town right now are the government and the rebels.''

Annie interjected. ''No matter how hard the Gavronese government's trying to distance itself from the United States, no government would threaten another's embassy. There'd be too many repercussions to their own embassies abroad.''

Tom nodded. ''Good point. It must've been the rebels, then.''

Annie frowned. ''What kind of armaments could the rebels possibly have that would smoke out the Americans so fast?''

The three men exchanged another one of those pregnant looks before Tom spoke. ''We didn't see everything the rebels have while we were out in the jungle. But what we did see made them just about the best outfitted terrorist group I've ever seen. I wouldn't put it past them to have anything up to and including cruise missiles in their arsenal.''

Annie recalled with a shudder the high-tech radar she'd dodged when she'd flown over the jungle and the shoulder-held missiles that had greeted her there. ''And we have to make our way past that arsenal to get out of here?''

Tom grinned. ''Don't sound so skeptical. Hardware is only as smart as the people using it. We'll just have to outthink them.'' Abruptly Tom changed the subject. ''Tex, does Annie still have time to get to the embassy before they're done evacuating?''

''It'd be tight. They looked like they were in a plenty big hurry.''

''Dammit!'' Tom exclaimed.

Annie piped up. "I won't go to the embassy, anyway. You need me here."

He glared at her. "You're crazy to risk yourself unnecessarily for me and my guys. We can handle ourselves. And besides, I need to get rid of you."

"Yes, but I can help. You and your men don't know Gavarone like I do."

She was nuts for saying it. Goodness only knew she was in over her head already. It was insane to swim even deeper into these shark-infested waters. But she couldn't just abandon them. She couldn't abandon Tom.

"I'm sure you could help us, Annie. But it's more important to me that you get out safely than it is for you to stay with us."

Tex and Dutch nodded. "We have to agree with the major, there, ma'am."

"Thanks for your concern, both of you. But my answer is still no." She folded her arms across her chest belligerently. "I'm not leaving."

"How long would it take you guys to get Annie to the embassy? Maybe it's worth a try."

Tex eyed her critically. "If she's in as good shape as she looks, we could make it in a half hour on foot. But that doesn't take into account getting around our friends outside. With them parked in front of your building, it could take a fair bit longer."

She interjected, "Excuse me, but what part of the word *no* didn't you guys understand?"

Tom ignored her outburst and asked her, "How many people will the embassy lift out?"

She scowled. "There were about twenty staff members there this morning, I'd guess about four will stay behind. And then there are the marines."

"How many of them are there?"

"A dozen or so."

Tex interjected, "All of the marines will stay to hold the fort until the staff weenies get out." He threw her an apologetic look. "No offense, ma'am."

"None taken. I am, in fact, mostly a staff weenie."

Tex grinned. "And a cute weenie, too, if I do say so myself."

Tom cleared his throat. It sounded suspiciously like a growl.

Tex threw a Who-me? look at Tom. "Hey, at least I didn't throw in any cracks about her buns, now, did I?"

Annie stifled a smile. So Tom was jealous of Tex flirting with her, was he? The notion warmed her insides.

Reality check, Annie. Tom's not for you.

Tom sighed. "Well, my dear Annie, you're in luck. I don't think we'll be able to get you to the embassy in time. Plus, if we make a mad dash across town, we'll draw way too much attention to ourselves. You're stuck undercover with us." His rapier-sharp gaze shifted to Tex. "And no cracks about getting under covers with the lady."

Tex threw out his hands. "Li'l ol' me? Why I'd never…"

Tom grinned. "Uh-huh. Why don't you go crash in the bed for a while, pal? You look like day-old roadkill."

"Gee, thanks, boss. I think I will. Wake me up before the sun goes down, will you?"

"Have you got somewhere to be tonight?"

"I need to relieve Howdy. I'll send him over here when he's done with his shift on the spyglass."

"What's he watching?" Tom asked.

"Rebel headquarters."

Annie gasped. "You're that close to the rebels? Are you nuts?"

Tex gave her a lazy, west-Texas grin. "Being nuts is our job, ma'am."

She shook her head. "You guys are certifiable."

"Guilty as charged, Miz Annie." Still grinning, Tex ambled off to bed.

Dutch rose and shrugged into a photographer's vest. He shouldered the camera he'd been carrying when he came in. "I need to shove off, sir. I'm supposed to be out covering the rebels and doing a piece on preparing yourself to survive in a war zone."

Tom grinned. "That'll be a real stretch for you to write."

Dutch shrugged. "It's a cover. And I can travel among rebels and government troops pretty freely with my press credentials."

"Which are beautifully forged, by the way."

"Thanks. They're some of my best work."

Annie looked at the laminated pass around his neck. She'd seen dozens of them at the American embassy. "You made that?"

The big man smiled proudly. "Yes, ma'am."

"Wow. I'd have never guessed it's not real."

"It is real. Just the name and pictures are fake."

Annie started. "How in the world did you get a real American press pass? If there's a breach in security at the embassy, I'd certainly like to know about it...."

Tom laughed. "I wouldn't worry about it, Annie. There's about to be a breach in the embassy's *wall*."

Chagrined, Annie watched Dutch leave, her thoughts with her colleagues as they fled for their lives. If she had half a brain she'd be doing the same thing.

Annie jumped as Tom's big body loomed close on the couch. He was so...male. Just being near him was a bit overwhelming.

Oh, come off it, Annie. He's only a man, she told herself. A little voice in her head whispered back, Yeah, but what a specimen.

"I'm sorry we couldn't get you out of here today, Annie. It leaves you in a bit of a pickle, doesn't it?"

He didn't know the half of it.

"You were about to tell me something when Tex showed up."

Annie gulped. The other half of her pickle. She couldn't afford to alienate him now by admitting that she'd withheld information from him. They needed to work together if they were going to get out of here alive. Nope. She dared not risk telling him about being the pilot who nearly killed him.

"It wasn't important, Tom. Never mind."

Those piercing blue eyes of his looked right through her. "You seemed to think it was important a few minutes ago."

Crud. He wasn't going to let her off the hook. "I, uh, just wanted to thank you for looking out for me. I know I'm a burden to you guys, and I appreciate what you're doing for me."

He reached up and smoothed her hair back from her face, following the strands down to her shoulder with his fingertips.

"It's my pleasure."

His smile sizzled Annie's already-raw nerves with more sexual promise than she could bear calmly.

"Why don't you try to get a little rest before nightfall, angel? It's going to be hot and heavy out there tonight, and you may not get much sleep."

"Great. And what about you? You were supposed to stay in bed today."

"I haven't gotten my kiss yet."

Annie bridled. "Then what do you call what we did over by the front door?"

"Oh, that? That was just a little welcome-back peck. That wasn't a real kiss."

Her eyes narrowed. "So then, you're telling me you can do better than that?"

His blue gaze danced. "Most definitely."

"This I've got to see."

Tom leaned toward her, and Annie's heart swelled alarmingly in her chest, pounding furiously as he drew near.

"Hey, boss!"

Annie jumped away from Tom as guiltily as he did from her. Tex stood in the doorway to the bedroom.

"I forgot to tell you the Navy arrived last night. The Independence carrier group is sitting off the coast, just over the international waters line."

"That's good news, Tex. All we have to do now is get out to it."

If her ears didn't deceive her, Tom was breathing a little hard. Good.

"Boss, the bed's too soft for me. If you'd like to grab a little shut-eye in it, I'm gonna sack out on the floor."

"Do I look like I need a cushy mattress? Am I turning into an old lady or something?"

Tex's usually smiling gaze went dead sober. "You nearly died not too long ago, sir. Doc said he'd never seen a guy who was hurt so bad pull through. And if you'll forgive me for pointin' it out, you've still got a little hitch in your git-along. I just thought you might want to rest a spell."

Tom accepted the rebuke gracefully. "I might at that, Tex. Now that you mention it, a little shut-eye does sound good."

As the two men retreated into the bedroom, Tom looked back over his shoulder at her and mouthed the words, "You owe me a kiss."

Grinning, she stuck out her tongue at him and stretched out on the sofa for the nap he'd suggested.

When Annie woke up, she felt wrung out, more tired than when she laid down. Between the blankets Tom had hung over the windows in preparation for the coming night and the unrelenting steam heat outside, the apartment was stifling.

Unbuttoning the top buttons of her dress as she went, she crossed the room to the refrigerator. A blast of chilled air hit her as she fanned the door back and forth. She fished a couple of ice cubes out of a cheap plastic tray in the freezer and pressed them against the back of her neck. The cold wrenched a gasp from her, but relief from the heat soothed her shock.

The ice cubes dripped between her fingers messily, sending cold rivulets down her wrist and between her shoulder blades. And then something hot touched her neck. She jumped and would have turned, but Tom's hands closed on her shoulders and held her where she stood.

His mouth traced the path of the melted ice, stealing the cold greedily from her skin, replacing it with a fire that made the room seem cool by comparison.

She let her head fall forward and gave her neck to him while goose bumps rose on her skin that had nothing to do with cold.

"I could eat you alive, sweetheart."

She twisted under his hands and came up against his chest. Her arms went around him, hugging until he took a sharp breath.

She released him instantly. "I forgot about your ribs, Tom. I'm so sorry!"

"Don't worry about it. I'm fine."

"You're not fine, and I wish you'd stop pretending you are."

"And I wish everyone would stop treating me like I'm going to break if I even take a deep breath."

"We're worried about you, Tom. Is that such a bad thing?"

He frowned, considering Annie's question. He could get used to having a beautiful, smart, funny woman around, especially one who gave a damn for his well-being. It was such a tempting distraction. And such a deadly one.

Annie relaxed him. When she was around, he couldn't stay wired tight. A man in his work had to stay sharp if he wanted to live long. But one thought of her coming apart in his arms, and all his self-discipline evaporated.

Not only was he going to get himself killed, but he was going to get her killed, too, if he didn't get control of himself. It was starting to fall into a deadly pattern he knew all too well. She'd get under his skin, seduce him and then lead him into disaster. Just like Jackie.

Reluctantly he set her away from him.

"Annie, is there any chance you could make Tex a bite to eat before he leaves? If he hasn't slept in a couple days, it's a good bet he hasn't eaten much, either."

"Good grief! Of course I'll fix him something."

"Protein and carbohydrates if you've got them, and lots of both. He may be lean, but he can really chow down."

Tex was up and around by the time she finished making an industrial-size batch of spaghetti and meatballs. The man called Howdy arrived just as they were sitting down to eat.

He was medium in height and lean of build, with light-brown hair and medium-brown eyes. Annie's gaze had a way of passing right over him, even though he sat beside her at the table.

She'd prepared enough food for at least six people, but between Tom, Tex, and Howdy it all disappeared in short order. At least Tom was getting his appetite back.

Throughout the meal, Tex was almost as quiet as Howdy. Immediately afterward, Howdy headed for the couch and went horizontal, and the lanky Texan slipped out of the apartment with no more than a murmured word of thanks.

She asked, "What was up with him, Tom? Did I do something to upset him?"

"Not at all. He was gearing up for tonight. Putting on

his game face, as it were. Behind all those down-home quips, he's actually a pretty serious guy. Best spotter I ever worked with.''

Annie reached across the table to squeeze Tom's hand briefly. ''You're worried about him, aren't you?''

He gave her a candid look and lines of worry etched themselves in his brow. ''Yes, I am. This is a dangerous situation, and my men are out there, split up and incommunicado.''

Tom helped Annie clean up after the meal while Howdy slept on the couch. The man had appeared to go unconscious the second his head hit the cushion. That worried Tom.

His guys looked and acted worn-out. While he'd been snoozing in a hospital, they'd been living under high-stress conditions, building impromptu covers and trying to watch a revolution unfold, all without getting caught.

They'd been in the jungle for a solid month before his accident and were tired the night he got hurt. Now, on top of that, they'd had to play spy for two more months. Espionage was not what his men were trained for. It had to be draining their nerves badly. He needed to get them out of Gavarone before one of them slipped up.

Tom sat at the kitchen table for an hour doodling on a piece of paper, trying to come up with ideas to get out of the country, but he couldn't concentrate for squat.

He watched in appreciation as Howdy woke up from his nap, gathered his gear soundlessly and slipped out, ghostlike. Tom had never known another person who could move so quietly and completely unnoticed.

He gave up trying to work and went into the bedroom. Troubled, he pulled back the corner of the blanket to observe the street outside. Even though he looked long and hard, he didn't catch so much as a glimpse of Howdy as the man left.

Annie banged around in the kitchen for a couple more minutes, and then her soft footsteps scuffed across the bedroom to his side.

The deep sense of isolation that had overcome him seemed to reach out to embrace Annie, too. She was unnaturally still and silent beside him. Maybe she'd been in a position of leadership before. Maybe she, too, knew what it was like to worry about her troops, hoping she'd taught them well enough to deal with what she'd sent them into.

Command sat heavy upon him tonight.

As Tom watched the people below hurry to finish their last errands before darkness and its dangers, a deep restlessness welled up inside him. He wanted to be out there with his men, to be in the thick of the action, to watch events unfolding before his eyes. Unfortunately, about all he was good for was looking out a window.

As the streets emptied, his mind shifted into high gear. His senses grew sharper with each passing moment, more alert, faster, lethal. It was the coming of the night. It brought out the hunter in him. Adrenaline surged in his veins, and he itched with the anticipation of pitting his strength and wits against the enemy's. It was addictive, this feeling.

Annie stirred beside him. "What do you see when you look out there?"

He opened the blanket wider to give her a view, as well.

"I see a city preparing itself for a war, without having any idea of what it's really going to be like."

"But *you* know, don't you?" Her voice was quiet, almost sad.

Maybe it *was* a bit sad that he knew precisely what was about to happen to this peaceful, prosperous city.

"This is going to be an ugly fight with no mercy," he said quietly.

He heard her sigh, a soft sound of compassion and regret. "Such a tragedy," she murmured.

How right she was. As they waited and watched, the silence outside deepened. By gradual degrees the stillness grew heavy with anticipation.

Annie began to fidget. "I almost wish the fighting would start," she remarked. "The waiting is killing me."

Tom chuckled. "I'll remind you of those words in about six hours. Never fear, the fighting's getting close."

She looked up at him sharply. "Can you hear it?"

"No, angel. I can feel it."

"How?"

He shrugged. "I don't know exactly. This fight is like being in the same room with a pair of secret lovers. They're circling around the room pretending to ignore each other, but the electricity between them is so thick you can almost touch it. Don't you feel it?"

She gave him a perplexed look.

He let the blanket drop so only a tiny crack was left to peer out of. "Come here." He pulled her in front of him and put his arms around her.

"You see over there on that high hill, the one with the church on it, how there's a bluish haze hanging in the air?" He pointed over her shoulder so she could sight along his arm.

"Yes, I guess so."

"That's the army. They've got a big convoy of armored vehicles and tanks parked in that area."

"Are they getting ready to roll?"

"No, it's too early. They'll wait until after dark. It's probably just mechanics checking out the equipment. But the tension's building."

Annie relaxed back against him as the sun began to set, and he savored her easy trust in him. Since they were so near the equator, the sun seemed to hang motionless in the sky, not far above the rooftops, for a long time. Then, all of a sudden, it dived toward the horizon as if it, too, fled the night to come.

Sunset bathed the city in blood red, and under Tom's hands goose bumps raised on Annie's cool flesh.

"It's not an omen, Annie. It's just a red sunset."

She sighed. "I know. But it's still creepy."

He smiled into her silky hair. "Our lovers are circling each other, drawing ever closer with each trip around the room. They're pretending they don't notice one another, but they're so vividly aware of each other they can hardly keep from rushing headlong into an embrace."

Annie shifted restlessly. Her body flowed like silk between his arms, fluid yet substantial at the same time.

He continued talking low into her ear. "Right now our lovers are savoring the anticipation. They're imagining their joining, the sight of it, the sound of it, the smell of it. The waiting is heady, almost better than the real thing. But then, that's the reason for taking a secret lover, isn't it? For the thrill of doing the unthinkable, of tasting the forbidden, of breaking the rules."

Annie's respiration was rapid, her skin hot to the touch. Sexual energy poured off her. She provoked every unthinkable, forbidden fantasy he'd ever had of a woman. He was as hard as a rock, and his own breathing accelerated to match hers.

"Are we still talking about the army and the rebels?" Her whispered words were ragged, shaky, even.

"You tell me."

There was a long silence, and her body alternately went rigid and relaxed in his arms as she wrestled with her answer. He waited her out.

"Is that why you choose this life? You get a thrill out of it?"

For some reason he felt talkative tonight. "No. I hate being out there."

"Then why?" she whispered. "What are you punishing yourself for?"

Her words tore a jagged wound in a piece of his heart he'd thought was long ago put to rest. The pain almost buckled his knees. He forced himself answer her, but his voice was ragged. "I do it for Simon. The guy Jackie got killed was named Simon Pettigrew. I led him into a trap that I was too blinded by lust to see. My first command," he choked out. "My fault—"

Annie's hand was suddenly on his mouth, holding back any more words. "Stop it, Tom. Stop tearing yourself up like this. It happened a long time ago. What's done is done."

He reached for her wrist and pulled her hand away. "It's never done, Annie. Don't you see? I go from one war to another, and when that one's done, another one's waiting for us."

"What I see is a brave man, a good commander, being too hard on himself."

He whirled away from her, staring, unseeing, out the window. She didn't get it. She'd never had to make life-and-death decisions. She'd never made the wrong choice and killed someone.

"Tell me what else you see out there, Tom."

He fought back his turbulent emotions until he could answer her reasonably calmly.

He sighed. "I see youth and eagerness straining to prove themselves. I see cynicism taking advantage of naive ideals. I see disappointment, disillusionment and disaster coming."

Annie turned around in his arms to face him.

"Is that how you see me? Young and naive? Are we headed for disaster?"

"Annie, just now I was talking about the boys out there who are being pointed at each other by politicians and told to kill each other. That's not what I see in you at all."

"What do you see when you look at me?"

"I see a beautiful woman circling the other side of the room from me, pretending she doesn't know I'm here. I can taste her right now. I can already hear her voice raised in ecstasy beneath me. I feel her body becoming part of mine. I'm willing her to look my way, to catch my eye and signal that she can't wait any longer to have me."

Annie's voice came out muffled against his chest. "Wow."

Right now he'd do just about anything to have her. He needed her touch worse than just about anything he'd ever needed before. He needed to be reminded that he was still a part of the human race. It had been so long since he'd allowed himself this.

"Be my secret lover, Annie. Break the rules with me. Do every forbidden thing with me that you've ever imagined."

"I know better," she groaned, "but I want you so much."

He couldn't keep the desperation out of his voice. "Then come with me. Let's leave the party and have our secret rendezvous. Let's make the anticipation pale by comparison to the real thing."

His hands roamed up and down her back. Her spine curved as tautly as a bow as she leaned back, staring up at him in terrible indecision.

He gave her a half smile. "Come on, angel. Sin a little with me."

The tension left her as a reluctant smile lit her face. "How can a girl say no to the Devil himself?"

"The Devil, am I?"

She was closer to the truth than she knew.

"Well then, I promise your fall shall be one to remember, my sweet angel."

He leaned down and claimed the kiss that hovered on her lips waiting to be taken. They turned away from the window, and the last, dying streaks of the crimson sunset wrapped around them as if the very gates of Hell yawned open, beckoning.

With a flick of his wrist, Tom pulled the blanket over the window completely, plunging the room into soft darkness.

Chapter 8

Annie sprawled on top of Tom with nary a stitch of clothing between them when the shelling started. She had no exact recollection of how she'd gotten into this position, other than a vague memory of Tom's clever hands moving all over her and her clothes magically disappearing.

His body was solid everywhere, all slabbed muscles and hard tendons, just like she remembered. Except he was so much more impressive awake and in motion. The very gentleness with which he handled her spoke volumes about his strength, and Annie reveled in his care.

The sound of the first mortars tickled the edges of her consciousness, building slowly to a growl, vibrating deep in the city's throat. Meanwhile Tom's hands explored every part of her body, and the tremors he set off were nearly indistinguishable from those outside their private world.

The subliminal rumbling gradually grew into thunder, low and powerful, rolling through her and sweeping her along in its majesty. Tom's mouth followed the path of his hands, capturing her in a separate storm of his own making.

He started at the tips of her toes and worked his way to the top of her head, feeling and tasting all of her. He lingered at the backs of her knees, nibbled the tender flesh of her inner thighs, kissed his way across the flat plane of her stomach to savor the trembling flesh of her breasts. His explorations didn't end there, though. He lifted her up and slid her down his body slowly, burying his face against her neck, sending a riot of sensations throughout her. She eased down his gorgeous body, returning the favor, relishing the feel and taste of him.

Bright flashes of heat lightning exploded within her to match the surging thunder of Tom's heartbeat under her ear. He rolled over, reversing their positions in one of those blindingly quick moves of his. He stared down at her, his eyes caverns of darkness in his shadowed face.

"I shouldn't be taking advantage of you like this."

"Like how?"

"You're scared, and you want to forget what's happening out there."

"That may be true, but I still want to be here tonight...with you."

An even deeper shadow crossed his face, one from inside his soul. "Look, Annie. I care about you. Enough to tell you right now that my life, my work, doesn't mix well with long-term commitments."

She stared up at him, undecided. This was the point of no return. He was offering her an out, and she ought to take it. She knew the kind of life he led, the way his job would always come first. Besides, she had no business falling into bed with a man she'd been prepared to kill. *Was* it guilt she felt or real affection for him? This wasn't the way to find out.

But he was everything she'd ever fantasized about in a man—intelligent, kind, strong, confident—and she couldn't bring herself to turn away from him. She'd thought about this moment practically from the first moment she'd been told he was going to live.

Each sponge bath she'd given gave him, each massage, each soothing touch to ease his pain had led her to this moment. For weeks she'd ached to have him wake up and respond to her touch. She was dying to know what it would be like to have him touch her back.

The rumbling outside grew louder, separating itself occasionally into distinct explosions. The bed shook slightly. Whether it was from the shelling or her own trembling desire, she couldn't tell.

The danger outside crept slowly but surely into their nest, a living thing creeping over the windowsills like fog and roiling along the floor to lick at their feet. There was no way of knowing if she'd live to see another morning.

She spoke softly. "Tom, you're right. I am afraid. But that has nothing to do with how I feel about you. I—" she hesitated a moment more and then took the plunge "—want you."

He let out his breath on a sigh. "I can't promise you anything beyond this moment, Annie."

She reached up and placed her palm on the smooth plane of his cheek. "I know the rules of engagement here. I have an idea of the kind of life you lead. This moment is enough for me."

His arms relaxed, and he sank down with her into the night. She welcomed him, cradling his body with hers, offering up solace and passion, comfort and dreams.

The flashes of light outside lit Tom's face in harsh relief. His jaw looked tight, as if he was holding himself back carefully. She didn't want careful on a night that could be her last.

"Tom, let go. I want all of you tonight."

Tom froze and then drew back, staring down at her. That was the last thing he'd expected his scared little innocent to say. A big explosion went off somewhere outside, and he barely registered it.

Panic wrapped itself around his throat. Old fears warned him that if he allowed himself this moment of pleasure—with a woman he cared about, in the middle of a mission—disaster would follow.

His throat was so tight he could only whisper, "Are you sure, angel?"

Her lips curved into the prettiest smile he'd ever seen. "I'm sure."

That was it. He had no more protests left, no more lofty ideals to stand by, no more strictures of gentlemanly behavior to stop him. Tonight he needed her worse than life itself, and she wanted him back. It was a miracle, and he wasn't going to turn away from it or from her.

As her mouth moved beneath his and her body arched up into him, feminine and wildly appealing, he was humbled by her gift. He pushed aside the last of his doubts and embraced the world of the living. For this one night he was going to be a man and not an emotionless shell.

She drove him beyond distraction, and he was almost in a daze. Her breasts filled his hands perfectly. He kissed them reverently, then kneaded and kissed her flesh until Annie writhed and moaned beneath him. Everywhere he touched her, she burned for him. His hands and mouth roamed over her body while he reveled in her passionate response.

Finally she dragged him higher, wrapped her legs around him and pulled him near. "I want you now," she whispered in confession and demand.

He smiled, beguiled by her innocence and abandon. "I wouldn't want to keep a lady waiting," he murmured back. He paused long enough to brush the hair back from her face, to look deeply into her emerald gaze, to memorize her vibrant joy.

Slowly, he sank into her, amazed by how her body stretched and gave to accommodate him. And then he was so deep inside her he could barely breathe. He felt every tremor and pulse of her growing ardor, and it drove him out of his mind. He forced himself not to pound into her mindlessly, but to move slowly and savor this miracle.

He enjoyed every sensation, from the velvet slide of her flesh against his, to the taste of mint toothpaste on her breath, to the way she wrapped her arms around his neck and held on as if she'd never let him go.

She brimmed with life, embracing it enthusiastically and sharing it generously. He'd spent so many years living on the edge of death, he'd almost forgotten this existed. He gulped it down greedily.

Annie met him, breath for breath, kiss for kiss, smile for smile, as their bodies and feelings became one. She was life itself. If he could've made her a part of himself he would have. He held her as if he'd do just that, twining their bodies together, flesh to flesh, heart to heart.

Somewhere outside, the flashes and explosions were growing louder, but the fireworks in his head and the pounding of his heart drowned most of it out. The sound and fury inside and out built to a nearly unbearable crescendo.

It all paused for a breathless, infinite second in time. And then, as the walls shook and the windows rattled, he and his angel broke free of their bodies and soared into another place for one perfect moment.

Peace.

Sensation returned slowly. Annie's glorious body pressed against his from his ankles to his ears. He roused himself enough to murmur, "Am I crushing you?"

A gentle laugh from Annie. "Not at all. Don't move a muscle."

She was perfect. That's all there was to it.

After a long, relaxed silence, she spoke again. "Is it just me or is there a war going on out there?"

He laughed and rolled over onto his back, taking her with him and tucking her under his arm. Her head rested comfortably on his shoulder.

"I haven't the slightest idea what's going on outside this bed."

Her hand caressed his chest lightly. "Me, neither."

Annie lurched awake sometime later. Tom's chest rose and fell slowly under her ear. It was silent outside. Dead quiet. The kind of quiet just before all hell breaks loose. She tried Tom's trick of sensing what was going on outside and was immediately overcome by a powerful premonition of bad things to come.

"Tom," she whispered.

He was awake instantly. He lay perfectly still, but suddenly his awareness filled the room.

She whispered, "What's going on out there?"

He listened for a moment and then swore quietly. He eased out from beneath her.

"Stay where you are."

She lay back and enjoyed the dim view of his naked body moving away from her. He drew back the curtain a bare inch and peered outside. His lean hips and muscular shoulders were outlined against an eerie, orange glow.

"Ah, hell," he said between clenched teeth.

"What is it?" She sat up in spite of Tom's instructions. She'd never heard tension like that in his voice before.

"Get down." His words were sharp, short. "On the floor, now."

She rolled out of bed and had the presence of mind to drag the covers with her. From beneath the bed she saw Tom's feet take a running leap in her direction and disappear as he dived behind the bed with her.

A slow whistle began, tearing the air apart, growing louder and louder until Annie thought her eardrums might split. Tom's hand cupped the back of her head, pushing her face against his chest as he rolled on top of her.

A tremendous explosion rocked the room. Plaster dust rained down from the ceiling, and Annie's ears rang.

His voice was wry in her ear. "Well, I promised you a memorable fall, angel."

"What was that?"

"That would be heavy artillery aimed at a target real damn close to us."

"Are we safe?"

His chest vibrated with a silent chuckle. "Not exactly."

"Should we leave?"

"Not tonight. There will be soldiers and rebels crawling all over the place. You don't know enough about covert movement to make it past them, and I'm not in good enough shape to take care of you."

"Don't worry about it, Tom. We'll be okay." Her hands roamed over the expanse of his chest. "You're in plenty good enough shape for me."

A grin tugged at his mouth. "Don't distract me. I'm trying to do my job here."

"Oh, you are, are you? It looks to me like you're lying naked on the floor with a woman who's in need of serious distraction."

"Annie…" his voice held a warning tone.

"There's nothing we can do for now, so why worry about it? We either make it through the night or we don't."

"An admirable attitude, angel."

She grinned and reached for him. "Come here, soldier."

With the dawn came real silence and, finally, sleep for Annie. She roused vaguely some hours later when Tom eased away from her and made his way to the bathroom.

Sounds of water filling the bathtub lulled her back toward sleep. She was just conscious enough to register that when Tom came back he smelled of French lilac.

"There's a bar of Ivory soap on the windowsill behind the curtain," she mumbled.

She opened one eye enough to see a priceless expression of incredulity on Tom's face.

"You think you're pretty funny, huh?" he demanded.

She jolted violently awake as her ribs were attacked by poking fingers.

She squealed and squirmed and was treated to a demonstration of just how good Tom's training was as he immobilized her instantly.

"No fair using your fancy-shmancy skills on me!" she complained through her laughter.

"Who said anything about fair? I play to win, angel."

She grinned up at him. "Did you at least save me some hot water?"

"I did."

She climbed to her feet, surprised to find she was a bit sore. But then, after all the gymnastics they'd performed on a hard floor while they distracted themselves last night, maybe she shouldn't be surprised.

Tom had pancakes waiting for her when she got out of the tub. As she ate, she watched him move around the kitchen. There was a grace in his movements she'd not seen before.

"You're moving better. Does that mean you're feeling stronger?"

He grinned over his shoulder while he flipped more pancakes. "After last night? I'm wiped out."

She ducked her head and studied the way the butter melted into the syrup. A plate plunked down on the table beside hers, and Tom sat down to eat.

"I feel much better, actually. I think the exercise did me a world of good."

"Oh, so I'm just exercise, am I?"

He leaned over and cupped her chin in his palm. He lifted her face and kissed her gently on the mouth. "Never, angel. I think you gave me my life back last night."

Annie froze. Oh, Lord. If he only knew she was the one who nearly took it from him in the first place.

"Hey, I didn't mean to upset you. I knew the rules of engagement, too. If you want last night to be a one-time deal, I'll understand. I'll be disappointed, but I'll understand."

"I, uh, no, that's not it at all. I don't want a one-night stand." She added hastily, "That is if you don't, either."

"Definitely not."

Annie smiled at the vehemence in his voice.

"Well, now that that's settled, we've got some work to do today, angel."

Annie looked up, surprised. "We do?"

"We need to find out what the rebels were shooting at last night and whether or not they hit it."

"Why?"

"Do you want to sleep directly in the line of fire again tonight?" he asked.

"I see your point."

"If the rebels didn't destroy their target, we're going to have to bug out and find somewhere else to hole up. I'm not putting you that close to the action again if I can help it."

A warm feeling bubbled up inside her. He was worried about her safety. The little voice in her head commented, *For Pete's sake, let's hope so. It was his job to get them out alive, after all.*

Yeah, but he sounded more than professionally concerned.

"So how are we going to do this reconnoitering, Tom?"

"Well, you're going to do your hooker impersonation again, and I'm going to take you out for a walk."

"For what hookers charge nowadays, that'll be a pretty expensive stroll in the park."

Tom chuckled. "I'll deduct your fee as a business expense on my travel voucher."

"In that case, remind me to charge you a fortune."

After the meal Annie watched with interest as Tom sprayed himself with clear liquid from a little bottle that emerged from his pack. She watched his hands glide over his bulging muscles in utter fascination.

"What's that stuff?"

He flashed a mischievous smile at her. "Give it about an hour and you'll see."

In less than an hour, Tom's skin began to change color, darkening to a deep tan. He pulled on a white cotton shirt and slacks Annie'd bought for him before she brought him home from the hospital. Those, in combination with his new complexion and dark hair, made him look surprisingly like a local.

Annie donned her dress and wig and used eyeliner and lip pencil to change the shapes of her eyes and mouth. As she stepped back to survey her work, Tom walked into the bathroom. His presence behind her was so intimate...so domestic.

She could get used to this.

Stop it, she thought. As soon as we're out of here, he'll disappear into the next jungle that's about to explode into war.

"Tom, are you sure you're strong enough to go out? I can find out what's happening by myself."

"I'm sure you can. But you don't have to prove to me that you can do the job as well as a man."

"I...it's not..."

He cut her off. "Isn't it?"

She frowned. "No, it's not."

"Sure it is. I've been in this business longer than you have, and you've got all the signs. You're scared to death, but you're determined to prove to somebody that you can hack this life. Who? Who is it you're trying so hard to impress?"

"You, I suppose."

He shook his head in the negative. "Maybe it's me you're focused on in the short term, but somebody else drove you to Gavarone, drove you to be my cover, drove you not to leave with the embassy personnel."

She considered his words. Was he right? Was some of this about showing her father she could be more than a schoolmarm in a rinky-dink town? Maybe Tom was partially right. But mostly she felt guilty. She felt a need to make up to him for what she'd done to him. Not only had he suffered terribly, but she might very well have ended his distinguished career. The very thought of it made her sick to her stomach.

She fought off the sensation. "You need to get your strength back. Why don't you stay here and rest while I go out and have a look around?"

"No way. I'm not letting you go out there alone again. It's too dangerous."

She let out the breath she'd been holding. "You have no idea how glad I am you feel that way. I was scared silly the last time I went out."

He smiled gently. "Yeah, I noticed. I'm sorry I put you through that."

"I got the job done, and that's what counts."

"No, it's not. What counts is that you're safe."

He thought her safety was more important than the mission? Annie blinked. The mission was everything to Special Forces guys.

She had no time to ponder what it meant as Tom led her to the door and opened it. This time when she stepped out into the city, she trusted Tom to keep her safe. Even though he had to take the steps slowly and she caught a couple of grimaces on his face, she had complete faith in his abilities. It was a wonderful feeling.

Tom, however, wasn't feeling wonderful at all. His left arm ached, and his balance still wasn't where it ought to be. If he had to sprint anywhere today, he'd be sucking wind in a matter of seconds. He had only his brains to rely on for this outing. Usually that was enough, but not always.

They reached the sidewalk and gazed upon the previous night's work. Broken glass, bricks and dust were everywhere, and the burned-out hull of a car partially blocked the road.

He murmured to Annie in Spanish, "Do you know any of the shopkeepers around here?"

"A few," she answered back in the same language.

"Let's drop in and see what they know."

They spent the next two hours cruising the few shops that were open, encouraging gossip among the proprietors and other customers. No reliable information was forthcoming, and Tom's arm was killing him. Not to mention that his legs were starting to ache, and he was feeling a bit light-headed.

"Love, is there somewhere we could sit down for a while?"

She took one look at him and tucked her arm under his. He was grateful for the help, but it galled him to be this weak. He had to get his strength back fast if they were going to make it out of the country.

"There's a delightful café right around the corner. How about a bite of lunch?"

"Sounds great. Lead on."

Tom cased out the large, shaded patio of the café. High,

stone walls, no marked exits except through the indoor dining room through which they'd come. Another door into the building, probably leading to the kitchen. Not an ideal scenario, but he didn't have much choice in the matter now. He'd have to teach Annie how to choose safer public places to hang out in from now on.

Gratefully Tom sank into his seat and rubbed his aching arm. He checked out the other diners under the guise of hunting for a waiter. Most of the two dozen tables were filled with couples, although a few groups of businessmen lounged over drinks. This place either had great food, or the clientele was determined to live it up while the living was good.

It turned out both were the case. Tom's garlic-drenched shark steak was succulent, and Annie savored her salmon with a relish that almost made him jealous of it. They took turns feeding each other bites of their respective meals. Annie's gaze grew limpid when he accidentally dribbled butter down her front. She followed the spill into her cleavage with one finger and drew it out languidly. She put her finger in her mouth and sucked the butter off it slowly. Tom's mouth went desert dry at the sight.

He motioned a waiter over and ordered a bottle of wine.

Annie frowned. "You're allowed to drink on the job?"

"Everyone else is drinking. I didn't want us to stand out from the crowd."

Annie smiled knowingly at him over the rim of her glass. "What's going on in that devious mind of yours, angel?"

"I was just thinking about those secret lovers circling the room and wondering how many of them are here today."

He looked around the place. "A lot."

"Why do you say that?"

"Some of these women are too pretty to be wives. They've got to be mistresses."

"Chauvinist."

Tom's attention snapped to Annie. "Me?"

She grinned. "Yup. Admit it. You think women are weak little things that need to be protected."

"Most are weak relative to me."

"Hmm, and you have a big ego, too."

He leaned close to her. "I'm stronger than you, even in my weakened state, and you know it. If you don't believe me, I'll arm wrestle you right now."

"Sorry, that's not the kind of wrestling I want with you."

Their gazes locked, and sparks crackled back and forth between them. Her hand touched his thigh under the table, and he almost jumped out of his skin. A smile curved Annie's mouth, and Tom met it with one of his own. He'd give his right arm to take her to bed right now, with all that sexual promise pouring off her.

Bang!

A blast from what his subconscious identified as a twelve-gauge shotgun rent the air.

"Nobody move!"

Tom froze and prayed Annie would do the same. Very slowly he moved his eyes and found the source of the voice. It was one of the waiters. He stood near the kitchen entrance, brandishing a smoking shotgun.

"We are the forces of liberation and we are here to claim a traitor!"

Tom's gaze darted left and right. Completely healthy, he could've made it up one of the walls and hauled Annie over, but not now. They were trapped. He gauged the thickness of the wooden tabletop. Not heavy enough to stop twelve-gauge rounds at close range. He'd tell them Annie was a hooker he'd picked up on the street. He was buying her lunch before they adjourned to her place. Maybe they'd only kill him.

How in the blazes had he let his guard down and gotten into a trap like this? They must have followed him and Annie. He'd been too busy romancing her to notice. How could he have been so stupid?

The waiter advanced across the porch and Tom's muscles tensed. Two more armed waiters stepped forward into his periphery vision. He couldn't overpower three men with guns, unarmed as he was. He ruled out a takedown and willed himself to relax.

The men moved closer and closer and finally stopped at a table about ten feet away.

"Minister Ramirez, you will come with us. Our leaders wish to speak with you."

A terrified looking man stood up and was escorted across the patio by the three rebels. They stepped inside.

As quickly as it began, the incident was over. The patio was silent for several long seconds, and then pandemonium erupted. Tom slumped in his seat as the adrenaline drained away.

It occurred to him that Annie was being awfully quiet. He looked up, and she was staring at him, her eyes huge and dark against pasty white skin.

He threw a couple of bills on the table and said, "Let's go. The police will be here any second and will question everyone."

"Right."

Annie roused herself with some difficulty and followed him out of the restaurant. Tom all but ran from the building. She had to hustle to keep up with him as he ducked into stores, crossed streets without warning and dived into alleys, all the while checking for tails.

Finally they slowed and turned toward home. Annie was startled when Tom veered in yet another direction. A crowd had gathered ahead of them. A building, or what was left of it, spilled into the street in a man-high jumble of cement and steel. A rubble brigade had been established as workers lifted away bricks and chunks of debris, while rescue workers searched for victims.

Tom studied the building, looked over his shoulder in the direction of their apartment and then noted the position of the sun.

"The mortars last night came over our apartment and would have landed right about here. Annie, what was this place?" he asked tersely.

"An office building."

"What companies were housed in it?"

She racked her brain while Tom stared expectantly at her. She'd sold him on her usefulness because she knew the city like the back of her hand. Now was the time to prove it.

Think! She looked around the wrecked street, reconstructing what it used to look like. Details started coming back to her.

"There was an insurance company and a bank. National One Television was here, and—"

Tom cut her off. "I think we found the target of last night's shelling. The government's TV station."

Annie nodded. It made sense. The network had been gushing anti-rebel propaganda like an oil well recently.

"C'mon. Let's get off the street."

To her surprise Tom steered her into a supermarket on their way home. He loaded their basket with piles of canned food. He added several large plastic containers, rolls of plastic wrap and duct tape, a cheap headset radio, batteries and a stack of candles big enough to elicit a rude comment from the checkout clerk. Annie didn't ask what they were for. Right now she just wanted to get behind the walls of their apartment.

Before long Annie's arms were killing her, and she wasn't carrying nearly as many bags of groceries as Tom. She was huffing when they got back to the apartment, but he seemed unaffected. She'd hate to see him at full strength if he was in such good shape after his complete inactivity the past two months.

She'd no sooner put down her groceries on the kitchen table than Tom said, "Go take a bath, Annie. Take your time and enjoy it. It's the last one you're going to get for a while."

Alarm sluiced through her. "But we found the target of the shelling, and it was destroyed. We don't have to leave now, do we?"

"No, we're staying put. But if the rebels were smart enough to go after the TV station, then surely they know to go after the utilities. I'd bet my next paycheck we're about to lose water and electricity."

The reality of living in a war zone struck Annie hard. "I hadn't thought of that, but it makes sense."

He nodded absently, his mind already at work on the next problem.

"Join me in the bath, Tom?"

His gaze jerked to her, startled. "I'd better not."

Deflated, she replied, "If you change your mind, you know where to find me."

His gaze softened and a reluctant smile lit his features. "I'll keep it in mind."

Tom watched her turn and head for the bathroom. Her hips swayed just enough to drive him crazy. He could still feel them undulating in perfect time with his.

And he could still see the stark terror on Annie's face in the restaurant. He'd really screwed up back there. He should have seen it coming. The rebels wielding the guns had been clumsy amateurs at terrorism. If he'd been even half alert, he'd have seen the signs of it. But he'd been so wrapped up in flirting with Annie that he'd missed it completely.

He was going to get them both killed if he didn't get his mind on business and keep it there. It had been sheer dumb luck they didn't get killed in the restaurant. Next time they might not be so lucky.

Last night was a huge mistake. He couldn't let it happen again.

How he was going to stop it from happening he had no idea. The mere thought of lying beside Annie, holding her and loving her, aroused him. He wanted her so badly he could hardly stand it. She was an addiction in his blood.

Resolutely he set water on the stove to boil. Once they'd both had a bath, he was going to sterilize the bathtub and fill it with drinking water for them. He would cover it with the plastic wrap and it should last them for a week or two.

He took a roll of duct tape to the bedroom and crisscrossed tape across the windows. If they were hit and shattered, the tape would keep pieces of glass from flying around and injuring them. Next he taped blankets in place over the windows for extra protection from shrapnel. He left tiny peepholes on each side of the windows at eye level.

He dragged the bed into the living room, somehow managing to wrestle it through the doorway. When he finally got it in place along an interior wall, he sat down on it in relief.

Exhaustion rolled over him in a heavy wave, sucking him downward, seducing him into inactivity. If nothing else, their outing had shown him he was not strong enough to attempt leaving Gavarone yet. He closed his eyes and marshaled his strength. There was still a lot to do before dark, and the probable end of electricity. He was gathering himself to stand again when Annie's voice sounded.

"Tom? Could you come here for a second?"

Immediately he was alert. "Are you all right?" he asked as he hurried to the bathroom.

He opened the door and a wave of steam rolled forth. Annie sat in the tub, covered to her neck in bubbles. Her hair was pinned up, and tendrils curled around her face, teasing her rosy cheeks. She looked like a centerfold about to reveal herself.

"I forgot my razor. Could you get it for me? It's on top of the dresser in the bedroom."

"Uh, yeah, sure."

He stepped outside, leaning against the wall beside the door. He had to stop it, here and now. For both their sakes. But the sight of her luxuriating in that tub, looking hopeful that he might join her...

He shoved away from the wall and got her damn razor. He carried it into the bathroom, prepared to deliver it along with a speech about how they had to cool it.

She was standing up. Suds clung to her in all the right places, and she put any centerfold he'd ever seen to shame. Rivulets of water ran down her body, erasing the suds in their path, revealing tantalizing streaks of feminine flesh.

She had one foot propped on the edge of the tub, apparently waiting for the razor. Dumbly he handed it to her. Before his knees went too weak to hold him, he sat down on the closed lid of the toilet. Helplessly he watched her shave her legs.

Her hand smoothed its way up her calf, behind her knee, and up the back of her thigh. He watched its path, mesmerized. Another long stroke of her hand, and another strip of smooth flesh was revealed. Over and over, her hand glided upward in long, lazy movements. He couldn't have gotten up and left if his life depended on it.

She gave the same treatment to her other leg, and Tom began to find it difficult to breathe. It must be all the heat and steam in the small space. He unbuttoned the top button of his shirt, fanning the fabric to cool himself. It didn't help. He slipped another button free. And then another. Before he knew it, the shirt was off.

Still, he was burning up. Annie straightened and turned to look at him. She smiled, and he was lost. He rose and went to his Venus rising from the sea. She reached for his belt buckle, but her fingers were slippery and fumbled with the fastener. He brushed them aside and tore it open himself. She helped him out of his remaining clothes, more in the way than not, but the feel of her hands on him was pure heaven.

Finally, as naked as she, he stepped into the tub and wrapped his arms around her soapy perfection. His hands slid over her skin, and he gloried in her delight. And when she did the same to him, his knees threatened to give way once more. He carried her down with him and twisted so he lay full length in the tub with her stretched out on top of him.

Annie squirmed away and sat up. He guided her knees to either side of his hips and placed her hands on his shoulders. Her whole being lit up with a smile that warmed his soul as they became one.

The pleasure was exquisite, almost painful. He bit his lip and managed not to lose control. His effort was well rewarded by the sight of Annie, her head flung back, her eyes closed, her throat taut with ecstasy.

They laughed when water sloshed all over the floor, and they laughed again when he emptied the rest of the bubble bath into the tub. The heady aroma of gardenias swirled around them, and Tom knew he'd never smell that scent again without thinking of this moment. He gave himself over to it, savoring it with the same abandon Annie did. There was no holding back, no secrets. He laid before her everything that he was, and she did the same for him.

The water was cold by the time they finally climbed out

of the tub. They took turns toweling each other dry, extending the moment as long as they could. Tom brushed out Annie's hair and kissed the back of her neck while she blow-dried it. She spread his shaving cream for him, but he handled his razor himself. Annie inspected his work with her mouth and declared it a satisfactory shave. But finally the moment arrived when they had to leave the magic of their tryst.

Even Annie seemed to sense they might not have another like it. Her eyes grew shiny with unshed tears.

"You know we shouldn't be doing this, Annie. I need to focus one hundred percent on getting us out of here."

"I know," she whispered.

Tom held her gently. "No regrets, angel. Promise me."

She drew a shaky breath. "I promise. But you promise you won't forget me."

"I couldn't if I tried. There's never been another woman like you in my life."

She leaned back to look up at him. "I bet you say that to all the girls."

"I most certainly do not."

"You don't have to lie to me. I've seen the way groupie chicks hang all over you Special Forces types in bars while you lie your butts off to them about what you can do."

He scowled at her. "I knew there was a reason why I never date military women. I can't snow them with tales of my heroic deeds."

Her expression turned serious. "I bet if you did tell people the truth, they wouldn't believe you."

He matched her serious turn. "That's been my experience. We do some wild stuff. Sometimes even I don't believe we pull off some of our missions."

"Is this one of them?"

"It's getting there. I'll let you know when we're sitting in a debriefing room telling the tale."

She gave him a tremulous smile, the gesture both endearing and heart wrenching. "That's a deal."

"Meanwhile," he said, clearing his throat to loosen the tightness in his chest, "We've got a war to get ready for. Our survival may depend on the preparations we make in the next few hours."

Annie straightened her spine. It nearly broke her heart to see him so determined to take care of her and his men while he was still so hurt himself. The least she could do for him was to stand beside him and match his bravery. "Let's get to it, then."

Chapter 9

Two weeks into their enforced hiding, Annie woke up after a routine night of gunfire to the sight of Tom sitting on the edge of the bed, cutting the cast off his left arm.

She rolled over and spooned herself around his naked back. "Are you sure your arm's ready for that?"

He relaxed against her momentarily before the inevitable shift away from her. "Annie, we shouldn't have—"

She rolled away from him, exasperated. "You say that every single time, Tom. I know we shouldn't have. But we did. Nobody got hurt, nobody knows but us, and we both know the rules when we leave here. Can't you just relax and enjoy what we have right now?"

He frowned down at her. "It's not that simple. I can't explain it, but I have a gut feeling something bad's going to come of our relationship."

"Then we'll deal with it when it happens. You worry too much."

"And you don't worry enough."

She sighed. They'd been over that ground before. "Any particular reason you're taking your cast off today?"

"Yeah. We're getting out of here tomorrow, and it would be in my way."

Annie sat bolt upright in bed. "Tomorrow?"

"That's the plan. We're all going walk out of here and leave Gavarone to its war."

"You make it sound easy."

He frowned. "It'll be anything but easy. Which reminds me. Get plenty of rest today. No hard workouts."

She'd followed his lead and exercised rigorously for the past two weeks. It had been a nightmare for her. Watching the pain and suffering Tom had to put himself through to recover from the injuries she'd inflicted upon him had been pure torture. With every session, every muffled groan, every carefully disguised flinch from him, her guilt grew. Her need to do something—anything—to make amends to him or even just to suffer in like fashion grew nearly unbearable. She was as trapped in her own way by Tom's injuries as he was.

His voice interrupted her spinning thoughts. "Are you ready to get back to civilization?"

The idea captured her complete attention. She smiled dreamily. "Just think. I could be taking a nice hot bath the day after tomorrow."

Tom answered lightly, "Sorry to disappoint you, but Navy ships don't have bathtubs. You'll have to wait until we get stateside for that."

"Hey, I'd settle for a cold shower right about now."

Tom smiled. "Me, too. If it makes you feel better, the longest I've ever gone without washing, except for rain and occasional mud puddles, was sixty-three days. So you're not even close to my record."

Annie laughed. "That's disgusting! I bet you stood in the shower for an hour after you got back to civilization."

"Yup. Scrubbed myself with steel wool and Lysol."

"Your workouts these past two weeks may have proved you're tough, but you're not *that* tough!"

His response was casual. "I've been taking it easy on myself."

Annie shook her head. For all she knew, he might have been. But his exercise regimen had been awe inspiring nonetheless.

"The whole team's meeting here tonight, angel. Do we have enough food left to give them a decent meal?"

"We still have a fair bit. But the way you guys eat, I'm not sure it'll qualify as a decent meal."

"You know us growing boys."

She grinned. "*Boys* being the operative word."

Tom's eyes gleamed. "Oh, yeah?"

Annie managed one zig before Tom zagged and immobilized her completely. She didn't stand a chance of winning the tickling match that followed. But she did win the internal struggle between Tom and his conscience when he finally kissed her and then made love to her.

Tom's men started trickling in at dusk. They didn't eat the cupboards completely bare, but it was a close call.

Doc was the last to arrive. Annie sat with him while he gulped down a can of chili she'd heated over a couple of candles. When he finished, she followed him into the bedroom. The others were peering by flashlight at the six-foot-tall map of St. George that Tom had drawn on her lovely yellow wall.

Tom spoke over his shoulder, "So, Doc. What's the word from rebel headquarters?"

Over the past two weeks, Doc had earned the complete trust of the rebel leaders by treating their wounded brilliantly, compliments of Uncle Sam's fine training.

"They're moving into this eastern sector tomorrow night." He pointed at the map.

"Where are the troops coming from?"

"This area here." Doc pointed at a historic neighborhood in the center of the city known as Old Town.

Dutch spoke up. "The rebels don't have all that many soldiers there now. If they pull a large force out to attack to the east, Old Town's going to be covered pretty thin."

Annie mentally sighed in relief. It was just the opening they needed.

Tom frowned. "Does the government know about this? If they do, they'll move on Old Town tomorrow night to take it back."

Annie's spirits fell. Darn. He was right.

Mac spoke up. "I haven't heard anything about an offensive at the Gavronese Army's headquarters. But then I only work in their supply office. I'm not wiping generals' a—pardon me, ma'am—behinds like Doc is."

Tom turned to the silent member of his team, Howdy. The other men stilled and listened intently when he finally spoke.

"This afternoon the government repositioned a lot of heavy, rolling equipment for an attack of some kind. They're in place to hit either the sector Doc's talking about or this area to the northwest. Both targets are lightly defended by the rebels. Unfortunately, they're also our two best bets for egress routes."

"Could the government attack both positions simultaneously?"

Howdy shook his head. "Not enough firepower. They'll do one or the other."

Annie groaned silently. Great. So if they picked the right route, they'd have an easy walk out. If they picked the wrong one they'd land smack dab in the middle of a firefight. A hot one.

Tom frowned. "Any thoughts on which route we take, anyone?"

There were shrugs all around.

"Annie?"

She started. "What?"

"Which route would you suggest?"

Her cheeks grew hot as all the men stared intently at her. "Me? I don't know anything about this tactical stuff."

"Which section of the city are you more familiar with?"

"Old Town. It's tricky to navigate, though. Lots of narrow winding streets. The other area you guys are looking at is more modern with wide boulevards that run in compass grid lines."

"Well then, Old Town it is."

All the guys nodded in agreement with Tom.

Alarmed, she said, "Look, don't make this decision based on my lowly opinions. You guys do your expert thing and choose."

"We just did. Tanks maneuver lousy in tight spaces. And the more little alleys and side streets there are, the more hiding places there'll be for us." Tom shifted topics. "Okay, so how are we doing for firepower?"

Howdy rolled open a large bundle he'd carried in with him and dumped at least twenty assorted pistols, shotguns and rifles on the floor.

Eagerly the other men reached for the weapons, inspecting and commenting on the arsenal. In a matter of minutes there were gun parts all over the floor as the guys cleaned and tinkered with the weapons.

Tom gestured for her to sit on the floor beside him. She did so, leaning her back against the couch and savoring his nearness.

"Have you ever used any of these, Annie?"

"Well, I've shot .38 revolvers and 9 mm Berettas in my annual marksmanship training."

"Are you any good?"

She threw him a sideways look and murmured, "You mean with a gun?"

One corner of his mouth turned up and he murmured back, "I know what you can do without one, angel."

"I can shred the heck out of a paper bull's-eye."

"Ever shot at a live target?"

"Nope."

"Ever done any hunting?"

"Goodness, no! I wouldn't shoot at a poor, defenseless animal!"

The other men looked up at her outburst and grinned. Tex drawled, "I chase little bunnies, but I don't shoot 'em, either. It ain't sporting to hunt with a gun."

Mac laughed. "The only bunnies you chase are Playboy bunnies, Tex."

Tom leaned over until his shoulder touched hers and his breath was warm on her neck. She hardly noticed when he dropped a pistol in her lap. Its weight wasn't nearly as heavy as the thudding of her heart.

The timbre of his voice sent goose bumps down her spine as he said, "This is a SIG-Sauer P229 semiautomatic pistol. Its clip holds ten rounds...."

He rattled off a series of specifications, muzzle velocities, trigger pull weights and other assorted statistics. What registered with Annie was the way the corners of his eyes crinkled when he smiled and how kissable his mouth looked.

When his recitation ended, she said regretfully, "Tom, I'm terribly impressed by your display of knowledge, but I don't have the slightest idea what any of that means."

Snickers turned into coughs behind her.

Tex piped up, "Why, it means you point that li'l ol' thing at the bad guy and pull the trigger. Then hang on, 'cause it'll knock you on your derriere if you don't."

Tom's voice was dry. "Thanks for the translation into Stupid, Tex."

"Anytime, boss."

Tom demonstrated loading and aiming the pistol once, then placed the angular, heavy weapon in her hands. She scooted forward while he slid behind her and circled her with his arms. He placed his hands over hers and guided her through the motions.

Maybe it was the dark lethality of the guns and men around her, or maybe it was the leashed energy bursting in the room, but being with Tom like this the night before a mission was exciting and edgy and sexy.

He murmured in her ear, "Angel, if you get any more turned on than you are right now, I'm gonna have to take you into the bedroom and make love to you."

"What about your men?" she whispered back.

"What about them?"

"You wouldn't."

She felt his grin against her ear. "Don't dare me or I may have to."

Shivers raced from her scalp to the arches of her feet. The appeal of what he suggested melted her from the inside out. She considered tossing out the dare.

"Angel, don't tempt me."

She half turned and laughed at him. "I thought seeing to my downfall was your job."

"What job was that?"

Tom glanced up. "Nothing, Mac. How's that minigun shaping up?"

"Just fine, Hoss. The firing pin needs filing, but she'll be a sweet weapon when I'm done with her."

"How many rounds will it deliver before it melts?"

"Six thousand, give or take."

Annie glanced up, surprised. "A gun can melt?"

"Gatling guns like this generate huge amounts of heat. If you fire them continuously, the barrels eventually melt."

Dutch added, "But they lay down the prettiest carpet of lead you ever saw. One of these babies can take out fifty men in ten seconds."

She was impressed in a dubious sort of way. "I guess that'd even the odds in a fight pretty fast, wouldn't it?"

Tom nodded. "That's the idea."

Annie turned to Howdy. "Where'd you get all these weapons?"

"I liberated them from their owners."

"You stole them?"

"Not exactly, ma'am."

Annie frowned, confused.

Tom said gently, "The owners were dead."

"How come the other soldiers in their squads didn't take the guns? I've heard you guys talk about how there's a shortage of firearms for both armies right now."

Tom exhaled heavily. "Nobody else took the guns because Howdy killed the owners. He's our sniper."

"Oh." Sometimes she forgot the nature of Tom's work. Or, more accurately, she tried to forget the nature of Tom's work. She just couldn't equate killing and violence with the passionate, considerate, gentle lover of the past two weeks.

She stopped herself from staring at the silent, polite killer across the room.

When the nightly gunfire started outside, they extinguished all but one candle. To Annie's surprise, everyone else spread bedrolls on the floor and stretched out to sleep.

They seemed to expect her to use the bed, so she crawled into it and stripped down to her T-shirt under the covers. As soon as she was settled, Tom blew out the candle and the room plunged into blackness.

When Tom's arms went around her from behind and his body pressed against hers a minute or two later, she about jumped out of her skin. Not only hadn't she heard him get into bed, but she hadn't *felt* it.

"How did you do that?" she whispered.

He whispered back, "Patience and stealth, my dear."

"Sheesh. I guess. So do any of these guys snore?"

To her chagrin, Tex answered out of the dark. "Not hardly. If we did we'd be dead quick in our line of work."

"You guys would have to have great hearing, wouldn't you?" she groused in a normal speaking voice.

Quiet chuckles floated out of the darkness.

Tom pulled her close, spooning her body into his. "Get some sleep, Annie. You're going to need it in a day or two."

Why had Tom joined her in bed? Was it his way of giving her one last night with him? Or was it nothing more than his desire to sleep in a comfortable bed? Whatever his motive, she wasn't about to kick him out.

She relaxed against the solid bulwark of his body, enjoying the easy comfort between them. It was funny how the circle of Tom's arms had become home to her.

As she drifted toward sleep, images of flying over the jungle came to her. The feel of his body slamming into trees below her was one she'd never forget. It was strange how a single split-second decision had sent her life careening off in this direction, to this place and time, with this man.

How could she ever have made the decision to sacrifice his life to save her own? The thought made her cold all over. She'd never forgive herself for it. She'd do whatever it took to make it up to him.

Annie fell asleep quickly, but Tom wasn't so lucky. He lay in the dark for a long time, feeling the gentle rise and fall of her ribs beneath his arm.

Every time he touched her like this, it took something from him, something he feared he would never get back.

Maybe it was loneliness he felt slipping away. He feared it was something worse. Like the sense of detachment and nonchalance about dying so vital to his line of work.

Every time he made love to her, he swore it would be the last time. He'd steel himself to resist the pull between them, and then she'd smile at him or touch him or look at him in a certain way and his self-discipline unraveled all over again. He'd always prided himself on his control, but he had none at all when it came to Annie. It ate away at him, eroding his walls bit by bit.

It was a long, sweet fall toward hell. And no matter how hard he tried, he just couldn't stop the descent.

It was raining when they woke up the next morning, much to Tom's satisfaction. Rain covered the noise of men moving and tended to keep armies indoors.

They spent the day finishing off the remainder of the food, checking their equipment and picking Annie's brains about the layout of the Old Town area of the city. To Tom's disgust, the rain stopped just before sunset.

"Annie, could you come into the bedroom? There's something I want to show you."

She followed him to the window.

"Look outside."

She pressed her eye to the peephole. "What am I supposed to see?"

"The sunset." He'd already looked at it to know that every color from purple to brilliant orange tinged a layer of high, rippling clouds, and the sun backlit a lone thunderhead, spraying golden rays outward in all directions.

"Wow," she breathed. "That's gorgeous."

"I always watch the sunset before I go on a mission."

"Why?"

"Superstition, I guess. In case something happens to me, I won't die without having stopped to watch it."

"Well, if this sunset did end up being your last, it'd be a good one to go out on. But," she added fiercely, "nothing bad is going to happen to you, Tom."

He shrugged. "You never know."

"That's what I'd hate most about doing your kind of work. I can't be casual about the possibility of not seeing another sunset. I *want* to survive to see another one."

And therein lay the heart of his problem. He'd never cared one way or the other until she'd come into his life. Now he had something besides the mission to live for. And that changed everything.

The last colors faded from the sky, and he turned her around to face him. "We need to talk, Annie."

"About what?"

He thought he detected a tremor in her voice.

Tom didn't answer her question directly. Instead he asked, "How are you holding up, angel?"

"Okay, I guess. Nervous. Well, scared, actually. Excited."

He nodded. "Typical premission jitters. You'll need to be alert when we go. Try to relax as best you can and don't tire yourself out now. In the meantime I have another request. Actually, it's an order."

She frowned.

"I need you to promise me you won't push yourself too hard when we leave here."

"I don't understand," she said.

"Ever since I've known you, you've been out to prove something. I don't know who or what it is that drives you, but over and over I've watched you put yourself in situations that were way beyond your experience or training. You've scared yourself silly a number of times and nearly gotten yourself killed a time or two. I want you to operate within your capabilities tonight."

"I'm still standing here, so apparently everything I've done so far was within my capabilities," she retorted.

He grabbed her by both shoulders. "Listen to me. I know what I'm talking about. I've seen this dozens of times before. What I'm telling you is don't bite off more than you can chew. I can't afford to have you choke on me."

"I won't choke," she declared.

"You will. You're so caught up in being a hero you don't know your own limits. That makes you dangerous to me and my team."

She tore out of his grasp and paced angrily across the room and back. "I don't give a damn about being a hero, Tom Folly. And I don't need your amateur psychoanalysis."

He sighed, exasperated. Didn't she realize her angry outburst was proving his point? She was so busy being macho she wasn't listening to him. Whether it was proving to her father or to herself or to the powers-that-be in the Air Force that she could do the same job as a man, he had no idea. Maybe she was determined to be a hero. Maybe she was just looking for the mountain she couldn't climb. Regardless of its source, she was going to be a liability to him and his guys if she didn't get over it.

He spoke quietly. "Just promise me you won't do anything stupid and you'll follow all my orders immediately and to the letter."

She looked at him long and hard but finally nodded. "I promise."

"Good. Then my first order is for you to relax. Don't wear yourself out with all this nervous energy now. You'll need it later."

She stopped her pacing, but her hands still fidgeted.

"Come here." He held out his arms, and she stepped into them.

"Was there anything else you wanted to talk about?"

He sighed. The nasty thing about time was that it passed relentlessly. As much as he wanted to hold off leaving their hideout—and their tryst—he couldn't any longer.

"I suppose I should warn you. Once we leave here tonight, Annie, I expect to be in high gear and thinking on all cylinders."

"I should hope so."

"What I'm trying to say is I'll be in Special Forces team commander mode."

"Tom, that's what you'll be doing. Of course that's the mode you'll be in."

"I'm trying to warn you that I'm going to have to treat you like just another team member."

"And?"

"And you're okay with that?"

"I *am* a military officer, Tom. I understand how these things work."

"I've never...I don't know..." He frowned, at a loss for words. "Dammit, I've never had *feelings* for one of my team members, and I don't know how to handle having you working with me." Of course, he *had* been on a mission where he'd had feelings for the woman with him—a disastrous mission where he'd failed his men in the worst possible way.

He felt her grin against his chest as she said, "You'll never know how glad I am to hear you've never had *feelings* for one of your guys."

"I'm serious, Annie. I'm worried about tonight."

She looked up at him soberly. "So am I, Tom. I'm scared to death I'm going to get in the way or do something dumb and get all of you killed. I could never live with myself if that happened again."

"Again?"

He felt Annie freeze up like a deer caught in headlights. What was *that* all about?

She mumbled, "Well, uh, you nearly died once. I don't want to see you flirt with death again. That's what I meant."

"I'm not exactly eager to tempt fate a second time myself."

She stepped away from him, wringing her hands in agitation. He caught them between his own palms, stilling them gently.

"Look, Tom. I've never worked with anyone I cared about in a personal sense, either. We're just going to have to play it by ear. If you give me an order, I'll follow it. The rest of the time I'll try to stay out of trouble and help you guys as much as I can. That's the best I can do."

"Then that will have to be enough. I'll get us out of here safe and sound somehow, Annie. I promise."

He exhaled slowly. He had no idea how he was going to fulfill that promise. But he'd find a way. He always did.

"I know you will. I have complete confidence in you."

Her faith in him twisted his gut into a dozen little knots. She was so innocent. She didn't have a clue how bad a spot they were in or how many things could go wrong with this mission.

He sighed. He wished he shared her optimism.

Annie's premission nerves had deteriorated to abject fear by the time they slipped out into the street several hours later. The moon wasn't due to rise until almost 4 a.m., so they had roughly six hours of what Tom termed "good darkness" in which to move.

They waited in the alley behind the apartment building for a solid twenty minutes while their night vision adapted. Meanwhile Tom checked over everyone's black clothing and gear one more time for anything that might catch or reflect light.

Annie looked at the blackened faces of her comrades and

wondered if the greasepaint wiped all expression from her face, as well. Their gazes were ice-cold.

Tom had taught her enough of their sign language for her to understand when he gestured for Howdy to take the point and Tex and Mac to back him up. Tom went next with Annie behind him. Doc followed her, and Dutch brought up the rear.

Tom had instructed her in how to move silently along walls, sliding through shadows whenever possible. She followed his black-clad shape closely, mimicking his gliding progress as best she could.

They made decent time for the first hour, which was just as well. Annie was too jumpy to have sat still for long. They wended their cautious way well into Old Town before they heard any gunfire.

It started as a gentle buzzing noise, like a bee busily collection pollen. It grew into an angry wasp, and then into a raging attack of sound upon the senses. After two weeks of nightly warfare outside her window, she'd have thought she'd be used to it by now. But she wasn't.

Suddenly the fighting erupted all around them, with zinging sounds over their heads and bits of mortar pelting them from all sides. Annie was already on her way down to the dirt when Tom landed on top of her. Fast hand signals sent Tex and Mac slithering off on their bellies, and Tom signaled her to be still.

She was more than happy to comply. She felt like a cornered rabbit, her heart pounding so hard it nearly choked her. They were lying beside a pile of rubble at the mouth of a cavernous, black alley. A car partially obscured the street in front of them, and the corner of a building jutted out, protecting their left flank.

As she watched, one of the car's tires went flat with a sickening thud of lead on rubber. Despite herself, she flinched. Tom's arm tightened painfully against her shoulders, pressing her even flatter against the pavement, pinning her until she could barely breathe.

"I said, *don't move*," he hissed during the next volley of bullets.

She waited until the next blast of noise to mutter back, "Sorry." Sheesh. He didn't have to be so snippy about it.

Her train of thought derailed abruptly. Of course he had every right to be snippy. What was she thinking? This was what he'd been talking about earlier. He wasn't her lover anymore. He was her commanding officer. In a war zone. With bullets flying overhead.

She was startled when a hand touched her ankle, but she managed not to jump in fright.

A black form eased its way along her body inch by agonizingly slow inch until it lay beside her.

Tex murmured in her ear, "Tell Hoss there's an exit out the back of the alley."

She started to turn her head to relay the message when Tex hissed, "Slowly. Move slowly. You'll draw their attention if you move too fast."

By gradual degrees, she eased her head to the left until her mouth rested practically on Tom's ear.

"Tex says there's an exit out the back of the alley."

Tom's response was short. "Let's go."

She felt Tom's hand move on her shoulder as he signaled across her body to Tex.

The lanky soldier moved back down her side as slowly as he had before. Tex tugged on her ankle, and she took a deep breath. When the next flurry of gunfire erupted, she dug in with her toes and fingers and did her best to imitate his cold molasses style of movement.

Her arms ached and her calves were cramping by the time she moved a single body length back into the sheltering darkness of the alley. She paused during a lull in the fighting, panting from fear and exertion.

Tex tugged again, and she gathered herself to keep pushing on. Her nails were chipped and torn, and the palms of her hands felt raw from pushing against the rough asphalt. The smell of fuel oil permeating the ground beneath her head was faintly nauseating, but she tried to block it out.

Bit by torturous bit, they made their way backward into the inky bowels of the alley.

Annie thought she was going to cry before Tex finally tapped on her ankle for her to stop. Tom's dark form rose to a crouch in front of her. He grabbed her shoulders and lifted her to a half crouch.

She plastered herself against the cold wall at her back and crept after Tex's retreating form. Her thighs screamed in protest, but she pushed doggedly onward.

As she scaled new heights of pain, Annie decided she was never again going to think her aerobics instructor back home led a sadistic workout.

Just when Annie thought her legs were going to buckle out from under her, Tex slid around a corner and disappeared. She followed suit and nearly collapsed in relief when he motioned her to stand up. Tom joined them a moment later.

Annie jumped when a voice spoke into the tiny earpiece they'd fitted her with. She recognized Mac's whispered brogue. "This alley dumps out on El Segundo Street at the east end and Reynaldo Street at the other. Where to now?"

Tom answered with a question of his own. "Where's Howdy?"

Tex replied. "He's back at the mouth of the alley. Last I saw he was heading into a building across the street from our position."

Annie gasped. What in the world was Howdy doing heading toward the fighting instead of away from it?

She started when she heard Tom saying her name over the radio.

"Annie, does the street we just left intersect El Segundo or Reynaldo?"

She drew a blank. Oh, God. Howdy's life might depend on her knowing the answer, and she couldn't remember. Think, Annie, *think.*

She envisioned strolling down the avenue they'd left behind. There was department store with big, glass display windows. And a luggage store. The street took shape in her mind. It curved to the south and sloped downhill toward…

…toward Reynaldo Street.

Thank God.

"Reynaldo," she whispered urgently. "If Howdy goes west for about two blocks from the alley, the street hits Reynaldo. There's a stop light."

Annie was startled when Howdy's voice murmured a single word in her ear.

"Landmarks?"

She thought fast. "There's a bicycle shop on the northeast corner and a drugstore on the southeast corner."

Tom again. "Report when you're in the clear, Howdy."

"Clear. Four down."

He undoubtedly meant four men down. Howdy'd taken out four men all by himself? Already? Holy smokes.

As Tom took her elbow to urge her forward, he spoke once more. "Howdy, we'll meet you at the corner in ten."

"Roger."

This time Dutch took point as they made their way down the alley toward their rendezvous. They moved in fits and spurts, timing their movements with the sounds of the gunfighting to camouflage the noise of their movement.

By her reckoning, they must be getting close to Reynaldo Street. A faint glimmer of light glowed ahead where the alley ended. She'd started to breathe in relief when, suddenly, Dutch motioned them sharply to freeze.

That had been the first signal Tom taught her, and she

obeyed it instantly now. The sound of voices carried to her in a moment of relative quiet. Several male voices were muttering in quiet snips of Spanish.

In horror she watched a patrol of three soldiers turn into the alley from the opening ahead of them. No. Oh, no. She and Tom and the others were all going to die. The soldiers would see them and open fire. In this narrow concrete canyon, there was no cover, nowhere to hide. They were sitting ducks. Sick fear glutted her stomach.

At least she was going to die with Tom.

She watched the soldiers' progress through slitted eyes as Tom had taught her to. The whites of eyes reflect light easily, he'd said, so she should close her eyes or barely open them if she was trying to be invisible.

This qualified as a good time to be invisible.

The soldiers strolled forward, somehow completely unaware of the six people frozen in front of them. Disbelievingly, she followed their forward progress. The men were so close now that Dutch could reach out and touch them.

The soldiers took several more steps, drawing parallel to Tex. How in the world were these guys not seeing the team?

Another few steps. The soldiers were right in the middle of them.

And then it was over.

With a blur of motion so fast and silent she hardly believed she'd seen it, Tom and his men leaped on the soldiers from all directions. With barely a rustle of sound, the three hapless soldiers went down.

As Tom dragged her quickly past the bodies, Doc lifted his hand away from the last throat with a silent nod at Tom, who nodded back. The medic picked up the soldiers' rifles, shouldering one and passing the other two off to Mac and Dutch.

In shock Annie stumbled forward beside Tom.

She'd just witnessed the death of three men. The efficient brutality of it numbed her mind. Tom and his men had just committed cold-blooded murder and responded to it with no more than a nod to one another.

What kinds of monsters were they?

Chapter 10

In a daze, Annie allowed Tom to lead her to the alley's exit. She crouched when he told her to and stayed put when he told her to. She watched numbly as Tex and Mac sidled out of the alley and disappeared for what seemed like an eternity.

When they came back, Howdy was with them. Detached, she listened to the whispered conversation as Tom ordered Howdy and Tex to reconnoiter the area.

The two men disappeared, and Doc unfolded a tarp that appeared from somewhere on his person. It was made of loose netting with random strips of cloth woven through it.

Doc and Dutch stretched out on the ground under the edge of the tarp, their feet touching as they faced opposite directions. They peered through the scopes of rifles propped under their chins. Each murmured an all-clear into their collar microphones.

Tom's arm went around her middle and pulled her down beside him where he'd stretched out between the other men and a brick wall. Her head landed on his shoulder. She couldn't help it. She went rigid against him.

The warmth of his mouth touched her earlobe, and she jumped.

"What's wrong?" he murmured.

"Nothing."

"Bull. Tell me what's wrong."

"It doesn't matter. I don't want to distract you."

He shrugged. "Your call."

Ominous silence settled around them like a burial shroud.

Tom murmured, "We're going to be here awhile. You should get some rest. Sleep if you can."

"You've *got* to be kidding."

A silent chuckle shook his chest beneath her arm. "Nope. It'll be an hour or more before Tex and Howdy get back. What's got you so tense?"

"I told you I don't want to talk about it."

His voice was quiet. Final. "Look. I want you to relax, and you're not going to do that until you tell me what's wrong."

"No."

"Talk. Now. That's an order."

She considered arguing, but memory of what she'd just witnessed spurred her to shut up and obey.

"You and your team just killed three men. Don't you feel anything? Any remorse?"

He went very still. "No, I don't. It was them or us. Would you rather I'd let them kill us instead?"

"No."

"So what's the problem?"

"It was just so…"

His voice was a low growl. "Go ahead. Say it."

"…cold-blooded."

"That's my job, Annie. I do what is necessary to complete the mission. You know that."

She'd known in the abstract what Tom and his men did, but it was so much more graphic seeing it with her own eyes. How did this kind, gentle, decent man manage to kill without batting an eyelash, yet still retain his humanity? How could she love a man capable of such casual violence?

"Annie, I don't enjoy killing. But if it's necessary, wouldn't you rather have someone like me doing it than someone who gets pleasure out of it?"

He had a point.

"I suppose so. I just wish it weren't necessary."

"We try to minimize deaths, but it's not always possible. I'm sorry you had to see that, angel, but it couldn't be helped."

He rolled on his side and hugged her close.

"Try to get some rest."

She snuggled against the warmth of his body and closed her eyes. But visions of three men falling in a twisted heap kept playing over and over in her head. Sleep refused to come.

After several minutes she whispered, "Tom?"

"Hmm?"

"How come those soldiers didn't see us?"

"We were lucky. They probably hadn't been outside long enough for their night vision to be optimum. Also, as long as none of us moved, there wasn't much but a few black shadows to see."

"Why are we sitting here if there's not any fighting?"

"That's why. It's too quiet. Howdy and Tex are checking it out. I want to know where the army and the rebels are."

Annie frowned. She trusted Tom's judgment, but it still seemed as if they ought to be moving when there weren't any soldiers around.

Tom murmured, "If the rebels pulled out their main force to attack the east sector, they should have left at least a few patrols behind."

Annie murmured back, "What about those guys behind us?"

Tom's one-word reply chilled her. "Army."

"What were *they* doing here?" Annie asked.

His reply was grim. "That's what we're hoping Howdy and Tex can find out."

Their vigil was long and cold, but Tom had sat through worse. Until Annie's hand started roaming across his chest. She was probably cold and looking for a warm spot to put it. He tucked it under his armpit.

But that pulled her body against his, the fullness of her breasts pushing impudently against him. It also brought her mouth disturbingly close to his neck.

She behaved for a few minutes, but then her lips began to move against the sensitive spot at the base of his neck. She undulated slowly against him in the way that always drove him over the edge, while her mouth's explorations moved from his neck to his earlobe.

His respiration jumped, as did the nether regions of his body. His body temperature spiked, and suddenly the night's chill was no longer a problem. Nothing much was going on while they waited. Maybe if he indulged Annie in her flirting she'd calm down and get a little rest.

His free hand roamed down her back to cup her behind the way he'd been itching to ever since he first saw her in the sassy black slacks that outlined her derriere so enticingly. He pressed her close. Her thigh rode up his until her it caressed the hardening bulge of his trousers.

He almost groaned aloud, almost surged up over her, reversing their positions, almost tore off her pants and pulled her beneath him.

And then Doc's whispered voice shocked him like a bucket of ice water.

"You okay, Hoss? You're breathing hard."

Oh, hell.

He was in the middle of a war zone, and he'd completely lost his concentration.

Annie's leg jerked back down. She stilled abruptly beside him.

"I'll be okay. Bad dream, I guess. Ready for me to take a turn at the watch?"

"Sure."

Tom shrugged away from Annie and wriggled forward while Doc wriggled back. He settled into place, the position as familiar as breathing to him. He pressed his cheek against the machine gun that had been his companion for the past ten years. Its cold caress focused his mind, reminded him of who and what he was.

He hadn't liked the reflection of himself he'd seen in Annie's eyes earlier. *Had* he become a cold-blooded killer? It was a sobering thought.

A movement caught his attention, and he zoomed in the high-powered night scope. His finger caressed the weapon's trigger with a delicacy that would have sent Annie into screaming ecstasy, had it been her instead of the gun he stroked. *Stop it!*

Panic clawed at Tom's throat. Had he completely lost his ability to do his job? Should he declare himself unfit and turn leadership of the team over right now? What had Annie done to him? He was going to get them killed if he couldn't keep his mind on his work.

He registered a tabby cat picking its way across a pile of rubble on the far side of the intersection.

His threat reaction subsided, but not the out-of-control feeling hovering just beyond his grasp. He had to pull himself together for all their sakes. He concentrated fiercely on emptying his mind of everything but himself, the rifle and the street before him.

Whatever he was, murderer or otherwise, he wasn't

about to psychoanalyze himself tonight. He'd do whatever it took to get Annie and his men out of Gavarone alive. The chips would just have to fall where they would later.

And in the meantime he had to stay the hell away from Annie.

It was close to two hours later when Howdy eased into Tom's line of sight. It had taken Tom most of his watch to get control of himself again, but he believed, he hoped, he'd achieved a proper frame of mind.

The sniper dashed across the street and slid under the netting beside Tom.

In a rare state of agitation, Howdy whispered, "The whole damn army's headed this way. They're moving tanks, armored personnel carriers, artillery, the works. They've got a good two thousand troops with them on foot moving door to door. We've got to get out of here now."

"How much time till contact?"

"Fifteen, maybe twenty minutes. They're converging on our position from the south and the west."

Dutch murmured, "If we bug out now, we'll lose Tex. He doesn't know this sector well enough to find us. There's no rendezvous point arranged."

"Is Tex in radio contact?" Tom asked tersely.

"No," Dutch replied.

Tom's gaze swept the street through his scope while he thought furiously. Without Annie they could afford to stick around and wait a while longer for Tex to return. But with her slowing down their departure, they needed to leave now.

Dammit! How was he supposed to choose between endangering her and endangering his entire team? The next half second suspended itself around him in a slow-motion eternity of hell. This was the moment of crisis he'd felt building and had dreaded for the past month. He'd known in his gut it would come down to something like this.

It was an ironclad creed among their kind never, ever, to leave one of their own behind, alive or dead. Were it not for Annie, there'd be no choice at all. They'd stay. But how could he live with himself if she couldn't hack the pace or dangers of a hairy egress and got killed? There was no way to choose between her good and the good of his team.

Howdy murmured, "Hoss, Annie's going to be a liability. We need to roll now."

Tom turned his head to stare at the man who'd been at his side for the past decade. Their gazes locked. Howdy understood. Tom saw it in the fathomless grief of Howdy's gaze. They were going to have to sacrifice Tex—their friend and brother. Tom closed his eyes for a moment, praying that Tex could take care of himself. Then he reached deep for the strength to call the retreat.

Annie spoke as he opened his mouth, cutting him off. "We're not leaving until Tex gets back, and that's all there is to it." Her tone was belligerent.

Tom replied gently, "We have to, angel."

"I won't leave one of you guys behind again. I refuse to be responsible for choosing to let one of you die." Her tone was adamant, final.

"Now look here…"

"Tom, unless you plan to sling me over your shoulder and carry me out of here, that's the only way I'm budging."

He frowned, weighing the steel in her tone. "The longer we wait, Annie, the rougher the egress is going to be. You may not be able to keep up…."

"If you guys can act like superheroes when the chips are down, so can I. I'll take responsibility for keeping up with you guys. If I can't, it'll be on my head."

Dammit! This was just the sort of behavior he'd warned

her about. "Annie, you promised you'd follow my orders. And I'm ordering you to leave with us now."

Her reply was simple. "No. I don't consider that to be a lawful order."

It bloody well was a lawful order, and he'd see her court-martialed and hanged from a yardarm for disobeying if they got out of here alive. But right now what he needed was for her to get her butt in gear and move out.

"I *will* carry you if I have to..." he started.

Howdy touched him on the sleeve, stopping his budding tirade. Tom frowned at his old friend.

The sniper said softly, "Don't argue with her, Tom. Honor her right to make this choice. She's a duly commissioned military officer, and she knows the risk she's accepting."

Tom closed his eyes, hating the truth of Howdy's words. He nodded once.

Howdy squeezed his arm briefly, while Annie's sigh of relief tickled his eardrum.

Wrung out to the core of his being, Tom prayed fervently for Tex to appear.

Ten endless minutes ticked past. Annie's survivability grew more and more precarious with each passing second. Tom was on the verge of ordering the retreat when, suddenly, a man-size black shape loomed in front of him.

Tex didn't waste time on niceties.

He panted, "It's a trap. The rebels didn't leave this sector. They're on foot and in vehicles, waiting in force about three blocks northeast of here to ambush the army."

Tom was equally terse. "Are they moving?"

"No."

"Is there a clear route?"

"Maybe. We can move up Reynaldo Street about two blocks and cut west six or eight blocks. We may be able to punch north from there."

Howdy interjected. "Nope. That'd land us in the army's lap. They're maybe three blocks west of us, now."

Tom spoke over Tex's vehement curse. "We need to take cover. Did either of you see someplace safe where we can ride this out?"

The two men shook their heads in the negative.

Tom jumped when Annie's voice came up on headset. "I know a place. It's just a couple of blocks north of here. Neither side would dare touch it."

Tom ordered instantly, "Take us there."

They all jumped to their feet, abandoning the gillie net as they shouldered their weapons.

"Tex, is stealth necessary?" Tom asked hurriedly.

"Not if we hoof it."

Tom grabbed Annie's arm and hauled her with him as he ran forward, his rifle slung at the ready by his hip. "Where to?"

"Turn right out of the alley and go north on Reynaldo."

Following her directions, they broke into a run and burst out into the street. They sprinted down the sidewalk, heedless of any noise they might be making. Speed was of the essence now.

The group set a blistering pace, and Tom's respiration expanded and deepened into a stitch in his side. Thank goodness he'd been working out as hard as he had.

Annie ran beside him, breathing heavily. As much as he wanted to reach out and help her, it took all his energy to keep up with the team.

They pounded through an intersection, and then the street curved and climbed a sharp incline. Annie's breathing turned to rasping.

"Keep pushing," he panted. "Breathe deep. Exhale hard." It was all the advice he could squeeze out of his own burning lungs.

A rumbling noise intruded on the silence around them.

Tanks. The metallic clang of treads on pavement grew audible behind them.

They neared the top of a longer, steeper hill and Annie gasped, ''Left. Turn at the next street. It looks like a dead end—'' she took a wheezing breath ''—but it's not.''

The shifting of engine gears drew near. The tanks were maybe a block behind them, one curve away from spotting their fleeing forms.

Annie's steps began to slow.

''Run, Annie! You can make it. We're almost there!''

''I...can't...last building...on left...''

Tom reached over and ripped the small pack from Annie's shoulders, flinging it to the ground. He grabbed her elbow and dragged her forward with the last bit of his strength.

''I'm not leaving you behind. I'll die beside you if I have to,'' he gasped.

The headlights of the tank behind them lit the buildings at the base of the hill as the vehicle started a ponderous turn up the curving street behind them. The white beam of death gained on them mercilessly as Tom reached for the last ounce of strength in his being.

They weren't going to make it.

And then strong arms came under his elbows as Dutch and Mac dropped back beside him, propelling him forward. Annie seemed lifted from his hand as Tex and Doc grabbed her. As one, they sprinted for their lives.

Howdy already crouched ahead at the corner Annie'd indicated, calmly sighting the minigun at the street behind them.

They dived for the corner as the tank rounded the curve behind them. Bare instants after they hit the ground, the whining fury of Howdy's gatling gun deafened them.

Machine gun fire rat-a-tatted in response as Tom rolled

to his feet and took a quick head count. All present and accounted for.

"Fighting retreat! Annie to the rear."

Instantly the team fanned out. Annie went with Tex and Doc as they sprinted a hundred yards down the street. Dutch stayed with Howdy at the gun, and Mac went with Tom. They leapfrogged backward as the team farthest back sprinted its retreat and the other teams covered them.

Apparently the minigun had performed its equalizing task admirably, for no troops pursued them down the narrow, black street.

Each time a team passed Annie, they grabbed her and hauled her along, always keeping her with the hindmost team. They'd gone several hundred yards when Annie tugged at Tom's sleeve.

"That's it." She pointed at a large, ornate stone building behind a tall wrought-iron fence.

"Everyone inside," Tom ordered.

They retreated in good order through the garden and into the shadows of the deep, arched vestibule of the front entrance.

While Annie knocked urgently on the door, Tom asked, "What is this place? A church?"

The front door opened to reveal deep gloom. They slipped inside while the heavy wood portal closed out the sounds of gunfire behind them.

Annie's amused voice answered him out of the darkness. "Nope. This isn't a church. It's the best brothel in Gavarone."

A light flipped on to reveal a gaudy, wallpapered hallway lined with a series of gilt-framed mirrors. Tom gaped blankly at Annie.

"You brought us to a brothel?"

"It's the one place neither side would dare attack."

The muscular bouncer who'd opened the door for them

piped up in flawless English, "We have declared strict neutrality in the current unpleasantness. We are the Switzerland of Gavarone, as it were."

Tom didn't know whether to laugh or be appalled.

"I sure hope so, because there are tanks right around the corner from you."

"The fighting will not come down our little street. The proprietor has had solemn promises on that from the commanding generals of both armies."

Howdy grinned. "Now that you mention it, it did seem a little too easy how we made it that last stretch without any pursuit."

Tom shook his head. "I'll be damned."

The bouncer looked at them disapprovingly. "You will have to clean up and relinquish your weapons if you wish to partake of the delights of the house."

Like hell he was giving up his weapons. Tom opened his mouth to say just that when Doc's hand landed casually on his shoulder. The medic spoke to the bouncer.

"Is this by any chance Señora Armando's House of Fine Relaxation?"

The fellow flashed a broad grin. "It is."

Doc fairly gushed, "Thank goodness. I was beginning to despair of ever finding this place. We have come from far away to visit you. Your reputation extends well beyond the borders of your country."

The bouncer's chest expanded. "Does it now?"

Doc laid on the flattery thick and fast, while Tom watched him, bemused. His brows shot up when Doc explained that they'd be glad to compensate the proprietor at double the usual fees, due to the current climate of uncertainty.

That seemed to thaw out their host mightily.

The bouncer was distracted momentarily when a girl approached from the other direction and whispered in his ear.

Doc used the interruption to murmur, "This guy is 'Señora' Armando. If he likes you, he won't report you to the authorities. But if you cross him…"

The owner turned back to them.

Doc shifted topics instantly, "I was just congratulating my friends on braving a veritable war zone to partake of your fabled delights."

"You came, knowing the war was about to start?"

Tom interjected solemnly, "We did. You see, we're a little club of…connoisseurs. We scour the world in search of ultimate pleasure."

Tex grinned and looked over his shoulder at Tom. "That's us, all right."

Tom scowled back at Tex, but addressed himself to the owner. "We'd just like to sleep tonight. It was a rather arduous trip. Tomorrow when we've rested up, then we can sample the ladies. No delights are necessary this evening."

The fellow's demeanor changed abruptly. "No girls, no rooms. We're not a hotel. If you don't partake, you're out of here."

Tom noted sourly that all his guys grinned widely at that. Crud. If they went back outside, they'd be mowed down in the crossfire of two armies. He sighed.

"If we must, I suppose we can find the strength to partake this evening. After all, we've gone through so much to get here. Perhaps you could show us to several bathrooms so we might wash up a bit first?"

Tex slapped him on the shoulder. "Ahh, the sacrifices we make in the line of duty."

Mac chimed in, "It'll be rough, but I'll do my best to be *up* to it."

Even Doc chuckled and mumbled, "How are we ever going to explain this on our expense reimbursement forms?"

Their host cut in. "The woman will be extra."

Tom frowned. "I beg your pardon?"

"You want a three-way with your girlfriend, yes?"

Tom's gaze swiveled to Annie, who looked shocked to her toes. "Uh, yes, I guess so."

His guys were abruptly silent, all gaping at him. Annie blinked and swallowed convulsively before she nodded, looking dazed.

He glanced at his men and murmured, "Not a word or I'll break your necks. Is that understood?"

They all nodded meekly.

Resolutely he followed "Señora" Armando's six-and-a-half-foot tall frame down the hallway to a rest room, where he scrubbed off the black greasepaint and cleaned himself up for he knew not what next.

Chapter 11

Annie looked around the bedroom the languid blonde was showing them. Whatever she'd expected, this wasn't it. The room was decorated with beautiful antiques and heavy, mahogany furniture. Several small, fringed lamps lit the space artfully, casting shadows across the enormous bed that dominated the room.

"What now?" Annie asked.

She looked on, relieved, as Tom pulled out a wad of Gavronese money and instructed the prostitute who was supposed to entertain them to go away and hide until morning. The blonde seemed more than happy to comply.

"Start a normal conversation," he murmured.

Normal? In a brothel in the middle of a war zone? Sure. Let's see. She and Tom and the guys were supposed to be connoisseurs sampling the pleasures of fine bordellos around the world.

"Honestly, Tom. Did we have to come here tonight? Couldn't we have waited until this stupid revolution was over to try out this particular gourmet brothel?"

He walked the length of the walls, using a handheld, electronic gadget to search their surfaces for bugs or cameras.

He answered her over his shoulder, "But it's the danger that gives it spice. Our customers wouldn't have paid half as much as they did for this excursion if they hadn't had to duck bullets to get here."

The sound of bullets flying past her ears was one Annie would never forget. The ominous zinging of ricocheting lead made her flinch just to think about it.

Tom gestured her to talk more while he inspected the furniture. Someone would no doubt burst in and shoot them if she didn't keep up the pretense. The panic that had been clawing at her for the past hour blanked her thoughts. She blurted out the first thing that came to mind.

"So who gets to be on top tonight?"

Tom abruptly stopped what he was doing and looked up at her. A predatory grin split his features. "I think it's your turn."

That was the same smile he'd flashed briefly at his men after they cut down the soldiers in the alley—the wolf congratulating his pack on a clean kill. Annie shuddered. It had been sheer luck they didn't get gunned down themselves in that alley. She still smelled the death there, sharp and metallic, as blood had spurted.

He finished his search with a last glance around the room.

"All clear," he announced.

Annie exhaled a sigh of relief, but that brought her back to her original question. "So what now? Do we rappel out the window and keep pressing on toward the ocean?"

"Nope. Now we hunker down and get a good night's sleep."

Annie stared at him. "You're kidding, right? I couldn't sleep if my life depended on it."

His expression turned serious. "It may. You'll need your rest before this is over. We're not clear of this country by a long shot."

A shudder swept through her. "Great."

"Have a little faith, angel. We made it this far, and that's a minor miracle." He swept a critical look down her body. "In the meantime, you need to get out of those clothes. Unless I miss my mark, you broke a sweat running from that tank and you're damp. Your clothes need to be dry before we leave here tomorrow. The last thing we need is for you to get sick."

The cotton turtleneck *was* sticking to her body steamily. And then suddenly, she was choking, unable to take a deep breath. A band of terror closed itself more and more tightly around her ribs. She couldn't think of anything she wanted more than to be out of that shirt. She tore it off over her head, taking the throat mike with it. She kicked off her shoes and socks and peeled off her pants for good measure, too.

Annie scrubbed her hands hard over her skin to remove the cloying, filthy feeling blanketing her.

And then Tom grabbed her, pulling her against his chest and holding her so tight she could barely breathe.

"It's okay, angel. We made it."

But not by much, they hadn't. Annie still felt the tank's spotlights gaining on them, still tasted the helplessness of knowing she wasn't strong enough or fast enough to outrun its promise of death. Her heart pounded anew.

Tom's clothes were rough against her bare skin, his arms iron bands surrounding her. Everywhere she touched him tonight, he was a soldier. From his sculpted granite shoulders to the ammo pouches on his belt to the bulge of a pistol on his hip, all of it spoke of lethal skill.

This side of him frightened her, but it also fascinated her. It was primitive and wild, barely controlled, and all the more dangerous because it was tightly leashed. When he'd warned her he'd be in commando mode tonight, she'd never dreamed this was what he'd meant. Nothing she'd seen of him before had hinted at this.

She suspected any less of a warrior would have failed her tonight. But he hadn't. They were all safe—for the moment.

The fear and creeping horror of the past several hours finally caught up with Annie, and she began to shake. Adrenaline surged through her veins, making her tremble uncontrollably.

She burrowed her face in his shoulder and let the aftershocks run their course. He murmured comforting sounds into her hair, gradually calming her. Tom's solid body absorbed her quivering until she finally stilled.

"I thought we were going to die," she whispered.

"Nah, not us. We're the best."

Annie reached up and placed a hand on each of his lean cheeks. "Nobody's invincible, Tom. Not even you. Promise me you won't forget that and try something only a superhero could pull off."

His eyes went dark and hard. "I know my limits. But make no mistake about it. I'm in this to win. We *will* get out of here alive."

Annie flinched at the sharp edge in his voice. Restless, she paced the confines of the room, doing laps around the big bed that dominated the center of the space.

When Tom turned out the light and plunged the room into inky blackness, she was forced to halt. She listened, her senses on edge, and just managed to hear him move to the bed and stretch out on it.

His voice came out of the darkness, a low growl of command. "Come to bed, Annie."

She fumbled her way to the bed and climbed between

the crisp coolness of satin sheets. Reaching for Tom, she was surprised to discover he was still fully clothed.

"Expecting to make a quick departure?"

"Nope. Just a precaution."

Her hands found his chest and roamed across its delicious expanse.

"A precaution against what?" she asked.

"You."

"Me?"

She propped herself up on one elbow and explored the far side of Tom's neck.

His response was stoic. "Yup."

He held himself rigid, refusing to respond to her touch.

"I don't understand, Tom."

"I do. You're wired tighter than a two-minute bomb. All that tension is going to turn to lust any minute. I know the signs."

Now that he mentioned it, she was feeling a certain tightly coiled need deep in her belly.

"So what's the problem?" She threw a leg across his, rubbing the arch of her foot against the cool fabric of his pants. "Are you too tired to, uh, rise to the occasion?"

A noise that sounded like half snort and half laughter came from his side of the bed.

"Let's just say the combination of your adrenaline and mine could be a bad thing."

She rolled over until she lay partially on top of him. A bad thing? What was he talking about? He felt pretty darn good to her right about now, all bulging steel muscles and masculine appeal. Sexual vibes poured off him like steam from a sauna.

Heck. She was alive. He was alive. That's what mattered. They'd barely escaped with their necks, but they'd *done it*. The rush of having avoided death surged through her veins.

He felt it, too. She knew it in the way he went stiff beneath her.

"How can this be a bad thing?" she murmured as her hands roamed over his shoulders and arms. The soft cotton of his turtleneck belied the power beneath.

Tom's hands gripped hers painfully tight, stilling them against his chest. "Sex can get a little…intense…after a brush with death. Trust me. You don't want this."

Heat flared in her at the violence in his voice. Something restless and wild was loose inside her tonight, and it was in dire need of taming. There was no doubt about it. She most certainly *did* want this.

Her thigh moved across his, and she writhed sinuously against him. The way his clothes rubbed against her naked skin was maddening. She was woman, and he was man. Why was he holding back?

He lay rigid beneath her, breathing heavily, his heart thudding beneath her ear.

"Come on, Tom. Let it go."

He gritted out a single word from between clenched teeth. "No."

She rolled fully on top of him, demanding that he acknowledge her, demanding that he feel her desire. She rubbed shamelessly against the hard bulge in his trousers, knowing she could make him give in to her, needing him to give in.

"I want you, Tom."

"You don't know what you'd be getting into."

"Show me."

Abruptly he surged beneath her, reversing their positions in an instant. His leg lay across hers, his foot hooked around her far calf as he pinned her to the bed. He yanked her roaming hands away from him and thrust them up over her head.

"I just came off a mission. It takes me a while to wind down. Tonight I'd play rough."

Her voice dripped with challenge. "And?"

His voice was a low growl. "Annie, I don't want to hurt you."

She tested the strength of his hold on her. "You think I can't handle it? Is that it? Didn't it occur to you I might feel the same way?"

He went still against her. There was a long pause. She could all but hear him wrestling with himself.

"Are you sure, angel? I can't promise to be gentle...."

She cut him off, kissing him wildly, with her whole body. She wrapped her arms and legs around him and surged up into him, searching for the release she knew he could give her.

He pulled back, disentangling himself for a brief moment.

His voice came to her out of the velvet blackness of the night, taut and edgy. "You do like to live dangerously, don't you?"

The dark tone of his words sent a thrill down her spine. He was part of the night. He enveloped her in his arms, his demanding weight pinning her in place. His callused hands roamed over her naked flesh just shy of painfully, taking pleasure where they willed.

The night's desperation broke over her, and she returned his caresses. She tore at his clothing, maddened by a need to feel his naked skin against hers.

"Slow down, sweetheart," he murmured. "We can't afford to lose any of this equipment."

He snagged her wrists and dragged them upward. He wrapped her fingers around two spindles of the headboard. "Don't let go," he ordered.

He rolled away and his weight left the bed.

She waited impatiently while he shed his throat microphone, his ear piece, binoculars, pouches and pocketfuls of bits and pieces of explosives, assorted knives and his spare pistols. Annie noted that one of those went under his pillow.

Finally she heard the whisper of clothes hitting the floor, and the mattress moved beneath her.

Then his mouth captured hers. He kissed her rapaciously, biting her lower lip, plunging his tongue inside her mouth aggressively, burning her cheeks and chin with his beard.

His hands trailed down her arms until they encountered her bra. He all but tore the garment off her body, baring her to his greedy mouth. He twirled and flicked her nipples with his thumbs, sending her surging up off the mattress into the almost painful pleasure that seared through her.

He did tear off her underwear, and then his knee intruded between hers, opening her for his invasion. It came first from his hand, his fingers plucking mercilessly at the very core of her until she thought she'd scream in pleasure and frustration. He followed with an assault by mouth and tongue, driving her beyond thought, beyond anything but an all-consuming need to have him inside of her.

He made her beg until she nearly wept for him, and then he rose over her, lifting her hips to him. He filled her with a single violent stroke that brought her to an immediate, shattering release.

He gave her no quarter.

While she was still shuddering around his burning heat, he began to ride her, plunging again and again into her, stoking the fires of her desire, demanding more and yet more from her.

She could no more deny him than she could deny her unfettered exultation at being alive.

Again and then again she scaled the heights of ecstasy, while Tom dragged her ever higher until she could no longer breathe, overcome by such an excess of rapture, she thought she'd die from it. She twined her legs around his waist, urging him wordlessly to take every last bit of her.

He wrapped his hands over hers where she gripped the headboard, his vise-like grasp barely noticeable as he pounded into her. At the last second before she screamed aloud with the glory of it, his mouth closed over hers, drinking in her cries as if he would suck the very life from her.

For a single, endless second, she and Tom became one. They breathed and felt as one in a union of bodies. Everything else ceased to exist as they experienced a moment of pure sensation, a moment of quintessential perfection.

In that single second Annie knew exactly what it felt like to be truly alive, down to the very last fiber of her being.

If there had been any doubt in her mind about whether or not they'd really made it through the night's perils, that doubt was erased as Tom's perspiration-slicked body pressed intimately against hers.

And then he rolled away, taking her with him and tucking her under his shoulder.

His whisper was rough, yet infinitely tender. "Are you all right, angel?"

Shuddering pleasure still rippled through her body. With effort she found the strength to answer.

"'All right' doesn't quite capture how I'm doing."

Concern laced his voice. "I didn't hurt you, did I?"

She snuggled closer to him, smiling against his chest. "Do I seem hurt to you?"

He answered with a low chuckle. "I guess not. If anything, you seem…well pleasured."

"And you? Are you all right?"

"I'm better than all right, angel. Although, I've got to tell you—I can't imagine there will ever be another egress to top this. This is one for the record books."

She smiled. She had to agree with him on that score.

* * *

A dull flash of steel glinted off a bloody knife as it descended toward her. A rebel soldier with skeleton face and a gaping, bloody hole in his chest wielded it. She turned to flee from him and ran out into a street where a tank was waiting to cut her down. She ran and ran, but she couldn't find Tom anywhere. A dark mist closed in around her and she was trapped, unable to see her way out of the maze.

Very gradually Annie became aware of a hand on her shoulder shaking her. An urgent voice murmured, "Wake up, Annie. Wake up!"

She lurched awake abruptly. It was very dark. She was in a strange bed, and she was not alone.

Tom.

He was with her in the bed. The nightmare loosened its grip a little at the thought of him coming to her rescue. Tanks and knives and crumpled bodies began to jumble together in her head in a grisly tableau.

Instantly Tom's arms were around her, almost as if he'd been waiting for this moment. "I've got you now. You're safe."

She huddled against him, grateful for his solid comfort.

Her body felt bruised and sore, not only from their lovemaking, but also from hours spent lying on the ground and then that frantic sprint for their lives. The thought of it still made her shudder. Were it not for the last second help by Tom's men, she'd have died out there in the street.

She savored the slow, steady beat of Tom's heart beneath her ear.

"I had a nightmare," Annie finally whispered.

"So I gather. I was expecting it."

She pulled back enough to look at his darkly shadowed face. "You were?"

"I do this for a living, remember? I've rescued a few civilians in my time."

She turned her head away from him, ashamed. "But I'm not a civilian. I'm a military officer."

"Who's never seen combat, if I don't miss my guess."

"I've been shot at before." Her tone was defensive.

She felt his smile against her forehead.

"Oh, yeah? When?"

Annie went stiff. When she nearly got him killed, that's when. She changed the subject and prayed he wouldn't become suspicious. "I hope you're not mad at me for bringing you and your team to a brothel. It was all I could think of in the heat of the moment."

His voice caressed her out of the silken darkness. "We're alive. How could I possibly be mad at you for that?" Humor crept into his voice. "Besides, it's a rare mission where we get to spend the night in a comfortable, safe bed."

"Not to mention the hookers provided for all your men."

Silent laughter shook him. "I'll never live this mission down. Try to get some sleep. Tomorrow will probably be worse than today."

She stiffened, lifting her head in a futile attempt to see his face in the darkness. "Why?"

"We're going to have to get past whoever wins tonight's fight."

"Oh." She already felt naked and exposed just thinking about it.

"Don't think about tomorrow, Annie. It'll take care of itself. Sleep now."

She shook her head. "I'm too wired to sleep."

Tom sighed. "I know the feeling."

They lay comfortably entwined for several minutes. He remarked quietly, "You did good tonight. That was a nice run you made."

"I almost didn't make it."

He tightened his arms around her. "But you got the job done. You gutted it out. I'm proud of you."

A warm glow spread through her until she remembered the tightness in her chest, the heaviness of her feet, the awful certainty of failure. She willed away encroaching memories of the narrowness of their escape. "I'd have died without your guys' help."

His voice was velvety soft, soothing. She focused on it. "That's what teamwork is all about. They helped you run a little faster, and you found us a safe place to stay."

"Well, for tonight at any rate." She paused. She truly didn't want to hear the answer to her next question. "Tom, what do we do next?"

He sighed, his voice shifting into a tone of military command. "Tomorrow we'll scout the area and find a way past whatever army ends up controlling this sector."

Hating herself for asking, but needing to nonetheless, she said, "I'm going to be in the way again, aren't I?"

"Of course not!"

"I nearly got you guys killed tonight."

"No, you didn't. I nearly got us killed. I'm the one who decided to stick around and wait for Tex."

She could hear the self-recrimination in his voice. "You'd have left if I hadn't made you stay, though."

He shook his head, his chin brushing lightly against her brow. "You didn't make me do anything, angel. I was in command, and I'm responsible for what happened. We waited for Tex, he had the information we needed, and we all made it out. That's what matters."

Annie listened to the steady beat of Tom's heart beneath her ear. He'd made the courageous decision that she hadn't when she'd been faced with the same dilemma over the jungle. He'd understood the value of saving one person, even if it meant risking the whole team to do it.

And yet, he'd been willing to turn his back on Tex for her. He'd been willing to abandon that very sense of teamwork that was the glue holding them all together. She might be a noncombatant, but she knew exactly what had happened in that alley. He'd been about to destroy his team for her.

"Tom?"

"Hmmm?" He sounded relaxed, on the verge of sleep.

"Why were you going to choose my safety over keeping your team together?"

He was silent a very long time. So long she thought he wasn't going to answer. But finally he spoke. His words sounded ripped from the depths of his being. "Do you really have to ask why I chose you?"

Annie squeezed her eyes shut. Maybe that was the difference. Maybe if she'd known Tom before she decided to sacrifice him by dragging him through the jungle, maybe if she'd loved him then, she'd have had the courage to risk herself and all his men for him.

But maybe she wouldn't have.

"I don't deserve you, Tom."

Abruptly he rolled her on her back. She felt him looming over her, his expression dark and forbidding.

"And why not?"

She bit her lip, knowing he'd make her say it out loud. "I'm not a good enough person for you."

He settled back to the bed, pulling her into the crook of his arm. A sigh lifted his chest beneath her ear.

"Then answer me this, angel. Why did you insist on waiting for Tex?"

"You guys are a family. He's like a brother to you. I couldn't ask you to sacrifice Tex and to break your most solemn vow to the others for me. You'd never have forgiven me if I cost you their trust, not to mention if something bad had happened to Tex."

His tone was matter of fact. "They'd have understood."

"But *you* could never have lived with it."

"What are you talking about?" he asked suspiciously.

She knew well enough by now that brutal honesty was usually the best approach with him. "Tom, running from war to war until you get yourself killed is no way to make up for Simon Pettigrew's death."

Utter silence was his only reply.

Finally she broke the ominous stillness. "I'm sorry if that makes you mad to hear, but it's the truth. Somebody needed to say it to you. You don't have to die to make amends for Simon's death. He signed up for this. He knew the risks. He was in the wrong place at the wrong time. A mission went bad, and a bullet with his name on it found him."

Tom ground out, "The mission went wrong because I screwed up."

"Since when are you held to a higher standard of perfection than the rest of us? Everybody makes mistakes. You've got to let go of this guilt you've been hauling around. It's going to get you killed."

His next question startled her. "Why do you care if I kill myself with a guilt complex?"

Why indeed? She could run from the answer as she had from the tank, but in the end it would catch up with her. Resigned, she finally admitted the truth to herself. She loved Tom.

He stirred beside her. No doubt he was waiting for an answer.

She whispered, "Do you really need to ask?" She turned to him, needing to say it once out loud. "I lo—"

His mouth closed over hers, stopping the words before she could say them. Grief speared through her. Even now, when they'd nearly died together, he wouldn't acknowledge what was happening between them. His defenses were so entrenched, she'd never get through to him.

He might not let her say it aloud, but that didn't change

anything. She'd known it deep down in her heart for a long time, but she'd fought admitting it until now.

Tonight she was too raw, too exposed from the terror of the night's events to hide from it any longer.

Her arms closed around the strong column of his neck, drawing him down to her. Tonight, with a war raging outside, his presence was vastly reassuring. There was, indeed, a time and a place for men who could and would kill on an instant's notice.

The room was warm, but a chill of anticipation raced across her skin. Once more, her warrior-lover came to her and taught her the exhilaration of cheating death.

He might refuse to say the words, but there was no doubt as he chased away her nightmares about how he really felt about her.

Chapter 12

A sunbeam fell across his feet as Tom sat absolutely still in a high-backed armchair in the downstairs sitting room. His men lounged on the far side of the room, trading quiet comments with one another. They knew to give him space when he was this tense.

Annie, on the other hand, was pacing like a caged tiger. She was no doubt wired for the same reason he was.

He'd sent out Doc and Dutch to reconnoiter hours ago, and they still weren't back. He'd chosen them because they had the best covers for moving around in daylight.

They'd left well before 10 a.m., but lunch had come and gone without a sign of them.

He repeated the same litany to himself that he'd been reciting in his head for more than an hour. They were good at what they did. They knew the city, and they knew how to handle themselves in a tight situation. He should have faith in them and be patient a little while longer.

At least worrying about his men kept his mind off what

had happened last night between him and Annie. He shouldn't have given in to her. It was a complication he seriously didn't need.

He'd barely managed to do his job during last night's maneuvers with Annie present. And now, with their feelings for each other becoming more and more obvious, his distraction was only going to get worse. He should've known better than to make love to her. He was the worst kind of fool.

"Boss?"

Tom looked up, startled, at Tex.

"Have you taken a good look at Annie this morning?"

Tom frowned. He'd seen her up close and very personal when they woke up, as a matter of fact. "What are you talking about?"

"Doesn't it strike you that she's acting jumpy, kinda like a cornered jackrabbit?"

Tom gazed closely at her. Now that Tex mentioned it, she did look on the verge of panic.

"Not that it's any of my say-so, Hoss, but I think the filly's gonna need some settling before we try to run her again."

Generally, the more folksy Tex waxed, the more attention Tom paid to him. Besides, the lean Texan was an outstanding judge of human nature. If he thought something was up with Annie, Tom was certainly going to listen. Lord knew, he wasn't having much success at dealing objectively with her. His own judgment couldn't get much more clouded where she was concerned.

"What do you suggest, Tex?"

"Looks to me like she's lost her gumption. She needs her feathers ruffled a little to stiffen her spine. There's nothing like a good fight to make a woman grit her teeth and come out swingin'."

Tom looked at Tex, surprised. "You're suggesting I pick a fight with her?"

"Yup. Like Hell Week with the new recruits."

Tom knew exactly what Tex was referring to. The first week of Special Forces school was designed to weed out all but the most dedicated and mentally tough volunteers. A common technique by the instructors when the recruits got close to quitting was to make them mad. The good recruits would dig deep when provoked and find strength they didn't know they had. That, too, was an important part of their training.

A fight, huh?

He had a pretty good idea of what buttons to push to get a rise out of Annie. He stood up and flashed Tex a rueful grin.

"This could get ugly."

"It needs to be done, Major. We've still got a lot of war ahead of us."

Tom sighed. "Yeah, I know."

He strolled over to where Annie stared out a window at a small, uninspired garden. He'd never seen her this tense before. Her shoulders were bunched up around her ears, and she looked about ready to bust a seam.

He looked out the window until he knew her attention was on him. Casually he pulled out his pocket pager to check for a signal from his men.

"Anything?" she asked.

"Why do you care? They're not your men," he snapped. "Besides, you know I'd tell everyone if there were any news."

"I was just trying to make polite conversation."

"Don't. If I want to trade pleasantries with diplomats, I'll visit Washington."

She crossed her arms and turned her back on him. Good. She looked irritated.

But knowing her, she'd try to make peace. She was too much the attaché to go for long without trying to fix the misunderstanding. Sure enough, she turned back to face him.

Her tone was soothing. "Dutch and Doc will be fine, Tom. They know what they're doing and they have good covers."

He glared at her. "Nothing's fine in a scenario like this. It's too damn unstable. I shouldn't have put men in the field until after dark."

He spun away and noticed Howdy and Mac staring at him. Hopefully Annie wouldn't see their expressions and catch on. He glared at his men until Tex whispered something to the others and they all turned away.

Annie tried again. He had to give her credit for persistence.

"We agreed they'd blend in with the civilians who'll be moving around in daylight. Dutch's press credentials fooled even me, and Doc looks and speaks like a native. You made the right decision."

He whirled on her. "How would you know? You've never made a real combat decision in your life."

She glared back at him, clearly stung. "Wanna bet?"

"You've spent your whole cushy career sipping cocktails by swimming pools and shmoozing generals. You haven't faced a single life-or-death situation in your entire career. You wouldn't know a tough call if it reached out and bit you in the butt."

"You think I couldn't make that kind of call?"

"I know you couldn't. You don't have the nerves for this kind of work."

"I'm not the one checking my pager every ten minutes for a signal from Dutch and Doc."

His gaze narrowed dangerously. "Don't push me. I'm in no mood for games."

She planted her fists solidly on her hips. "Neither am I. And I'd appreciate it if you didn't patronize me."

Her hands balled into fists. Good. She probably needed to be a little more ticked off, though, to get to the point where she'd go through hell and high water to show him how wrong he was. He pushed another button.

"Face it. You'd have died without me last night. Women can't hack it in the field."

"You'd have died without me three months ago!"

He snorted in disdain. "Look, I appreciate what you did to help me. But feeding me painkillers in a hospital and holing up in an apartment with me for a month does not make you a combat veteran. Hell, the night janitor at the embassy could've done what you did for me."

Ahh. There it came. A flush of red creeping up her neck. She definitely didn't like the janitor comparison.

"Why, you sanctimonious...condescending...ungrateful...chauvinist..." she sputtered.

She apparently couldn't think of a word foul enough for him.

"If it weren't for my helping you, I could be sitting by a swimming pool sipping a cocktail with a general this very minute!"

She'd found her voice again and was gathering steam fast. He leaned a hip against the windowsill to ride out the forthcoming explosion.

"I risked my entire crew to pull you and your guys out of the jungle. I got shot at saving your arrogant butt. I stayed until the rebels had missiles locked on me so you could get hoisted out of the jungle. I dodged radar sites and all but flew through the damn trees with a shot-up engine to get you back to a hospital. And you're comparing me to a janitor?"

He went very still. *She'd* pulled him out of the jungle?

She'd been the pilot who dragged him almost to his death? *She'd* been the pilot who decided to sacrifice him to save herself, her crew and his men?

He pushed away from the windowsill, his spine rigid. He spoke very, very calmly. "Would you repeat what you just said?"

"You heard me! Who do you think flew the helicopter that pulled you guys out of the jungle three months ago? I'm the American embassy's only helicopter-rated air attaché."

Tex interjected from across the room. "I knew I recognized your voice from somewhere! You're the lady captain I talked to on the radio. You ain't kidding. That *was* a dicey piece of flying."

Tom glared at him.

The Texan smiled back lazily and drawled, "I think you got her feathers where you wanted 'em, Hoss."

"Stay out of this, Tex," Tom snarled.

He grabbed Annie's arm, marched her out into the hallway and opened a random door to reveal a small empty office. He shoved her inside. This was one conversation they were going to continue in private.

"I've got to warn you, Annie. You've pushed me real close to the edge of violence, here."

Trepidation glinted in her eyes, but she stuck her chin out defiantly.

"*You* flew that helicopter," Tom growled.

"Yeah."

"*You're* the pilot who bugged out while I was still hanging beneath your bird and dragged me damn near to my death."

"That was me."

His voice was low and deadly. "And when were you planning to share this little tidbit with me?"

Some of her bravado faded in the face of his cold fury.

"Well, I was going to tell you before the Americans evacuated the embassy, but they left so unexpectedly I didn't get a chance. And once they were gone, you were my only way out of Gavarone. I thought it might be best not to make you mad at me right then."

He cocked a skeptical eyebrow. "Oh, so you *were* planning to tell me someday?"

"Well, I was planning to at first. But then we started to get close to each other, and I decided there really was no need to mention it to you."

"You didn't think I'd be interested in the fact that you almost killed me?"

"I didn't almost kill *you*. Well, I did, but I didn't know *you* back then. You were just some nameless soldier hanging on a cable."

"Why'd you do it? Why'd you leave me hanging?"

"We were taking ground fire, and our radar picked up shoulder-held missiles. The rebels got lock on and were going to fire at us. I either had to sacrifice you and hope to get everyone else out alive or get shot down for sure and kill the rest of your team and my crew."

His wrath abated momentarily at the sound logic of her decision, then flared anew. "Didn't you think I'd understand that? Why did you have to lie to me about it?"

"I didn't exactly lie to you. I just didn't tell you everything."

He glared at her, and she glared right back. "It wasn't anything personal, Tom. A decision had to get made, so I made it."

She paced the cramped office.

"You and your men are always preaching about how you never leave anyone behind. About how you live or die together. I should have stayed and died with you and your men. I didn't tell you about it because I knew you wouldn't understand why I did it."

"Just because we live to a higher code than everyone else doesn't mean we expect other people to do it."

She stopped abruptly and spun to face him, a scowl on her face, her hands on her hips. "You think I can't hack your 'higher' code of honor? It just so happens I can, Tom Folly. That's why I didn't tell you. I wanted you to respect me. I wanted to be someone who lived up to your damn code."

He turned on his heel and stared blindly at the wall while he struggled with himself. He could've forgiven her just about anything but a lie. Anything but a betrayal like this. He smacked the wall with his open palm.

He *knew* he shouldn't have let her inside his head or his heart! He'd seen the results of misplaced trust before. He'd known better. Damn her. Visions of a cat-eyed, black-haired beauty swirled through his mind's eye, tangling with images of Annie writhing in pleasure beneath him. Flashes of Simon Pettigrew's bloodied body mingled with memories of his own horrible ride through the jungle on the end of a cable. Annie's cable.

When he turned back to her, his face felt chiseled from granite. Granite that was cracking under the strain of holding back his emotions.

"What else have you lied to me about, Annie? Has everything that's happened between us been just a ploy to make sure I got your precious butt out of here in one piece?"

She stared at him in shock. "Give me a break. You know darn well I wasn't faking what happened between us."

"Do I?"

She stared him down defiantly. "You tell me, Tom Folly."

He closed his eyes for a pained moment. "That's the problem with trying to live up to our code. We trust completely until you blow our trust, and then we distrust completely.''

A look of panic spread slowly across her lovely, deceitful features. The Special Forces commander within him noted that she was breathing too fast and way too shallow.

Everything they had between them was slipping away like sand between his fingers. How was he supposed to stand here and watch the death of the only real relationship he'd ever had? It was worse than that hellish ride underneath her helicopter.

From a distance he heard her say, ''Okay, Tom. So I should have told you. I made a mistake. One little mistake. But it's not the end of the world. Are you going to throw away everything we have because of that?''

He gave her the only answer he could with his throat locked up the way it was. Silence.

In the face of his nonresponse, her flash of anger seemed to fade. ''I have never lied to you about anything else, and I swear…I *swear*…I'll never lie to you about anything again.''

He couldn't trust his voice to remain steady, so he took refuge in further silence.

Tears were running down her face. ''Can't you forgive me a single mistake? Is your precious code so inflexible that one screw-up is the kiss of death? Are you telling me neither you nor any of your men have ever made an error?''

She didn't get it. This wasn't about mistakes or forgiveness. It was about trust. It was about loving a woman and being betrayed by her.

He tried to explain it to her in a way she would understand. ''If I sent you out on a recon mission and asked what you saw when you were out there, I'd base my decision to proceed on what you told me. I'd have to have absolute faith that you'd tell me the whole truth and nothing but the truth. But I don't know if I can do that with you anymore.''

"Well, of course you can—"

The door opened and Tex stuck his head around the jamb. "Sorry to interrupt folks, but Dutch and Doc just got back."

Tom whirled and left the room. There was no more to say, anyway. She'd lied to him and he wouldn't—couldn't—forgive and forget.

The government had retaken the Old Town sector but had been stopped about two miles north of the brothel.

They were going to have to cross the battle lines again tonight. Annie cringed at the thought of dodging more bullets and tanks, but she'd be damned if she was going to complain about it. Not after Tom's insults about her not having the nerves to handle combat.

She'd show him.

Why did she care what he thought, anyway? He was a first-class jerk.

Except she understood his reaction. As an aircraft commander, she relied on her crew members to be honest with her, too. She also made life and death decisions based on what her crews told her.

Still, he could've forgiven her a single mistake. Everyone was entitled to one, weren't they?

She was relieved when Doc wired her microphones and radios for her at sunset. She didn't think she could've handled having Tom's hands under her shirt and caressing her bare skin the way he had the first time he'd threaded all her gear through her clothing.

They waited until full dark to step outside, and then they spent another twenty minutes lurking on the bordello's front porch while their eyes acclimated to the night.

And then it was time to move again.

Unlike last night the group stayed close together this time. Howdy took the point, as usual, but he was always well within visual range of the group. They moved in quick spurts from shadow to shadow, doorway to doorway, their weapons drawn.

Fear rode Annie heavier than any pack of gear could have. Her stomach wobbled like Jell-O, and her knees weren't much steadier. Every little noise or movement made her jump, and she flinched every time she stepped on a patch of gravel. Only her spitting fury at Tom kept her moving forward.

Their journey took on a surreal quality, like a scene in a movie scrolling past her.

They'd been traveling for about an hour when they heard a quiet, distant rattling, like rain on a rooftop. The battle. Annie's heart leaped into her throat.

The sounds of fighting grew clearer and steadily louder as they moved forward.

Suddenly Howdy gestured them to get down and then disappeared from sight himself. Tom grabbed Annie's arm and jerked her down beside him in an alley. They waited motionless for an endless minute until they were sure they hadn't been seen. Tom stood up, and Annie followed suit.

"Take this." He shoved a pistol in her hand. She recognized the SIG-Sauer he'd shown her several days before.

"What am I supposed to do with it?" she whispered back.

His answer dripped with sarcasm. "Shoot it."

She scowled at him. He'd been sharp and short-tempered with her ever since their little scene in the brothel. And it was starting to get on her nerves.

"And just who do you propose I shoot it at?"

"At whoever's shooting at us."

Shooting *him* was starting to sound pretty appealing.

"If we're spotted, we all need to look armed and ready to respond with force. It'll make you less of a target. Just do what I said and carry the damn gun."

"Yes, *sir!*"

His hands shot out and grabbed her upper arms with frightening strength. He yanked her close to his nose. His eyes were dark and furious.

"I do *not* have the time to deal with an attitude out of you tonight. You do what I say when I say it and keep the crap to yourself. Got it?"

He was the one copping an attitude, but seeing as how they were in the middle of a war zone, and he *was* in command, she wasn't going to argue the point. Not to mention she could get shot in the back as easily as he could.

The thought no sooner occurred to her than she dismissed it as preposterous. No matter how ticked off Tom was at her, he was honorable right down to his toes. She didn't doubt for a second that he'd die for her this very minute, regardless of how mad he was at her.

Her irritation subsided. "I'm sorry. You're right. I'll stay out of your way and follow orders."

He gave her a surprised look and then a short nod.

From her experience with men, that might be as close as he ever got to acknowledging her apology. She accepted it for the small victory that it was.

Howdy's whispered voice interrupted her thoughts. "We've run up on the tail of an army patrol. They're clearing buildings about three hundred meters in front of us."

Tom murmured back, "Are they posting a tail-end Charlie to watch their six?"

"Nope."

Tom muttered, "Idiots. Can we tag along behind them?"

"If we're quiet, we…"

Howdy's transmission stopped and Annie's heart jumped in fear. The sound of a single shot rang out somewhere ahead of them.

Tom whispered, "Howdy?"

"Sniper. Aiming at our army patrol. Sorry 'bout that. Had to take him out," Howdy answered casually.

"How much cover are these boys going to need?"

"Truckloads," Howdy answered. "I could use another pair of eyeballs up here. These army troops are real green. They're going to need a lot of help from us to stay alive."

"Tex?" Tom murmured.

"On my way, boss."

They held their position for another ten minutes or so and then began a strange game of tag with the army patrol in front of them. The Gavronese Army soldiers acted as unwitting bait to draw out lurking rebels, whom Howdy and Tex then knocked out with cool efficiency.

Annie wondered if the army patrol had any idea how many times they should have died over the course of the next hour. Probably not.

It was nearly midnight when the army patrol peeled off, leaving Annie and the others perched on the edge of the front lines. Howdy and Tex rejoined the group as they huddled behind a burned-out minivan.

"How's it looking?" Tom asked.

Annie flinched. This was one of those moments he'd talked about earlier, where he was going to make life-and-death decisions based on what his guys told him.

Howdy and Tex exchanged glances, but it was Tex who answered. "We don't see any way through the lines except brute force. I think we're gonna have to shoot our way out of this one."

"Damn." Tom's gaze flickered her way for the barest instant. He sighed. "Well, we're in good shape for ammo as long as this doesn't take more than about ten minutes."

Tex drawled, "If we're not through in three minutes, we ain't gonna need more lead than that."

"Howdy, go find us a good spot to punch through. The rest of you, lock and load."

Annie watched on in disbelief as the men around her calmly prepared to engage in combat. It was really going to happen. She was about to land in the middle of a no-kidding firefight.

Tom pressed several clips for her pistol into her hand. "Take one shot at a time, nice and slow. Pick a target, let out a deep breath, aim and then pull smoothly through the trigger. Count to three before you pick another target. This isn't a John Wayne movie. Accuracy counts over speed. Got it?"

"Got it."

He asked her calmly, "Are you going to panic on me?"

She answered just as calmly. "In pilot training the folks who panicked in a pinch got washed out in a hurry. I'll hold it together."

She would hold it together until this was all over. *Then* she'd go to pieces.

Howdy's voice tickled her ear. "I've got it, gang. It's a sweet little alley with tons of cover and one dead rebel patrol at its far end."

He'd no doubt provided the latter convenience himself.

"I'm at your ten o'clock, range 150 meters. Stick to the storefronts on the left side of the street until you pass the busted-up personnel carrier. I'm about ten meters beyond that on your left."

"When's contact?" Tom asked.

Annie cast back through the lessons in lingo Tom had given her a lifetime ago in the apartment. He was asking when they'd have to start shooting.

"Other end of the alley. If we press ahead about two blocks, we should have smooth sailing from there."

"Let's move out."

Annie followed Tom's order and jumped to her feet. Terror tangled itself around her feet and she stumbled into him. He steadied her with a rough hand to the shoulder.

"You okay?"

She nodded at him.

"Stick to my back like glue. I'll take care of you."

It might be a war zone, and it might be his job, but those were possibly the nicest words she'd ever heard from Tom. A soothing warmth spread through her. He *would* take care of her, and they *would* get through this nightmare together.

Tom's crouching silhouette darted forward into the open. She took a deep breath and then she followed him into hell.

Chapter 13

Gunfire exploded and bullets rained around them the second they left the alley. Government troops peppered the air around them with gunfire. Annie was hard-pressed to keep up with Tom as he zigzagged his way along the sidewalk. How he managed to aim his rifle and return fire over his shoulder was beyond her.

She counted herself lucky not to have dropped her own weapon, let alone to have fired it. Only the thought of accidentally shooting Tom in the back kept her numb fingers clutched around the pistol's cold steel.

"Get down!" Tom shouted suddenly.

A whooshing noise streaked past her and an explosion rocked the building behind her. Fierce heat licked her back. She was knocked flat on her face.

Instantly Tom was beside her, half lying on top of her. His hands roamed frantically over her shoulders and arms, probing for injuries. "Are you hurt?"

There was no mistaking the ragged concern in his voice. The rest of her grew as warm as her back.

"I'm fine. How about you?"

"Me? I'm fine." He sounded surprised that she asked. "If you're ready, angel, let's go. We don't want to get left behind."

He'd called her angel. It was tempting to just lie here and make like an ostrich. But burying her head wouldn't make the war disappear. She nodded at him.

"On the count of three, run as fast as you can for that storefront over there."

She looked where he pointed and saw the dark cavern of a blown-out store.

"One. Two. Three!"

She leaped up and ran as fast as her legs would carry her. When bullets started popping into the concrete around her, her feet somehow moved even faster. She dived to the ground behind a wheelbarrow-sized chunk of concrete at the store's entrance.

Tom was already stretched out flat behind the large block, a machine gun propped against his cheek. An aura of eerie calm surrounded him. He was shooting methodically in short, controlled bursts. Annie's gaze followed the direction of his rifle barrel to where government soldiers were dropping systematically to the ground.

Eight soldiers had followed them. Five were still standing.

Annie grasped the pistol in both hands and steadied her grip on the edge of the concrete. Remembering Tom's instructions, she exhaled slowly, sighted a soldier and squeezed the trigger.

A red blossom exploded where the soldier's chest had been, and the guy dropped.

She blinked in disbelief. She'd actually hit her target. There was no time to think about anything else as she picked another soldier and tried again. This time she hit the fellow's leg, but he dropped to the ground, anyway.

She missed the third guy, but Tom dropped him a split second later.

And then there were no more soldiers running at them.

"Come on!" Tom ordered as he jumped up and sprinted off.

Annie followed him, breathing hard. Debris littered the ground, and she had to watch her footing. She ducked when shots rang out in front of them, but Tom yelled over his shoulder, "That's Howdy and Tex. Keep going!"

She hurdled a downed lamppost and grunted when Tom's arm snaked around her middle and yanked her practically out of midair.

"This way." He took off crawling on his hands and knees. "Stay down. Out of my guys' line of fire."

She followed suit while Tom's team shot over her head at the troops who'd followed them. The pavement scraped her palms raw, but she barely noticed the stinging pain.

Some thirty yards later she looked up and realized she'd crawled right into the middle of Tom's men. And they weren't shooting anymore. She rocked back on her heels.

"Man, am I glad to see you guys," she panted.

"What took ya so long?" Tex drawled. "You two stop to neck a little along the way?"

Tom snorted. "Had to knock out the hangers-on. Nice shooting, by the way, Annie," he remarked as he started reloading his weapons.

She blinked, stunned. He'd complimented her?

"How's it looking up ahead?" Tom asked.

Howdy answered, "Doc's checking it out."

Tom nodded. "Annie, put in a fresh clip and hand me the old one. I'll top it off for you."

Dazed, she complied. It hit her suddenly that she'd killed a man and wounded another. And she hadn't given it a second thought at the time. So that's how Tom did it. When it was her or the other guy, killing had come easy.

But the idea of having shot down a man was still overwhelming. Her control threatened to slip.

Then Doc was back among them, speaking urgently.

"We need to get out of here now. There's a big rebel force headed our way."

Tom nodded. "They probably heard our gunfire and are coming to check it out. Let's go."

The group moved out, running low and fast. Annie kept pace with them, but didn't have any leftover energy to look around. She locked her gaze on Tom's broad shoulders and concentrated on breathing deep and keeping up.

Fortunately, they only ran for about ten minutes. They stopped while Doc went ahead and identified himself to a rebel patrol.

His conversation was just on the edge of her hearing, but from what Annie gathered, Doc knew someone in the patrol and gave them directions to the fight they'd just left behind.

She used the pause to lean over and catch her breath.

Tom's face appeared, bent down beside her. "How are you holding up?"

"A little winded. I'll be okay in a minute or two."

"Are you going to be up to a couple more runs like we just did?"

Annie nodded and stood up straight. She thanked her lucky stars she'd been working out as hard as she had for the past weeks.

"Let me know if you need to stop, angel."

"Okay."

Tom touched her cheek. "Promise?"

She nodded. Why was he being so nice to her? Was he just doing his job, babying the flighty female through the mission, or did it mean more? Was he truly concerned about her? Had he forgiven her for not telling him who she was?

Doc rejoined them, and they moved out again.

The second time they paused, Dutch remarked, "You're not doing bad for a girl, Annie."

Even though her side hurt like hell, she smiled up at him. "Thanks." That was high praise indeed, coming from this group of soldiers.

They ran in short bursts for almost an hour. Annie was seriously considering telling Tom she couldn't go anymore when they stopped again.

She sagged against the wall of the building they stood beside and looked around. She'd been too busy suffering to notice that they'd run most of the way out of downtown St. George. They'd entered an industrial area she recognized as lying on the north side of the city.

Howdy left for a few minutes and then came back wearing a crocodile grin.

"Follow me," was all the sniper said.

There it was again. That absolute trust thing. Tom didn't even ask where they were going. He believed in his men utterly.

Howdy led them to a trailer on a construction site. He opened the door and ushered them inside. "It was unlocked, of all things," he commented.

Tom shook his head. "Thank heaven for small favors."

A bit of light seeping in through a window caught Howdy's grin. "Well, it doesn't come with high-class hookers, but there's a refrigerator full of food and some beds."

Tom laughed. "I'll take it, anyway."

Annie looked around at the trailer's dingy interior. Cheap paneling covered the walls, and the desks were all piled high with haphazard stacks of paper. Two cots were pushed against the back wall behind the desks. A dirty white refrigerator hummed at the far end of the room.

The team wasted no time making themselves at home.

In short order they'd emptied the refrigerator of everything but the beer.

Tom carried a sandwich over to where Annie sat on the edge of one of the cots.

"Here. I brought you a bite to eat before the guys inhale everything else."

She was too exhausted for hunger, but she knew she should eat, anyway. She'd need the energy later.

Annie looked up at Tom. "What next?"

He sat down beside her. "We're going to rest a bit. Then we're heading for the airport."

Annie sighed. That was a good five miles from their current location. "Why the airport?"

"When Doc talked to those rebels a while back, they said the fighting had pulled away from the airport to the main highway. We're hoping to slip past the rebels at their weakest point."

"I thought we were already past the rebels."

"We've gotten past the light urban fighting units. But the main rebel army still lies between us and the ocean."

A sinking feeling dragged at her.

"Hey, don't fall apart on me now. You've held up great so far."

Annie definitely felt like falling apart in a big way.

"How do you do it, Tom? How do you stay mentally strong through night after night of this?"

"We're trained and equipped for it, and we get used to it after a while. Everybody's scared the first time they get shot at. If it makes you feel any better, I was terrified my first mission or two."

"Really?"

He grinned. "I guess I should be complimented that you sound so surprised."

She smiled back. It seemed he'd declared a truce of sorts with her. She could live with that for now.

"Why don't you lie down for a few minutes, Annie? It's going to be a long night."

She took his advice and stretched out. It was pure bliss to let go of all the tension in her muscles. Her last thought before she went unconscious was that she understood now how Tom could sleep anywhere, anytime.

After Annie crashed on the cot behind him, Tom eased away. He joined his men at the other end of the room and let his upbeat facade slide.

Doc asked in concern, "How are you holding up, Major?"

"I'm surviving. If Annie can do it, so can I, dammit."

That brought chuckles all around.

Tom asked quietly, "What'd the rebels say about the forces between us and the ocean, Doc?"

"We were just talking about that."

"Without me?"

Tex piped up. "We figured you've got your hands full enough with Annie."

"She'll be okay until we're safe, and then she's gonna be a mess."

Dutch remarked, "She's a tough kid."

Yeah, she was. Tom nodded in agreement.

She'd borne up under circumstances that were trying, even to his seasoned team. When the chips were down, she'd come through. Just like that night over the jungle. When it had come down to a tough life-and-death decision, she'd stepped up to the plate and made it. He couldn't blame her for choosing the other nine people onboard that helicopter over himself. Hell, he'd probably have done the same thing in the same circumstances.

Maybe he'd come down on her too hard earlier. He would have to find a way to make it up to her somehow.

A rustling of paper drew his attention back to the table

they all stood around. Doc unrolled a blueprint he'd found on a desk and drew quickly on its blank back, talking as he worked.

"As I understand it, we've got large troop emplacements here and here. Believe it or not, straight through the middle of the airport sounds like our best bet."

Tom frowned. "There's no cover. It's all wide-open spaces. We'd never get Annie through there undetected."

Not to mention he didn't think he could low crawl two miles or more alongside a runway.

Doc continued to sketch in the details of terrain and troop emplacements around the airport.

Howdy leaned forward, studying the map. "I don't see any other choice, boss."

Tom groaned mentally. Howdy was right. The area around the airport was all open meadows and fields, and if that was where the rebels were concentrated, they'd have even less chance of getting through.

"How about a diversion?" Tom asked.

The others nodded.

"What if we set off a series of explosions? Maybe set a fuel tank or two on fire. That ought to draw everyone's attention."

Doc pulled out a new sheet of paper and sketched the airport in greater detail. He warned, "I may not have all this right, I only saw the aerials of the airport once in rebel headquarters."

Tom grinned. "That's better intelligence than what we get from Uncle Sam on occasion."

More grins all around.

That was better. The food was hitting everyone's systems and their morale was on the upswing. Annie'd kept them all from getting down prior to this. None of them were going to show weakness if the woman with them didn't.

"How many rebel soldiers are at the airport right now?" Tom asked.

Doc shrugged. "As I understand it, there's just a skeleton force in place to protect the airport workers."

That was good news, at any rate.

They finished a plan of attack, and then Tom set a watch rotation. They'd take turns standing watch and catch some sleep before they pressed on.

The night had turned cold when Tom woke Annie several hours later. The flimsy cot trembled with her shivering, and reluctantly he pulled her close.

"Put your hands in my armpits," he murmured.

She mumbled a protest, half-awake, but did as she was told.

He girded himself to resist the pleasure of holding her in his arms again and wrapped his arms around her. He'd thrown away her extra clothes when he'd ripped her pack off the night before so she could keep running from the tank. He owed her a spare bit of body heat.

As always, her body molded perfectly to his, her soft curves a perfect complement to his hard planes. There was no avoiding the fact that he was still ferociously attracted to her.

He sighed. Truth be told, he was a lot more than attracted to her. It wasn't himself he'd worried about out there tonight. His concern for her had gone far beyond professional interest. There was no denying it. He was in love with her, whether he liked it or not.

Annie's shivers subsided and she emerged into full consciousness.

"Angel, it's time to go."

She sighed, but stood up without a word of complaint.

Pride in her filled him. He announced, "I've got some good news for you, Annie. We don't have to run the next part."

"Hallelujah."

The other men chuckled at her heartfelt response.

They walked cautiously for several hours, everyone but Tom taking turns at the point position so they'd stay sharp up front. A rear guard was posted, and they moved in a leapfrog pattern from position to position. It was a standard maneuver, and his men fell into the rhythm of it without thought. After an hour or so even Annie had the hang of it.

The first streaks of color were lighting the gray sky in the east when Tex muttered into their earphones.

"Airport's dead ahead. Eight hundred meters of open terrain between us and it."

Damn. He'd been hoping they'd reach the airport perimeter while it was full dark. "Let's put a hustle on, gang," he ordered.

Simultaneously they all broke into a ground-eating run. He kept a close eye on Annie. She was obviously wiped out and stumbled several times. Each time he reached out and steadied her with a strong hand on her elbow.

She kept moving and managed to keep up until they reached the embankment that was their goal. Mac and Dutch were already working on the gillie nets, weaving in grass and plants from the hillside they were going to hide on.

Tom glanced up at the orange and pink streaks lighting the sky. It was nearly bright enough to see with the naked eye. He gestured the others to help with the camouflage process. Annie watched for a few seconds, and then she pitched in, too, grabbing handfuls of grass and poking it through the net's holes.

"Okay, let's get under cover."

Tom was the last man to crawl under the net. The others had finished propping up the cover with sticks, leaving them a three-foot-tall tent to move around in.

Annie's eyes were starting to glaze over. She looked ready to shatter into a thousand pieces.

He stretched out to one side of the enclosure. "Come here, Annie."

She crawled over to him on her hands and knees.

He opened his arms. "We're all done for the night. It's time to fall apart, now."

She hesitated for a split second, and then she collapsed against him. Silent sobs shook her shoulders, and he held her until she cried it out.

"You did good, kiddo," he whispered into her hair.

Her arm crept across his waist, and she snuggled a little closer against his shoulder.

"Now what?" she whispered back.

"Now we sleep. The other guys will take turns on watch first. We'll be here all day, so settle in and get as comfortable as you can."

Her arm tightened slightly around him. "I can't think of anyplace else I'd rather be right now," she whispered.

He squeezed her in return but didn't answer. His heart and head were in too much turmoil at the moment. And he had no bloody idea what he was going to do about either.

He fell asleep without finding an answer.

It was hot and muggy when Annie woke up. Her wristwatch proclaimed it to be late afternoon. Tom's shoulder under her head had been replaced at some point with a balled-up sweater. It smelled like Tom. She inhaled the spicy, masculine scent.

She started to roll over, but halted abruptly. She hurt from head to foot. Even turning her head caused stabbing pains to shoot down her back and across her shoulders.

Against her volition, she moaned.

Tom was beside her in an instant. "Where does it hurt, Annie?"

"Everywhere," she groaned. "Where's everyone else?"

"They're out having a look around. Doc will be back in a little while. Are you injured?"

"No. I'm just not in good enough shape to do what we did last night."

"Ahh. You're in luck. That affliction falls within my limited medical expertise. I'll be right back."

He crawled away and returned in a few moments with a canteen and four white pills. "Take these."

"What are they?"

"Muscle relaxants and painkillers."

"They won't knock me out, will they?"

"No. We need to be alert in the field. This medicine's made specially for us."

She took the pills and washed them down with water from a canteen Tom produced. After she shuddered away the bitter taste, she grinned at him.

"So. The truth comes out! You guys aren't superheroes after all. You use painkillers to keep you going!"

Tom grinned back at her. "You won't tell anyone, will you?"

"Your secret's safe with me, Clark."

"Thanks, Lois. Those pills should hit in about two minutes."

"Actually, now that you mention it, I am starting to feel a bit better."

Tom repositioned himself at her feet and reached for one of her calves. "This'll help, too."

He grasped her leg and very gently rubbed her calf with a circular motion. Gradually he built up the pressure until it was almost, but not quite, painful.

"A massage helps break up the lactic acid buildup in the muscles," he commented.

Melting warmth flowed outward from where his hands

caressed her. It started as relief from pain, but evolved into exquisite pleasure.

"I don't care if it paralyzes me. That feels wonderful. How long did you say your men were going to be gone?"

Tom chuckled. "Not that long, I'm afraid."

"Drat."

Silence stretched out between them as Tom worked his way all the way up her right leg and then started on her left foot.

Apparently his truce was progressing rapidly toward a full-blown peace treaty with her. She wished she could talk to him about it, but it would have to wait until they reached safety. She wasn't about to draw his attention away from keeping them alive.

"What's the plan, Tom?"

He crawled up to her side. "For you to roll over so I can loosen up your back."

His hands settled lightly on her shoulders and began to work their magic. She was putty in his hands by the time he spoke again.

"The guys are out picking spots to set explosives tonight. We'll wait until almost daybreak tomorrow and light the place up."

"Why wait so long?"

"People are the most tired between four and five in the morning. It'll create the most confusion to do it then."

Talk about confusion. Tom's hands were doing things to her that had nothing to do with sore muscles. Liquid heat was building low in her belly and spiraling outward at an alarming rate.

There was a slight rustling at the edge of the netting, and Tom whirled away from her, a pistol suddenly in his hand.

Tex poked his head into the tent. "Hi, honey. I'm home."

"Shut up, Tex," Tom growled.

Tex grinned and crawled inside. He shrugged out of a gillie suit made of the same material their tent was. He picked grass out of his hair and boots.

"So, how's it looking?" Tom asked.

"It's gonna be a right pretty fireworks show."

And it was.

Tom woke her up about a half hour before the charges had been set to detonate. Tom's men had peppered the airport with grenades, incendiaries, booby traps, and C-4 explosives.

When the first flash went, they were perched at the top of the embankment and ready to move. Moments later a secondary explosion shook the ground as a million-gallon fuel storage tank went up in flames.

"Too bad it was almost empty," Howdy commented blandly.

Annie thought the white-orange mushroom cloud rising into the night sky was spectacular enough. And it had the desired effect. Sirens went off, and fire trucks careened across the runways. Silhouettes of men scurried back and forth, black specks against the roaring flames of the fires.

A dozen more explosions went off, and the chaos was complete. Annie wriggled through the hole in the hurricane fence around the runways that the guys had cut earlier. She jumped to her feet and took off running after Tom's tall shape.

If she got out of this nightmare alive, she was never going to run another step as long as she lived.

Doggedly she pressed on. They hugged the far side of the runway away from the ramp where the fuel tank and several airplanes were on fire.

Shells started exploding randomly. Apparently one of the airplanes had been loaded with ammunition. Streaks of light zipped every which way, and several more airplanes caught on fire.

Annie was so engrossed in watching the show and running at the same time that she all but tripped over Tom, who was stretched out on the ground in front of her.

He grabbed her leg and yanked her to the ground.

Now what?

"Stay down flat," he hissed.

She was about to ask why, when a beam of cruelly bright light passed over their heads.

Mac swore from in front of them. "Dammit! The tower's got a floodlight. Should I take it out?"

"No!" Tom answered sharply. "You'd have to wait until it was pointed at us to hit it, and then they'd know there were snipers out here and what direction we were shooting from."

Annie risked a glance around. They were about three-quarters of the way down the runway. A bunch of airplanes were parked directly across from them.

"Get out the nets," Tom ordered.

Annie didn't know much about this kind of work, but this couldn't be good. Tom expected them to hunker down right out here in the open.

This time the nets lay directly on top of their bodies. There was no room to maneuver.

Tom murmured from beside her, "Don't move unless you absolutely have to, Annie. If you have to scratch your nose, move at the speed of a snail. Literally. Quick movements are easy for the enemy to spot."

The ground was cold, and before long, dew had seeped into her clothing, chilling her through. Her muscles cramped with inactivity, and she was downright miserable in a matter of minutes.

To make matters worse, the sun was rising, and it was getting light out. Black smoke billowed overhead from the fires, and it was torture trying to suppress the coughing fits a lungful of it caused.

Annie lay still and watched the airfield burn. She prayed for her and the team's safety and tried to breathe between gusts of smoke. The morning warmed up around them, and her damp chill was replaced by steamy, hot discomfort.

They'd been immobile for several hours when, out of the clear blue, something painfully obvious dawned on her.

It looked for all the world like a Huey helicopter was parked not too far from their position.

"Tom, do you have a pair of binoculars?" she whispered.

"Yeah."

"I need them."

"You've got to be kidding."

"No, I'm serious."

He sounded dubious. "This'll take a while."

She waited impatiently until he eased the binoculars out of a pouch and over to her. The action took a good two minutes to complete. She mimicked his extreme slow-motion movement and inched the binoculars up to her face.

She focused the lenses and scanned the airfield. Sure enough. It was a Huey. The tail number indicated it was from the same manufacturing year as the equipment she'd been trained on.

She tried to glimpse the instrument panel, but couldn't get a clean look at the whole console. But what she saw looked reasonably familiar.

"What's up, Annie?" Tom murmured into his throat mike.

"There's a Huey helicopter over there. I know how to fly it."

"And?"

"Why don't we go take it and fly out of here?"

"Are you out of your mind?" Tom demanded in a stentorian whisper.

Tex interjected. "Yeah, I see it from here. It's only about a hundred feet beyond the runway. That's about four hundred feet from our position."

"It would be way too dangerous."

Annie argued quietly, "If we can get into that bird unseen, I ought to be able to fly my way out of the airport."

The other team members jumped into the discussion. Two things emerged from the whispered argument. One, they couldn't stay here for long or they'd be discovered, and two, Annie's idea was as good as anything else they could think of.

With a heavy sigh Tom asked, "Annie, are you sure you can fly that helicopter? We're dead meat if we climb into it and you can't start it."

"Yes, Tom. I'm sure."

And there it was. The moment Tom had been talking about. Could he believe her now or not? Annie listened in agony as the silence stretched out. She could practically hear Tom wrestling with the decision in his head.

"I know what I'm doing, Tom. I'm telling you the God's honest truth. My neck depends on this one as much as yours does."

Of course, she was assuming the helicopter wasn't broken or out of gas or otherwise unflyable.

The silence lasted a few more seconds.

"Howdy, do we have enough ammo to blow up some planes and create another diversion?"

"Yeah. One more diversion. But that's it."

"Then pick your target wisely," was Tom's only reply.

The sniper slithered off into the grass, as stealthy as a snake.

Tom's voice interrupted her amazement at Howdy's silent departure. "Annie, how much time are you going to need in the seat before you can get off the ground?"

She reviewed the engine start procedures in her head, weeding out the unessential preflight checks. "Ninety seconds."

"We ought to be able to hold them off for that long. Okay here's the plan...."

Annie couldn't believe they were actually going to do this. They'd just laid all of their lives in her hands. What in the heck had she been thinking to volunteer for this crazy stunt? But before she could talk into her mike and call the whole thing off, an explosion rocked the ground.

She clicked the stop watch feature of her wristwatch and risked lifting her head to see what had happened.

Howdy had picked his diversion well. He'd shot a grenade down the intake of a fully fueled fighter jet. Flaming JP-4 fuel spewed all over the far end of the ramp, and the plane's ammunition was starting to ignite and fire off in random directions. Annie took off running.

It was arguably the fastest four-hundred-foot sprint ever recorded by a woman. She crouched down beside the Huey's door and reached up to open the latch.

It was locked.

Oh, God.

Chapter 14

Tom skidded to a halt beside her. He took up a crouching stance and started firing.

"Let's go, Annie," he urged between bursts of gunfire.

What was she going to do now?

The SIG-Sauer pistol. She fumbled at her belt and pulled the gun out. She shot out the door latch and all but cried in relief as the door swung open.

She leaped into the seat and took a fast look around the cockpit. Everything critical to flight was in relatively the same place she was used to seeing it. She started flipping switches as fast as her hands would go.

Ping. Ping, ping.

She ducked.

A spray of bullets flew into the cockpit, piercing the tempered glass windshield on the copilot's side, leaving three small round holes with spider cracks spreading outward in jagged radials.

She sat upright again and flew through the engine start

sequence. The overhead rotor started to turn sluggishly in an arc overhead.

"Hurry, hurry," she begged the helicopter.

The back door slid open. She reached for the pistol at her belt. It was Dutch and Mac.

The two men stood in the rear door of the Huey and took turns firing while the other reloaded. They were laying down a veritable curtain of lead. At that rate, their ammunition wouldn't last long.

But then, if her plan failed they wouldn't have long, anyway. Thirty seconds were left on her stopwatch of the ninety that Tom had promised her.

She only prayed there was a reasonable amount of fuel in the Huey's tanks.

Dutch and Mac fell back into the helicopter's interior, and Doc and Tex took their places in the door.

The RPMs started winding up on the engine, and the tail rotor began to hum. The fuel gauge wound up. A full tank, thank goodness.

Howdy materialized in the doorway.

Where was Tom? She wasn't leaving without him. She looked out her door, and he wasn't anywhere to be seen.

The overhead rotor revved up to full speed, and she flipped on the radios and remaining navigation equipment. None of it would be properly aligned, but she could glean enough information to get them north to the ocean.

"Tom!" she called into her throat mike. "Come on! Let's get out of here!"

She started violently when the copilot's door slammed open. The dark-skinned face and red beret of a rebel soldier appeared, along with the muzzle of his rifle.

Hate glinted in his eyes, and Annie stared into the face of Death incarnate.

He was going to shoot her, and nobody else would be

able to fly this bird out of here. The whole team was going to die because she went and got herself killed.

And then there was a flash of steel under the soldier's chin. A fountain of blood sprayed all over the inside of the cockpit. Its warm wetness splashed her face and she tasted blood.

The soldier's body fell aside, and Tom stood in his place. He leaped into the cockpit, shouting, "Let's go!"

Annie was pulling back on the collective before he even closed his door.

"Strap in," she ordered. "And close that door back there, guys. This is gonna get rough, and I don't want to dump any of you out."

Her own door wouldn't latch, but she'd taken a precious few seconds to buckle herself in already.

Ping, ping.

Bullets ripped through the floor.

Annie slammed the throttle forward, and the helicopter picked up speed. Its tail tilted up sharply as she flung the craft forward, barely clearing the airplanes below her.

The ground skimmed past in a dizzying blur as the helicopter's engine screamed. She shoved the throttles all the way to the forward stop, not caring if she oversped the engine.

The airport fell behind in a matter of seconds, and she yanked up hard to clear a treeline that rushed toward them at 150 miles per hour.

"God, Annie, that was close," Tom gasped as the trees flew past barely beneath their feet.

"I know how to fly, Tom."

He leaned back in the seat. "Thank God for that."

"Where to?"

"North. The *U.S.S. Independence* is twelve miles offshore. I don't know exactly where, but we ought to be able to find an aircraft carrier, don't you think?"

Annie banked the helicopter to the left and started a lazy 180-degree turn that carried them well wide of the airport and toward safety.

She commented, "I'll crank up the radios and get the Navy to vector us in."

She didn't know the standard Navy frequencies, so she tuned the VHF radio to a general emergency frequency.

Chatter abruptly filled the cockpit.

It was American voices. Panicked ones. Yelling about their position being overrun by rebels. Screaming for help.

Tom picked up the microphone.

"Unknown rider, unknown rider, identify yourself. This is Major Tom Folly of the United States Air Force."

"This is U.S. Marine Squad Delta Tango. We're getting the snot shot out of us! We're outgunned and outnumbered ten to one."

Annie gasped. "That's the marine detachment at the American Embassy!"

"Say your location, Delta Tango," Tom ordered tersely.

"We're on the roof of the American embassy in St. George. We've got some sandbags and furniture up here for cover, but they're about to come through the emergency hatch on to the roof. We're done once they get up here with us."

Annie looked over at Tom.

"How long?" he asked.

She didn't have to ask what he was talking about. She glanced outside for reference points to orient herself.

"Five, maybe six minutes, at top speed."

"Firewall it."

Annie nodded and shoved the throttle all the way forward again. She banked hard back in the direction they'd just come from and flew like a bat out of hell across the tree-tops.

Tom transmitted to the marine, "We'll be at your position in five minutes. Conserve your ammo and hang on. We're about to even the odds for you.''

The voice answered, ''If you don't mind my asking, just who in the hell are you, sir?''

''Special Forces. We'll be coming in on a Gavronese Army painted Huey...'' He released the mike button. ''What's the tail number, Annie?''

''Four Five November Yankee.''

''...on a Gavronese helicopter, tail number Four Five November Yankee,'' Tom finished.

''Roger. We'll be glad for the assist.''

Tom keyed his throat mike to his men in the back. ''You guys copy what's up?''

''Yes, sir,'' Tex answered. ''We're loading up. There's a nice little fifty-caliber machine gun back here with a crate of clips, compliments of the Gavronese Army.''

Annie breathed a sigh of relief at that news. Tom and his men had to be getting way low on ammunition after the gun battle back at the airport.

Tom looked over at her. ''Have you ever practiced combat maneuvers in one of these things?''

''I'm familiar with the basic idea. Run parallel to the threat so the gunner can do his thing out the side door. Any of your guys ever work out of a helicopter with a machine gun?''

''Standard issue training for us.''

She grinned. ''I sure am glad you guys are on my side.''

He grinned back. ''Let's go rescue us some marines.''

She streaked across St. George, painfully aware that every second was crucial. She took more than a few risks, but she got there in five minutes and ten seconds.

The embassy was hard to miss. As they neared the building, a column of black smoke rose from the residence building next door.

''The bastards are trying to burn the marines out,'' Tom growled.

''The main building's stone. They'll have a hard time lighting it up,'' Annie replied.

''Excellent.'' Tom voice was steady, reassuring. ''Here we go, guys. Get the fifty-cal ready back there.''

The back door slid open, and Howdy swung out the door in a gunner's harness.

''Bank it up,'' Tom directed her.

Annie slowed the craft and banked toward her open door, giving Howdy the best possible angle to shoot from. The helicopter shuddered as he loosed a barrage of lead at the rebels surrounding the embassy building.

Initially the soldiers scattered and ran every which way, unsure of where the hail of bullets was coming from. Annie flew a 360 around the building.

''Better get over the roof, Annie. They'll start shooting back any second,'' Tom directed.

She did as he suggested. A handful of marines waved wildly as she brought the Huey to a hover over the far side of the building from them. She didn't want her downwash to blow any of the marines off the roof.

''Set it down, angel.''

She landed quickly but gently.

Tom and his men leaped out, ducking under the rotor and heading for the marine position. Annie watched as a short conversation ensued. Tom's voice came up on her earphone.

''How many men can we get in that bird, Annie?''

She glanced back at the cargo space and calculated her maximum possible takeoff weight fast. ''Fourteen, if they're all gonna die if I don't pull them out.''

''There are sixteen people here including me and my guys.''

Annie's heart dropped. "Sorry, Tom. Fourteen's gonna be pushing it as it is."

"Understood."

Oh, Lord. Was she going to have to leave people behind to die? Again? The thought made her sick to her stomach. She couldn't do it. She just couldn't.

And then something odd caught her attention. The marines and Tom's men were shedding their weapons and laying them down in a neat row in the makeshift sandbag bunker. What in the world were they doing?

And then, the soldiers sprinted in her direction. A single man in a white dress shirt and gray slacks caught her attention as he stood up from behind the sandbags.

Good grief, it was Ambassador Kettering. What was *he* still doing here?

Tom and the ambassador ran up to her door while Tom's men tossed out the fifty caliber gun and ammo and herded the others into the back of her bird.

"Captain O'Donnell. So glad you could join us!"

She nodded back at the ambassador.

Tom shouted over the noise of the helicopter, "The ambassador and I will be staying behind. Take the rest of them out to the *Independence*."

Horror filled Annie. *No. Not Tom.* She couldn't leave him again. She wouldn't!

"Tom, I can't!"

"Yes, you can, Annie. It's the two of us or all of them. This is the way it has to be."

"No!" she screamed over the noise of the helicopter.

"This is an order, angel. Get those men out of here."

The nightmare was repeating itself. Time slowed around her as disbelief turned to shock. "No-o-o," she moaned.

Tom leaned through her open door and grabbed her shoulders. "Listen to me, Annie. We've got a decent arsenal up here, and we'll be able to hold them off for a while. Maybe long enough to negotiate a surrender. I don't think they'll kill Ambassador Kettering if they realize who he is.''

Annie appealed to the silver-haired gentleman in question. ''Don't do this, sir! It's suicide.''

He nodded resolutely. ''You're probably right, young lady. But just as a captain's place is with his sinking ship, this is my post. This is American soil, and by God, I'm not handing it over to anybody without a fight. The major and I will let these bastards know they've had a tough time before we go down. Now you go on and get those boys out of here.''

She couldn't believe this was happening.

''Tom…''

''Honey, you need to leave. We'll buy you enough time to get out of here.''

Tears streamed down her face. ''Tom, I can't leave you again. I love you!''

''I know, angel. Now go on.''

Tom and the ambassador backed away from her toward the makeshift bunker that had been set up around the flagpole.

Sobbing so hard she could barely see, Annie eased back gently on the controls. The helicopter groaned as it struggled to lift the weight of all the souls onboard.

Inch by bare inch, she lifted away from the ground.

She looked back to see Tom arming himself with an array of weapons while the ambassador stood ramrod straight beside him. The rotor wash caught the American flag on the pole beside the two men and whipped it around their legs.

Without warning, Tom snapped to attention, and threw her a full-blown military salute while Old Glory's stars and stripes wrapped themselves around him.

She saluted back as tears streamed down her face. Her

heart was breaking in two. She finally gained enough altitude to bank away. She took one last look down at Tom—her own private hero.

He lifted his hand in a final wave of farewell and mouthed the words, ''I love you.''

Moaning in agony, Annie banked away and accelerated into the morning sun.

She pushed the helicopter to the very limits of its performance and raced north as if the Devil himself was nipping at her heels.

She blatantly ignored the Navy air traffic controller's repeated requests to slow down her approach to the *Independence,* and she flung her craft to the deck of the ship with reckless abandon.

Her passengers, who'd been packed in like sardines, tumbled out the door the second it was opened. A flight-deck officer pulled open her damaged door.

''Welcome aboard, Captain O'Donnell. Congratula—''

''Back up, sir.''

''I beg your pardon?''

''Stand clear, sir. I'm taking off again.''

''You're what? You don't have clearance to do that!''

''I don't recall asking for clearance!'' she shouted back over the roar of her engine. She checked her gauges and throttled up.

Another voice shouted over the radio. ''Captain, you are ordered to shut down. You do not have takeoff clearance.''

She picked up the microphone. ''Well then, with all due respect, you better give it to me fast. I left Ambassador Kettering and the man I love behind at the American Embassy, and I'm going back for them.''

''This is an order, Captain—''

She turned off the radio.

Flight-deck crewmen scattered all over as she lifted off

unexpectedly. She backed the helicopter away from the conning tower and, as soon as she was clear, banked hard left.

''One more time, baby,'' she coaxed the helicopter as she pushed the engine well beyond its design limits yet again.

She flew high enough to keep salt spray from fouling the engine, but as soon as she hit the coast, she dropped down to treetop level again.

A strange calm came over her. There was no more fear, no more questioning of right and wrong. She was not leaving Tom behind. They lived or died together, and that's all there was to it.

She did have the presence of mind to swing wide and approach the embassy from the opposite side this time. There was no sense getting shot down because she was too panicked to think straight.

She was horrified as the building came into sight. Soldiers in red berets were scaling the sides of the embassy itself on ropes.

But then the implications of that dawned on her. Tom and the ambassador hadn't been killed yet!

Exultation shot through her.

She could do a little something about those rebels on the ropes. She positioned the helicopter over the edge of the building, then she pulled back hard on the collective and hit the throttle simultaneously. The helicopter leaped straight up in the air and sent a tremendous surge of wind downward at close to two hundred miles per hour. She banked for a second to see the effect of her maneuver.

A bunch of guys in red berets sprawled on the ground like dead ants.

She repeated the maneuver on the other side of the building.

She glanced quickly toward the makeshift bunker on the

roof, looking for any signs of movement, but she saw none. Smoke obscured too much of the view, and she was too occupied trying not to hit the flagpole to take a better look.

At least the immediate threat to anyone still on the roof had subsided for a minute or two. That ought to be all she'd need to find Tom, dead or alive. She landed as near the flagpole as she dared and leaped out of the cockpit, leaving the engine running.

She sprinted across the open space. A hail of bullets flew at her from a neighboring rooftop, and she zigzagged at a dead run while firing her pistol over her shoulder, just like she'd seen Tom do.

The sandbags loomed before her. She took a running leap and prayed she didn't land on Tom and squash him.

She landed beside him.

He was covered in blood from head to foot. The ambassador leaned over him, pressing down hard on a wound to Tom's thigh, and on another high on Tom's chest.

"Oh, God. Don't tell me I'm too late."

The ambassador didn't mince any words. "Not yet, but we're going to lose him soon. Can you lift his legs if I get his head?"

"Sir!" Annie protested.

"We're all going to die if we stay here. Do you propose to leave this fine soldier behind after he saved all our lives, Captain?"

"No, sir."

"Then help me pick this boy up."

Annie jumped to obey.

They managed to half drag, half carry Tom to the helicopter and dump him inside. A pool of blood formed under him in a matter of seconds.

Annie's heart flew into her throat.

She raced around the helicopter and climbed into the seat. A red beret poked over the wall in front of her.

Oh, no.

She didn't even wait to strap in, but yanked back on the controls. The helicopter lurched into the air. To her utter shock, gunfire started from the back of the helicopter. She glanced back to see the ambassador—and Tom—wielding pistols.

Their burst forced the rebels to duck for a split second. But it was enough. She was up and away from the roof.

A hail of gunfire raked their belly, but Annie was too focused on flying to notice the holes in the floor, inches from her feet.

The helicopter lurched. She pushed the craft forward faster and climbed higher. It bucked again.

A quick glance at the engine gauges showed the hydraulic system was hit. Her flight controls were going to be compromised soon. She wouldn't be able to command the Huey to go up or down, left or right.

She couldn't come this close to saving Tom only to crash now.

He climbed up into the cockpit beside her, and she stared at him in shock.

"What are you doing up here? Get back there and lie down so the ambassador can help you."

"I'll be okay. What in the hell were you thinking, coming back for me? That was insane!"

"Do you want me to turn around and drop you back on that roof?" She didn't wait for him to answer. "Inside this bird, I'm in command. So cut the small talk."

A pause. One side of his mouth turned up in a grin. "Yes, ma'am."

She wrestled with the cantankerous helicopter for several minutes in silence.

Tom spoke from beside her. She couldn't tell if he knew what he was saying or not. His head lolled drunkenly on his shoulders and his color was terrible. "I told you to leave the embassy. You disobeyed my direct order!"

"I did leave. And you never ordered me not to come back."

"I didn't think I had to. This was a damn fool maneuver."

The coastline came into view. The helicopter bucked harder this time and fell off to the right slightly.

She corrected with the rudder and eased back on the throttle. The helicopter shuddered again.

"Look, Tom, I don't have time to argue with you. This bird's getting unruly, and we've still got a few minutes to go. Go lie down."

"Like hell—"

"I give the orders here. Get back there, get horizontal, and don't you die on me. Got it?"

He lifted an eyebrow at her. "Got it."

He crawled out of the seat and into the back of the helicopter. A sudden lurch threw him against the back wall, and he grunted in pain as he collapsed onto the floor.

Annie muttered to herself, "I went to a lot of trouble to fetch that lout's worthless hide. If he dies, I swear, I'll—"

"You'll what?" Tom's voice came over her earphone, amused.

She started. She hadn't realized she was transmitting over her throat microphone and that it was still set to the same frequency as Tom's gear.

"You've got a stuck mike, darlin'. That dive you took into the fox hole must've jostled something."

"Great."

She didn't have any more time to argue with him because the silhouette of the *Independence* carrier leaped over the horizon in front of her.

The helicopter was really becoming a handful. It crow hopped and jigged like a bronco trying to toss an unwelcome rider. She babied the controls and coaxed it to co-operate long enough to get them over the carrier's deck.

But setting the bird down was another matter. Her vertical control was all but gone, and she swooped and dipped like a swallow in flight. Her tail winged around in a sickening 360-degree arc, almost taking out two flight-deck crewmen. But finally her right skid impacted the deck. For a second the helicopter tipped up on its right side. She chopped the throttle, and it rocked down to the deck with a hard thud.

Annie cut the engine and leaped out of the craft, screaming for a medic.

A team must've been standing close by because in seconds Tom's unconscious form was surrounded by paramedics. Some of them poked needles into him and hung bags of blood and plasma around him, while others worked on stemming the flow of blood from his wounds.

Annie hovered protectively over the whole proceeding, keeping up a constant stream of conversation with Tom, begging him to stay alive and keep fighting. She held on to his hand with bruising force, as if she could will her own life energy into him.

When he was stabilized enough to move, four men picked up the stretcher and lifted him out of the helicopter. They took off running for a doorway with Annie still grasping Tom's cold fingers.

"Excuse me, Captain. You need to come with me."

Annie shrugged off the hand that tapped her shoulder. "I'm staying with him," she replied.

"I'm sorry but that won't be possible. The admiral wants to see you right away. And besides, the doctors won't let you stay with him while they work on him."

"I'm not leaving him!" Her voice climbed on a hysterical note.

The flight-deck officer took her upper arm in a strong

grasp and forcibly guided her away from the stretcher. Tom's fingers fell away from hers, and it was as if a piece of her heart had been ripped out. He couldn't die. He just couldn't.

The officer spoke forcefully to her. "You've got to let him go, Captain! He needs medical attention, and you'd be in the way. Besides, you have an appointment with the admiral."

She tried one more time to follow Tom's retreating form, but the flight-deck officer was having none of it. Like it or not, he steered her across the deck and into a different part of the ship.

In a daze she allowed herself to be led through a maze of corridors and hatches. She only vaguely registered the flight-deck officer's tirade about snot-nosed pilots who disobeyed orders and endangered his crewmen. Fortunately, he wound down before they got to the admiral's office.

She was directed to a wooden chair in the admiral's outer office to wait. Slowly awareness of her surroundings came back to her. It was all well and good to have disobeyed orders and to have done her darnedest to save Tom's life, but now it was time to pay the piper.

Sick dread filled her. She'd worked hard to be a good officer and, to date, had led a distinguished career. But this episode had pretty much blown it.

A sailor finally led her into the admiral's beautifully appointed office and left, closing the door behind him with an ominous click. She stood glumly at attention.

Her knees were shaking. It wasn't from fear of the butt-chewing she was about to get, though. It must be shock setting in.

As she'd expected, the admiral worked up a good head of steam and ripped into her hard for disobeying his officers. She put on an appropriately remorseful expression and rode out the storm in silence.

Her thoughts wandered. Getting court-martialed would be worth it if Tom lived. Even if she spent the next ten years in jail at Fort Leavenworth, at least she'd know he was alive. She could live with that.

Finally the admiral stopped shouting and came around from behind his desk, his face thunderous. She braced herself.

But then he broke into a big grin. And walked right past her to greet someone who stepped into the room behind her. She looked over her shoulder.

Ambassador Kettering shook hands warmly with the Navy flag officer. "George, long time no see! How the hell are you?"

"I'm fine, Jack. But what in the hell were you doing in a firefight on top of the embassy?"

"Just doing my job. Defending the good old U.S. of A."

"Hell, you got out of the Navy thirty years ago. Aren't you a little old for playing soldier?"

Annie stood by quietly as the two men traded quips.

Finally the admiral remembered her presence and turned to the ambassador. "So what am I supposed to do with this young captain? She disobeyed a direct order from my flight-deck crew not to take off and go rescue your crusty old hide."

"Actually, sir," Annie replied, "I disobeyed several direct orders."

The ambassador's mouth twitched, but the admiral looked stony.

"I ought to have you court-martialed and strung up from the yardarm, Captain."

"Yes sir, you should," she answered.

"But seeing as how you just pulled off one of the most damned heroic pieces of flying I've ever seen, I think I'm going to have to shake your hand and tell you to get yourself down to the infirmary to visit the man you love."

Annie blushed. He'd heard about that, had he?

"Uh, thank you, sir. If you'll excuse me, gentlemen…" She looked back and forth between the two men, not sure which one would give her permission to leave.

"Go. Go." The admiral waved his hand at the door.

She whirled and managed not to sprint from the room. The admiral's executive officer showed her through the maze of passageways to the infirmary.

A sailor gestured her to a seat in the outer office.

"Is he all right?" she asked.

"They're still working on him, ma'am" was the impassive reply.

Each minute that passed was agony for her. He had to be all right. He just had to be. They'd been through so much together. They'd made it out, just as he promised they would.

Images of the past few weeks floated through her mind in a collage of memorable moments with Tom. It seemed unreal to be sitting in a sterile, quiet doctor's office as if nothing had ever happened. As if they'd never been shot at, as if they'd never had to fight tooth and nail for their very lives.

It all started to feel like some sort of dream, insubstantial and fleeting. Had her relationship with Tom been part of that unreal time? Was there anything left for them, now that the mission was over and they were out of Gavarone?

An officer stepped through the inner door and walked over to her, a sober expression on his face.

Dread clogged her throat. They had to have saved him. They just had to.

She wasn't very familiar with Navy uniform insignia, but she thought she recognized a medical corps badge.

"You must be Annie," the doctor said.

"I am. How did you know?"

"My patient's been demanding to see someone by that

name, whom I gather is a rather independent-minded pilot of the female persuasion.''

Tom was alive.

Annie smiled widely, relieved to the point of tears. ''Can I see him?''

''Please do. Maybe he'll stay in bed if you're here. He's been threatening to get up and search the ship until he found you.''

Annie stepped through the oval door. Tom lay in a bed, eyes closed. His chest was bare, and a white sheet was pulled up to his waist. His left shoulder was swathed in a white bandage.

She hesitated in the doorway, unsure of what to say to him. He looked different, somehow. More authoritative, more an officer. Less her lover and companion of the last weeks.

''Hi.''

His eyes opened. ''Hi.'' His voice was gruff.

''I hear there's a soldier in here who needs to be convinced to stay in bed,'' she said lightly.

He gave her a long, inscrutable look. His eyes were that stormy shade of gray blue they turned when he was angry.

''We need to talk, Annie.''

''About what?''

''About your suicidal tendencies.''

She blinked. ''My what?''

''You heard me.''

He wasn't joking. She stepped fully into the room and shut the door behind her.

He continued, ''I didn't put it all together until a few minutes ago. You've been running around trying to be Superwoman the last few months because you felt guilty about dragging me through the jungle.''

She frowned. ''And your point?''

He stared intently at her, his direct gaze cutting straight

into her soul. "You were right about Simon Pettigrew. I have been running around trying to be a hero to make amends for getting him killed."

Annie started. She hadn't expected ever to hear such an admission out of him.

"But you're doing the very same thing, Annie." His voice took on a sense of urgency. "You've got to stop it. You made a reasonable decision under the circumstances out in that jungle."

"But—"

He cut her off. "I didn't die. You *didn't screw up.*"

"But—"

He waved his good arm, silencing her protest. She stepped forward involuntarily when he winced at the movement.

"No buts. If we're going to have a future together, you've got to let go of your guilt. I forgive you. Now get over it."

She stared at him in silence. As hard as it was to hear his words, he was right. She had started doing the same thing that she'd watched him do to himself. He'd all but destroyed himself from the inside out. Was that really the path she wanted to go down, too?

She looked at Tom, lying in his hospital bed, his leg in an unwieldy cast, a gunshot wound in his chest, perilously near his heart. It was a miracle he'd survived as long as he had with a death wish ticking away inside him like a time bomb.

She stepped close, staring down at him intently. "Tell you what, Tom. I'll let go of my guilt if you'll let go of yours."

He frowned up at her. "Explain."

"You've been trying to get yourself killed ever since Simon died, right?"

He shrugged and then gasped in pain. She waited until

the white line around his lips disappeared before she continued.

"But you've been carrying around something else inside you even more deadly than that."

One dark eyebrow raised. "Do tell."

"Tom, you're afraid of love."

He reeled back, staring at her, a stunned expression in his eyes.

She plowed on. He'd given it to her straight; she owed him nothing less in return. "You fell in love once. With a woman who betrayed you and your men. Have you ever loved another woman since then?"

"I've been too busy," he protested.

She replied gently, "You'd have made time for love if you wanted it, Tom."

His gaze slid away, and he went very still. He'd gone to a place inside himself where she couldn't follow.

It was killing her to tear open his old wounds like this. It might very well cost her the man she loved. But he had to hear it. He had to face his demons once and for all.

She waited for several minutes, but he didn't speak. Finally she couldn't stand it anymore. "Tom, you've punished yourself worse than any one man deserves to be punished, by denying yourself love all these years."

His gaze finally turned back to her, clear, calm and completely unnerving.

She managed to speak past the lump in her throat, "I never met Simon Pettigrew. But surely he wouldn't have asked you to sacrifice everything—your life, your love, your very *soul* for him."

Tom shook his head slowly. "No, he wouldn't have."

She waited for him to put words to his thoughts, which he clearly was struggling to do.

"You know, ever since I woke up in the hospital three months ago I've been afraid of what was happening to me.

I didn't know what it was. It felt like I was losing control of myself, and no matter what I did, part of me just kept slipping through my fingers.''

Annie tilted her head quizzically.

He continued slowly, searching for words. "The funny thing is, I spent all that time convinced I was losing the most important part of myself, when in fact I was finding it again."

"What are you saying, Tom?"

"I'm saying you taught me how to feel again. You showed me that my well-being counted to somebody. That it mattered if I lived or died." His voice trailed off to a near whisper. "You taught me how to love again, angel."

A smile started deep down in her soul and burst forth throughout her entire being.

He held out his good arm to her. "Come here."

She moved into the circle of his arm, perching on the bed beside him.

"So where were you for the past hour while I was asking for you?" he asked lightly.

Annie grimaced. "Getting my butt royally chewed by the admiral."

"And a richly deserved butt-chewing it was," he growled. "If you *ever* pull a foolish stunt like that again, young lady, I'll kick whatever's left of your butt into next year. Is that understood?"

She glared back at him. "No, it's not. I'd make the same decision again any day of the week and twice on Sunday. There was no way I was leaving you to die. I nearly killed you once, and I won't have that on my conscience a second time. I love you, darn it."

"Is that a fact?"

She matched his belligerent tone. "Yeah. As a matter of fact it is."

He smiled at her. "Glad to hear it. I was worried that

when we got out of Gavarone and you were safe again, you'd realize you'd been clinging to me because you were scared and not because you truly cared for me.''

She laughed. "And here I was, worrying that I was just a convenient female and that you didn't really care for me.''

He snorted. "Trust me. You were *not* convenient by any stretch of the imagination.''

She stuck her tongue out at him while he grinned at her.

"Are you sure you can stand being around a beat-up old remnant like me, angel?''

She considered him thoughtfully. "I think I might just be able to stand having someone like you hanging around.''

A smile lit up his face and went all the way to the back of his eyes. "And have you got any bright ideas on how to bribe me to stay in bed while I recuperate?''

"Well, I could kiss you. That is, if you promise to stay in bed the rest of the day.''

He considered her in turn. "Hmm. I'd need a sample before I accepted a deal like that.''

"I think we could arrange that.'' Annie leaned down toward him but then stopped. She looked deeply into his midnight-blue eyes. "I thought I'd lost you today.''

For once, he didn't sound casual about a close call with death. "I thought I'd lost you, too, angel. Don't you ever do anything so heroic—or dangerous—again. You hear me?''

Annie laughed. "Only if you'll agree to the same.''

He looked at her seriously. "The doctor says my femur's shattered. I'm going to need surgery and some heavy-duty physical therapy to repair it. Today was it for me. My days as a field commander are over.''

She put her hand over his. "Oh, Tom. I'm so sorry.''

"You know, a few weeks ago, that would've torn me up pretty bad.''

"And now?"

"Now I'm hoping maybe you'll agree to take a nice, quiet staff position at a boring, out-of-the way Air Force base while I run Charlie Squad's command center."

Annie's heart skipped a beat. "What are you saying, Tom?"

He gave her a withering look. "What do you think I'm saying? I'm asking you to marry me!"

She started to fling herself at him and then remembered how badly he was injured. She stopped short of touching him.

"You'd better kiss me fast, angel, or I'm going to get out of bed and start doing calisthenics."

Gazing lovingly into his smoky-blue eyes, she drew close to him. Just before her lips touched his, she paused long enough to whisper, "Welcome back from hell, Tom."

* * * * *

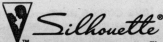

If you enjoyed what you just read,
then we've got an offer you can't resist!

Take 2 bestselling
love stories FREE!

Plus get a FREE surprise gift!

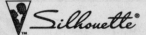

COMING NEXT MONTH

SIMCNM0902